11/16

P9-CQO-446

In-between Days

Also by Vikki Wakefield

Friday Never Leaving

In-between Days

VIKKI WAKEFIELD

SIMON & SCHUSTER BFYR

NEW YORK • LONDON • TORONTO • SYDNEY • NEW DELHI

An imprint of Simon & Schuster Children's Publishing Division
1230 Avenue of the Americas, New York, New York 10020

This book is a work of fiction. Any references to historical events, real people, or real places are used fictitiously. Other names, characters, places, and events are products of the author's imagination, and any resemblance to actual events or places or persons, living or dead, is entirely coincidental.
Text copyright © 2015 by Vikki Wakefield
Jacket illustration copyright © 2016 by Guy Shield
Originally published in Australia by The Text Publishing Company in 2015
First US edition 2016
All rights reserved, including the right of reproduction in whole or in part in any form.
SIMON & SCHUSTER BFYR is a trademark of Simon & Schuster, Inc.
For information about special discounts for bulk purchases, please contact Simon & Schuster Special Sales at 1-866-506-1949 or business@simonandschuster.com.
The Simon & Schuster Speakers Bureau can bring authors to your live event. For more information or to book an event, contact the Simon & Schuster Speakers Bureau at 1-866-248-3049 or visit our website at www.simonspeakers.com.
Jacket design by Krista Vossen
Interior design by Hilary Zarycky
The text for this book was set in Bembo.
Manufactured in the United States of America
2 4 6 8 10 9 7 5 3 1
Library of Congress Cataloging-in-Publication Data
Names: Wakefield, Vikki, author.
Title: In-between days / Vikki Wakefield.
Description: New York : Simon & Schuster Books for Young Readers, 2016. Originally published in Australia in 2015. | Summary: After dropping out of school and moving in with her free-spirited sister, seventeen-year-old Jacklin (Jack) maneuvers her way through a summer of family drama and first loves.
Identifiers: LCCN 2015039688 | ISBN 9781442486560 (hardback) | ISBN 9781442486584 (eBook)
Subjects: | CYAC: Love—Fiction. | Dropouts—Fiction. | Sisters—Fiction. | Coming of age—Fiction. | BISAC: JUVENILE FICTION / Social Issues / Dating & Sex. | JUVENILE FICTION / Social Issues / Adolescence. | JUVENILE FICTION / Family / General (see also headings under Social Issues).
Classification: LCC PZ7.W13355 In 2016 | DDC [Fic]—dc23
LC record available at http://lccn.loc.gov/2015039688

For Russ

In-between Days

1

The worst part was the waiting. I swear I spent half my life with my chin on my hands, looking out the bedroom window. The summer I turned seventeen we were all waiting—our town was waiting for death to bring it back to life; my sister Trudy was waiting for me to grow up so the rest of her life could happen; Ma was waiting for Trudy and me to disappear.

I waited for Sundays. Every other day was just an empty square on the calendar that I couldn't wait to put a line through.

Friday night: a pale crescent moon, no breeze. The air was so humid it was hard to breathe, and my pajamas clung to my skin. Even though it meant the world could see in, I switched on a light in every room. The sky was split open, and the stars were a blizzard; in the trees, the high-pitched buzz of the insects was like an electrical pulse. My blood kept time. Sunday was still too far away.

Just before eleven, a car had driven up the dirt road behind our house to the hanging forest. Now it was after midnight, and it hadn't come back down.

I was good at being alone. I listened to the radio, played who'll blink first with the possum in the gum tree, or wrote notes to Luke Cavanaugh that I'd never send. I had our old boxer Gypsy for company. She was twelve, arthritic, and half-blind, but her instincts were sharp. Her underbite was so bad we had to wipe her chin after she'd eaten.

Gypsy was lying in her corner of my room, blowing air and twitching in her sleep. I wondered if she was young in her dreams. Could she run again? Could she see?

I picked up my pen and opened my notebook. I wrote: *I love you.* Next to that I doodled his name over and over, in loops, in capitals, in daggers: *LukeLukeLukeLukeLuke.* Trudy always said you should never be the first to declare love, but by her reasoning it would never be declared at all. I crossed it out. I'd wait for Sunday and show him instead.

I slid open the window and plugged the hole in the screen with my finger. The air outside was still, but the ground moved—bugs, millions of them, drunk on light. A big Christmas beetle hit the window and landed on the sill, spinning on its back. A smaller beetle, maybe a male, clung to the mesh. I pressed my knuckles into the hole, working my fist until my arm went through, then flipped the big beetle over, unhooked the smaller one, and turned them to face each other.

"Here he is. Look." I nudged the big beetle with my finger. "He's right in front of you." The female turned a slow circle, shuddered her wings, and took off, lured back to the light.

How on earth did they find each other, fumbling around in the dark, half-stunned and blinking?

I saw headlights, but coming from the main road. Gypsy's reaction was lazy and late, so it had to be Trudy. I was relieved, but the other kind of relief would have been better. A minute later, Trudy's wheezy Mazda pulled into the driveway.

I closed the window. When she walked in the front door, I was waiting.

"You're late."

"Are you my mother?" She smirked.

"A car drove up."

Trudy's irises turned flat and black. She shrugged. "I'm exhausted. I'm going to bed. Max kept the bar open way past closing." She stretched, faked a yawn, and untied herself: hair, shoes, apron. She took too much care undressing, folding, and stacking her clothes on the arm of the couch. When she was down to her underwear, she frowned at the neat pile she'd made. "Were you waiting up for me?" Her tone was breezy, but a mad pulse in her throat gave her away.

"There was only one person in the car." It was a lie. I was half asleep when I heard it, and by the time I got to my window, the taillights were all I could see.

"You're obsessed," she said.

"We can't sit here and do nothing."

"That's what the ranger's for. Anyway, cars go up all the time."

"Not this late. I know. I listen."

I knew I wouldn't be able to sleep. I wanted Trudy to stay up. She would never come to look for the car with me, so the best I could do was wait out the dark. Morning arrived late to our town and night came early; it was ten by the time the sun made it over Pryor Ridge and around four when it ducked behind Mount Moon. Everything in Mobius stretched to reach the light: We built our houses on stilts; our trees grew tall and spindly; our shadows were long.

Trudy roughed up the pile of clothes, and they fell to the floor. She went to her bedroom, switching off lights along the way, and came back wrapped in her robe. She poured herself a glass of wine, and I knew she'd stay.

"Just one," she said. "Do you want to watch a movie?" She climbed onto the U-shaped couch we called the banana lounge and curled her legs under her.

"You pick," I said.

She chose *The Man from Snowy River*, like I knew she would. Trudy liked films. I preferred documentaries. It was our version of conversation, and letting the other choose was as close to kindness as we got.

I watched her watching the film. She always mouthed her favorite lines. Maybe she thought I didn't notice—more likely she didn't care.

Male company will be a pleasant relief in this hothouse of female emotions.

Trudy snorted. Wine spilled onto her lap.

I didn't think it was that funny.

It wasn't often we laughed at the same things, and, considering the man ban Trudy had imposed on our house, it was kind of tragic. Under her rule it was okay for me to come home raccoon-eyed and bowlegged, but I had to come home alone.

Something inhuman screamed out in the forest.

"Have you been feeding that damned cat?" Trudy snapped.

I shook my head.

She poured another glass of wine but fell asleep before the movie finished, still holding the full glass.

I prized it from her fingers and set it on the table.

When she was drunk or asleep, the lines around my sister's mouth disappeared. She unclenched her fists and smiled in her sleep. All of her spikes were laid flat. This was the Trudy I'd remembered and missed.

I lifted a stray rope of hair and placed it with the rest.

When the credits rolled, I turned the volume down and started the movie over. I draped a blanket over her.

Gypsy came out of my room. She shuffled to her spot by the back door and flopped down like someone had let go of her strings. Her eyes rolled back. I peeked through the curtains, but the moon had disappeared behind a cloud. The road stayed dark.

Mobius called itself a town, but it was really a populated dead end, a wrong turn, a sleepy hollow. Other towns had histories, natural wonders, monuments, and attractions, but Mobius was only famous for one thing: fifty-three people who had left their possessions in neat piles, gone deep into the forest, and never come out.

Ma used to say that it wasn't healthy for the moods and fortunes of a whole town to be dependent on that dirt road and what lay beyond it, but the forest didn't scare me. It was just a bunch of trees as old as time, and if there were ghosts, I'd never seen them.

People scared me.

Only Trudy could make coffee smell bad. My stomach lurched.

I pushed open the sliding door, stumbled onto the deck, and leaned over the railing, gulping air. After a night like the last, daylight always made me feel foolish—for being afraid, for thinking everything was bigger and darker and scarier than it really was.

"What's this?" Trudy called.

Her foot connected with something. She'd found the box.

"What the hell are we supposed to do with a hundred cans of tuna?"

I didn't give her an answer because I didn't have one. That box of tuna accounted for nine hours of overtime—I'd had a choice between taking the tuna and letting Alby feel bad that he couldn't afford to pay me again. It wasn't his fault the roadhouse was dying, like everything else in our town.

"Jack, they're almost expired." Trudy stood in the doorway. She waved a tin at me. "What about the pub? I'll ask Max if you can start some shifts in the kitchen."

"I don't want to work at the pub. Alby needs me even more now his dad's getting worse." That would be on my headstone: *Jacklin Bates. She minded the shop.*

Trudy shook her head then turned to stare at our falling-down back fence. "You're not going up there, are you?" Her gaze traced the line of trees up to the ridge. She looked back sharply. "Are you? It's not our business. You can't change anything. All you'll get is an image you won't be able to get out of your head for the rest of your life."

I shrugged and flicked a dead beetle off the railing, onto the lawn. The backyard needed weeding. If you weren't paying attention, the forest would take over; pull out one new shoot, and three more came up in its place.

I sighed. "I won't go, okay?"

"I heard Alby's old man was standing in the middle of Main Street the other day."

"When you have dementia you don't know what you're doing." I frowned at her.

"I heard he flashed Meredith Jolley and that's why she's in the psych ward. She's never seen one before." She laughed.

"She has a son. I'm pretty sure she's seen one."

"God, Jack, you have no sense of humor." Trudy spun on her heel. She stopped and turned suddenly, one hand on a hip, the can of tuna cupped in the other. "Are you still seeing that Luke?"

"Yes." I didn't have to lie to Trudy. Apart from the man ban, she gave me plenty of space.

"You should end it," she said. "He's not the one for you."

She had good reason for saying that, but it still hurt. We're kinder to strangers and people we don't live with. By the time I went inside, Trudy had gone back to bed. She worked so many late shifts, she was mostly nocturnal.

I stood in the shower until the water ran cold. I wouldn't see Luke until the next day, so I left my hair unwashed and ignored the stubble on my legs. I turned off the taps and stepped onto the bath mat. One of Trudy's hoop earrings was jammed between my toes. Strands of her long, white-blond hair were caught in my brush, tangled with my own darker, shorter hair. My tweezers were missing, my deodorant, too. I made a face at my reflection and, not a second later, forgave her again.

When my sister blew back into town a year ago, it was like she'd let the light back in. I was desperate to live with her. Trudy made anything seem possible. She was six years older; she'd been to Europe, liked it, stayed. Five years had passed without a phone call or a postcard, but I couldn't blame her—I blamed Ma for making her go. I missed Trudy so much I slept in her bare room for three months. Ma had packed away her things within a week.

I loved Ma. She made me feel like all my edges were tucked in, but she had a hundred ways to make a person feel shame. Dad was always there but not quite present. I think we were all picturing Trudy's adventures in our imaginations, but we never talked about it—we simply gave in to the peace that settled when she left.

And I had to forgive Trudy when she came back. She refused to miss another second of my growing up, and if that meant being stuck in the same town as Ma, she could live with it.

I felt as if had to choose a side. It seemed impossible to have them both.

While Trudy was gone, Ma gave up trying to make me be all the things Trudy wasn't. The day I moved out, I had just turned sixteen, and Trudy and I shoved my few belongings into her car as quickly as we could. Trudy didn't go inside. Ma didn't come out. She just watched from the window, blank-faced, like she wasn't surprised I'd left her too. Ma always said the wrong thing and did the right thing; Trudy was the opposite. I occupied the space between, the unclaimed land between trenches.

I stopped going to school partway through Year Eleven, a few months after I moved in with Trudy—I kicked my schoolbag into a corner and never went back. I got myself a job at Bent Bowl Spoon, bought a second-hand queen-size bed with my first paycheck, went to Ma's, and picked up Gypsy.

For the first few weeks I was like a bird sitting on the floor of the cage, unsure what to do once the door was open. My dreams seemed close enough to touch now that my sister had come home. I was in a hurry to grow up, yearning for things I didn't understand. I craved epic love and my name in lights. I was tired of waiting. With Trudy, I would soar beyond my life so far.

I've never been careful what I wished for.

2

Sunday came. I woke early. I cocooned myself in the hammock on the front deck, swinging my bare legs on either side. Across the street, the neighbor's house was waking: one light, two, followed by the shrill whistle of a kettle. In a few hours I would meet Luke at Moseley's Reservoir. It was our six-month anniversary, and I wanted him to remember, to bring me something nice.

I waited for the butterfly feeling in my stomach, but for the first time it didn't come. The world seemed a little off, and there was a flicker at the edge of my vision, like a hair on an old film. The breeze smelled of snow, or how I imagined snow would smell—bright and cold and faintly sweet—but it had never snowed in Mobius. I shivered.

The stray black cat crept out from the shadows beneath the house. It had started showing up a couple of weeks before. Trudy called it Ringworm—giving something a horrible name, she said, was a sure way to make it leave. She said it worked for Ma.

"Cat." I clicked my fingers. It was close to starvation, all eyes and ribs and patchy fur. Trudy hated all cats and this one in particular. Its screaming kept her awake. "Come here, Cat," I cooed, but it slunk away.

I went inside, showered, and put on makeup. I rolled my jeans around in the dryer to make sure they were tight, then changed my mind and pulled on shorts instead. I killed two hours this way—changing clothes, putting my hair up and taking it down again, rewashing, redrying it—until Trudy stumbled out of her bedroom and yanked the hairdryer cord from the wall.

"Your hair is going to fall out."

"Thanks a lot, *Gertrude*."

"Watch it, kid." She headlocked me and rubbed her knuckles on my scalp.

Through a curtain of hair I said, "I'm going up to the reservoir." Trudy let go. "Can't he come here? Please."

Her expression shifted into neutral. Neutral didn't suit her, since she was mostly either laughing or furious. "Not here. You know the deal. What you do out of the house is your business."

"Ma won't know," I pleaded. "She doesn't even care anymore."

"For once in my crazy stupid life I'm going to keep a promise."

"I love him," I muttered.

Her mouth flatlined the exact same way Ma's did. "You told him."

"I didn't."

She followed me to my room and stood with her arms folded, watching me fuss in front of the mirror.

There was a time when I wanted to be Trudy. I wanted her waist-length, sun-striped hair and her spitfire personality, her ability to be completely wasted and still in control, her chameleon eye color, and her dance moves. My eyes stayed middle blue in any light. My hair was darker blond and six inches shorter, and I would never get the hang of dancing without watching my feet. That day we looked more like sisters than ever, but Trudy's boobs hung lower than mine, and her tummy rolled over the top of her shorts a bit more. If you looked closely, her hair was frizzing, and her teeth were slightly crooked, and, for the first time, she seemed shorter than me. I hated myself for noticing, and for liking the feeling.

"You love too easy. You know what they say about giving the milk for free," Trudy said.

I could tell that she realized as soon as the words left her: She sounded like Ma. She covered her mouth as if there might be more.

I let the silence linger, waiting for an apology. Instead, she yanked a tissue out of the box on my bedside table and swiped at the gloss on my lips.

I jerked back.

Gypsy barked, short and sharp.

"Have you been feeding that damned cat?" Trudy asked again. She balled up the tissue, tossed it onto the floor, and strode out.

A whole year and we were still getting to know each other. Somehow we'd gone from a family who said too much to one who said hardly anything at all.

I remembered the box in the kitchen. I made a decision: For the next ninety-nine days I would open a can of tuna and set it on the spare-room windowsill, on the dead side of the house, where Trudy couldn't see.

I kick-started my trail bike and left an arc of churned-up gravel on the driveway. It was two kilometers to town and work, two and a half to my friend Astrid's house, and just over three to the reservoir. I went everywhere on my Yamaha. Since I wasn't licensed to ride on the road, I had worn a path parallel to the highway. The town cop had cautioned me twice already. I rode too fast and without a helmet, but usually there was only local traffic. Ma said it wasn't ladylike. I told her I'd ride sidesaddle if it made her feel better.

Moseley's Reservoir was a hole that filled with pale green water bubbling up from an underground spring. Trees grew sideways from the sheer rock walls, clinging by shallow roots. It was always full, even in high summer, and so deep in the middle that nobody I knew had ever touched the bottom. If you floated on your back, it felt like the world was caving in. Treading water, within seconds anything below your waist went numb.

I'd seen old photos of Ma when she was about my age, posing in a bikini top and cutoff shorts beside the reservoir. Two decades later, there was our Trudy, in a similar pose. During the sixties there was a short pier, in the eighties, a pontoon. In 1994 the pontoon had sunk to join the reef of junk underneath, and Ma had stopped taking pictures a long time ago.

Trudy didn't know the half of it: I'd done my growing up while she was gone, spending drowsy summers at the reservoir, drinking stolen bottles of tequila, driving around looking for something—anything—to do within town limits. The boys found me early. I let a few do the things Ma warned me about, and I liked it, so I let them keep doing them. I didn't fit in with other girls. I didn't stand out, either. I'd made a few friends the hard way at school and lost them the same way when I left.

When I reached the reservoir, I left my bike parked in plain view so Luke would know I was waiting. I hiked through the scrub to the opposite side of the reservoir, shook out a blanket, and spread it under our tree. It was a private place, hidden in deep shade, with a patch of soft, sandy ground that still held the shape of our bodies from the Sunday before.

I waited for an hour. Luke was late. Sometimes he didn't show up at all—it depended on his football coach and his teammates and if he had to work or whether he could borrow his dad's car. I came anyway. I came early so I could drag out the anticipation, which was beginning to feel better than the arrival, the duration, and sure as hell the leaving.

Overhead, clouds skidded past. Midday heat had settled in the valley, and the steady hum of insects and whooping birdcalls made it too noisy to think. A dead carp was lying on the bank, its eye glassy and scales wet, still fresh. I would have thrown it back in to be eaten and at least have a chance of becoming part of another living creature, but when I got up and flipped it over with my foot, it was crawling with ants and hollow inside. As I stared, the lorikeets squawked and scattered, then the bush fell quiet.

I kicked sand over the carp, slugged from my water bottle, rinsed, and spat. When Luke pushed his way through the trees, I had arranged myself on the blanket, trying to look like he wasn't the last thought in my head every night.

"Hey," he said.

"Hey, yourself."

He took off his shirt.

At school I wasn't at the head of the line for somebody like Luke Cavanaugh. At school I'd stayed where I was put. Not in the library or behind the sheds, but near the center courts, on a splintered bench under a shadeless tree, or sometimes on the steps by the science lab. My skirts were regulation length because Ma checked. My lunches were homemade, no surprises.

But this was real life, and there were new rules. I was different. In real life I borrowed a short skirt and a fake ID from my new friend Astrid, who was twenty-four; I shot pool using an umbrella at the Burt Hotel and danced with Astrid on a table. I blew my weekly paycheck in a single night and Astrid sang with the band and we lost our shoes.

The next day I woke sprawled on Astrid's couch. I had a raw rash on my neck, my bra was on inside out, and Luke's name and phone number were scrawled on my arm. I had no memory of his face. I'd been reckless, buying rounds and dancing barefoot; I'd been somebody else, basking in Astrid's reflected light, and it had paid off.

Luke had long fingers I liked to tangle with my own, ribs I would trace with my lips, and a smile that turned down. But he always looked happy. I often wondered how that could be. He'd shaved his head for charity, and his hair was growing back darker, in different directions, as if he'd just crawled out of bed. My heart always twisted up with black envy of the family who had him six and a half days a week. People I'd never met: a mother and a father and a sister about my age.

Luke was twenty-one. To him, it made things complicated that I was only seventeen. I thought the difference between our ages wasn't as great as the distance between our towns and the long wait before Sundays, but it didn't matter—he wanted to lie low until I turned eighteen. It was almost a whole year away.

He threw himself down next to me. "What's been happening?"

I didn't answer. I kissed him and unzipped him, and he was groaning and grabbing me like I was all he'd been thinking about too. I got him off quickly—twice meant he'd stay longer. I could be distant when he was in the moment. I'd look at him with his eyes closed and play through a whole other life: him, buying flowers on his way home from work; me, making dinner with a set of matching plates.

The sex part was easy. I found the before and after more difficult—I never knew if I was supposed to talk or just lie back with the feelings and say nothing at all.

"Jesus, Jack, you're something."

Straight after, he could never look at me, as if it was too much like birth or death, those moments when you get so close to another human being you overlap. He'd always find something to say about the weather, or the football, or his mother's cooking.

"It's like a jungle up here."

"It's summer," I said. "What'd you expect?" I pressed my cheek to his heartbeat and drew lazy circles on his stomach with my fingertip. "I smelled snow today."

"I can't stay long. I have to help my cousin move into a new rental."

"I could help."

"Trust me, you don't want to do that."

"I've never seen snow."

"Jack . . ."

"So that's it, then?" I said it pleasantly and focused hard on drawing those circles. "Maybe one day we could do something normal together, like go to the movies?"

"Yeah. Sure. Why not?"

"Did you know it's been six months today since we met?"

"Jack . . ."

I sighed and ran my hand over the muscles of his thigh. Touch was the only language I could speak without stumbling; touch could always reel him back in. Luke wasn't somebody I could think out loud with. Sex was simple. Sex and love together left me confused—I would rather freeze, for fear of making the wrong move.

He wanted me again and that made me feel powerful. I pressed myself against him, and he couldn't help it—he responded, because guys have one thought in their head and another in their pants, and the one in their pants gets the deciding vote. So Trudy said.

"Good?" he asked after.

Always, that question.

"Good," I said, though he didn't seem to need an answer.

He lifted himself off me, dipped down to give me a hard, smacking kiss, and rolled onto his back. It was like he counted to ten in his head. He shimmied back into his jeans.

"So that's it," I said again.

"What do you mean?"

"Nothing."

He sighed and crooked his elbow over his eyes, so all I could see were his lips moving. "It's easy being with you. You don't expect anything, you're just—here," he said. "Other girls want everything. You're not sitting around waiting for me to call."

What other girls? I'm no different. I want everything.

But I couldn't say it. That would make me like other girls.

"Still, I wouldn't mind a change of scenery every now and then," I said carefully. "Sheets might be nice. But let's not think too far ahead."

He snorted. "See, I love that about you. You live for the moment."

He was wrong. *I love that about you.* He loved the one thing about me that wasn't even true. I couldn't understand why I craved him, yet he always left me empty.

We were both silent for so long the water birds resettled in the reeds. Luke appeared to fall asleep. A king-size crayfish crawled out of the mud and died, baking in the sun. Its skeleton turned from glossy black to chalk gray.

How quickly I got used to this: sex, the great mystery, him so close, and our skins slipping together. Six months of Sundays and love below the neck. Lopsided love. My eyes ached and my nose burned from keeping too many emotions in check. Grief, sadness, heartbreak—physically, they all felt the same. It was only that your mind gave the feeling a name. There should be a pill to numb the heart so it didn't hurt anymore.

And while I was thinking, looking at the water, a blank screen with my thoughts upon it like a moving picture, the surface of the reservoir lurched. There was no other way to describe it—it *lurched*, and a wave of nothing became a bubble, three meters across, that rolled and opened up in slow motion as if the water was thick as oil. In seconds it was gone, and I thought I'd imagined it, except for the sound: hissing and fizzing and a final gulp.

"What was that?" Luke said, and sat up.

"I don't know." I stared at what was left, just a few bubbles and a small wake that rolled to the edges of the reservoir. "I don't know."

We waited for something to happen, but nothing did.

I stayed there, by the reservoir, long after he had gone. Luke kissed me when he left. It meant we weren't over. Or did it? I could fake most things, but not a kiss.

Trudy was right: Ask for too much and you might end up with nothing.

More crayfish marched out of the mud, beaching themselves on the bank. I checked for the tinge of an algal bloom, but the water was always greenish. I wandered along the edges where the reeds were thin. An opalescent layer of scum swirled on the surface—proof that something foul could still make a rainbow.

I picked the crayfish up one by one, turned them around, and nudged them back toward the water. They were passive, hardly flapped their tails at all—it was like something had called to them, and they'd given up their lives for it in answering.

I did this for an hour until it was plain that throwing them back wouldn't save them. I didn't want to go home to the house, empty except for Gypsy, who didn't meet me at the door anymore.

I thought I was going mad. I could still smell snow.

3

There were probably a million Main Streets in a million small towns all over the world, and, until I got past the age of ten, I believed they were all just like ours. Our Main Street was the stubborn trunk of a dying tree: New shops sprang up to replace those that had closed, but they were feeble shoots feeding off cheap rent and novelty. They withered fast, sometimes so fast they recycled the same CLOSED sign, over and over.

The pub thrived, and the OTB, the newsagent, bakery, and pharmacy. That about summed up the locals: hard-drinking, pie-loving, pill-popping people who were born in Mobius and would most likely die there too—but not before they had read that day's newspaper and placed a bet. Since the gold-rush boom in the mid-1800s the only sure thing to draw tourists was the suicide forest and only then in the year of a fresh death. Hardly anything was open before ten o'clock. People drove in by accident and left on purpose.

At the four corners of Mobius, like goalposts, stood Pryor Ridge and Mount Moon, Moseley's Reservoir and the abandoned drive-in. With only one town cop—who didn't live in Mobius and who knocked off early so he could be home in time for dinner—it wasn't hard to dodge the law if we were up to no good.

I always got to work an hour before opening. Bent Bowl Spoon had a fruity, overripe smell that triggered old memories: me riding Ma's hip, Trudy stealing tampons (Ma would only let us use sanitary pads), me bribing the older kids to buy me cigarettes. The Burt Area School bus picked up outside. If I timed it just right, I'd park my bike as the bus was leaving to avoid running into anyone I used to know. Afternoons were a different matter. When the bus pulled in, I'd cross my fingers and hope that Ben Matthias wouldn't be craving his daily frozen lemonade, and Jenna Briggs, Cass Johnston, Will Opie, and Becca Farmer wouldn't follow him inside. I went so far as to sabotage the slushie machine by jamming a washer onto the spindle. It grated for a week but kept on turning. Astrid was resigned to me disappearing at quarter past four. I'd find something to do out the back so I wouldn't have to wonder if they looked up to me now, or if they were still looking down, or if what I suspected was true: that I didn't exist for them.

Originally, back when it was the general store and Mr. Broadbent's parents were running it, the neon sign had read BROADBENT'S COUNTRY BOWL & SPOON. Over the years the letters had stopped working and so had Mr. Broadbent's mind; Alby added a single stuttering gas pump that pumped more air than fuel, and locals started calling it Bent Bowl Spoon. Now he owned the bric-a-brac store and the Laundromat, too. Hardly anybody went to either, so he only opened them on weekends. By age four I knew there were exactly thirty-eight black vinyl diamonds between the entrance of Bent Bowl Spoon and the front counter; by the time I was nine I'd counted four hundred and sixteen in the whole store. I'd heard of people who counted obsessively, but it wasn't like that for me—I just liked to know that some things didn't change.

I set up Astrid's cash register because she was always late. By the time she strolled in, I'd wiped, swept, and counted, checked, stocked, and marked off everything on the morning to-do list, all with my hands and mind on autopilot.

"Oh," Astrid said, and threw her bag under the counter. "What happened?"

Ma called her "that one with legs up to her armpits." Trudy rarely mentioned her, though they were the same age. She thought Astrid was a bad influence—getting me into bars, introducing me to the wrong people.

Astrid was the kind of pretty that rubbed people the wrong way: flicky blond hair, heavy makeup, miles of skin showing below her neck and above her cowboy boots. Around her I stood taller, spoke louder, acted wilder, just to make space for myself.

The locals called her Wrong Turn Astrid—but never to her face—because if you gave her time to draw a breath, she would launch into her story about being on her way to Tamworth with a guitar and a dream, taking a wrong turn onto Mercy Loop, and getting stuck in Mobius. She had a habit of raising her chin after speaking, as if she was used to people finding her disagreeable, a laugh like an automatic weapon, and a five-year-old son called Adam. The way she spoke about Adam you'd think she'd found him by the side of the road, never a hint about where he came from or who else loved him but her. She'd been working at the roadhouse for a year—almost as long as I had—and spent more time picking her perfect teeth with a guitar pick than doing any work. Astrid knew everything about me because I had no one else to tell; she had a knack for divining truth without making it feel like confession. We had nothing in common, and I liked her. I liked her a lot. Astrid had arrived at around the same time it hit me that the Trudy who'd come back wasn't exactly what I'd wished for.

"What do you mean, what happened?"

Astrid took a banana from the pile I'd just restocked. She hoisted herself onto the counter, tuned her banana, and strummed an imaginary chord. "There's a heart-shaped hole right here." She put her hand on my chest.

"You've got to stop talking in song lyrics." I slapped her hand away. "My heart is fine."

"Can you do my shift on Friday?"

"No."

"Thanks. I've got plans." She winked.

"I said no. Where's Adam?" Astrid often brought Adam to work with her.

She peeled the banana and took a bite. "Orientation day," she said around a stuffed cheek. "He starts school in the new year."

"Oh. It'll be quiet around here."

Astrid looked past me, through the front windows. "Uh-oh. Houdini's out."

Across the street I caught a glimpse of a checkered terry-cloth robe. "It's your turn," I said.

"He likes you better."

I sighed and let myself out through the shop door.

It was true; I was less likely to be bitten or scratched. The trick was to let Mr. Broadbent know you were coming—keep talking, sweet and low, until you could convince him to turn around and go home, up the steps to the flat above the roadhouse.

Somehow he'd made it across Main Street.

Alby stuck his head out of the flat window and yelled, "You got him, Jack?"

"I've got him," I shouted back, but I wasn't even close.

Mr. Broadbent heard me coming. He took off in his strange smooth run—like he had a unicycle under his bathrobe—

always in the same direction, east. His robe fell open.

I crossed Main Street. Ahead, Mrs. Gates came out of her salon and held her broom across the walkway like a boom gate. This week her hair was so black there would be no going back, with a perfect zigzag of white scalp, as if she'd been struck by lightning.

Roland Bone pulled up in his old brown pickup, parking diagonally in a parallel space. He laughed, pointed, and honked the air horn.

Mr. Broadbent stopped dead and started spinning.

"Shut *up!*" I screeched. "You're scaring him." I caught him and tried to still his flapping hands. "Where are you going, Mr. Broadbent? Where are you headed this time? Look, Alby's up there. The kettle's on. You've got no clothes. Let's get your shoes and you can go wherever you're going. C'mon, I'll take you. This way, that's right . . ."

"Stopped him, didn't I?" Roly leaned out of the window and grinned. He always looked like an animated scarecrow, pieces of him sticking out everywhere: his shirt collar, cowlick, one front tooth, and a creased ear. "He belongs in an institution."

"Mind your manners," said Mrs. Gates, lowering her broom. "The man *is* a goddamned institution."

"Thanks for nothing, Roly," I muttered.

I ran my palm over the stalks of hair on Mr. Broadbent's head. Alby had shaved him again because his father had a habit of plucking when he was upset. Alby should have let him pull them out—it kept him busy for hours. I closed Mr. Broadbent's gaping robe and tied a bow, trying not to look. He seemed calm, but you could never really tell. His eyes were a milky blue, like the dead carp's, and they only ever seemed to focus on something far away. To me, Alby was already an old, old man at fifty. Mr. Broadbent was a child—a wrinkled, naughty, insane child who belonged to our whole town.

"You're a good girl, Jack," said Mrs. Gates, nodding. "Trudy says you saw a car go up."

"Probably just tourists," I said carefully. Mrs. Gates had a big mouth and reserved seating in the saloon bar. "I'll take him home now."

Mr. Broadbent came quietly. I led him across the street.

Roly reversed his pickup and did a U-turn—it was only then that I noticed Jeremiah Jolley in the passenger seat.

I steered Mr. Broadbent up the steps.

Alby met me at the door with more lines on his face than he'd had the week before. "You're an angel, Jack."

I nodded and went downstairs to open the shop.

"Who was the hulk with Funny Bone?" Astrid asked.

"The prodigy son, returned."

"You mean prodigal."

"I know what I mean. It was before you came." I didn't tell her that I used to catch Jeremiah Jolley looking at our bricks with a magnifying glass, or that he would taste everything, including our bricks. I just couldn't warm to a kid who licked things. "He lived two houses down when I lived with Ma and Dad. Then he went away."

Astrid started checking for cracked eggs in some cartons on consignment. She would find an even dozen every time and take them home since we couldn't sell them. "Quality control" she called it. I could never see the cracks, but she swore they were there.

"Now, how are we going to fix this?" Astrid placed her hand over my heart again.

"Oh please," I said, and shrugged her off.

Across the street, Mrs. Gates had hailed somebody passing the salon. She gestured at the oil stain Roly's pickup had left behind and pointed down the street. The ones who had stayed were always curious about the ones who came back.

That night I paced from room to room and counted the knots in the oak-colored floorboards. They looked real enough until you matched identical knots in every fourth board. It appealed to my sense of order but made the counting far too predictable.

Outside, the trees rubbed and squeaked.

Gypsy's breathing seemed too slow, and I found myself tallying her human years. If I ever got to a hundred, I decided, I would not sleep. I'd keep my eyes open until the moment my heart stopped. Dying in your sleep didn't sound peaceful; it sounded lonely. I'd want someone to know the exact moment I went.

At seven I put another can of tuna on the spare-room windowsill and threw the empty one out. At eight I opened a packet of cashews, ate them all, and drank half a glass of wine. By nine Trudy still wasn't home.

That afternoon Ma had strolled past the roadhouse without a glance. Her hair, once pale blond like Trudy's, was darker and threaded with gray. I couldn't remember the last time I'd seen her wear it down. I stared at her through the window, willing her to turn around, but she kept walking.

Astrid had been talking all day about how there was nothing for her and Adam in Mobius and she didn't know why they stayed. When I added that to Ma's snub and Luke's distance, I found myself touching wood to ward off a bad omen. Any change in routine made me feel as if the ground had moved beneath my feet. If Astrid left Mobius, the sun might as well not rise the next day.

I washed, dried, and put the wineglass away. I couldn't stand it anymore, being too close to the person up in the forest and whatever awful thoughts they were thinking or whatever terrible thing they'd already done. I picked up the wall-phone receiver and listened to the dead connection. Trudy hadn't paid the bill, even though I'd given her the money for half of it.

I rode out to the nearest phone booth, a kilometer away

on the outskirts of town, itching to climb out of my own skin.

The phone booth seemed like the only lighted window in town. Moths circled above, some fluttering and dying on the ground.

I couldn't decide who to call. Astrid would be furious if I woke Adam. Off in one direction, Trudy might have been wiping beer circles off the tables in the pub; maybe Ma was asleep almost exactly the same distance in the other direction. Dad would be in a different room from Ma. That was the only thing I could be sure of.

I was still in the middle, holding two sweaty coins in my palm. I slid down, my back pressed against the dirty glass.

I don't know what I expected from leaving home, living with Trudy, loving Luke. I'd slipped out of my old life and into a new one. I had memories—some so hazy they could have been secondhand—of sitting on the school steps, listening to the other girls sharing plans for the future, imagining my own. Mine seemed reasonable and uncomplicated: freedom, money in my pocket, my own space, love. Once, when I was a kid, I climbed huge humps of seaweed at the beach, kicked them, felt their solid promise of something underneath—a creature, a treasure, even a dead body—when in reality there was just more seaweed. I had expected my world to open up, but somehow it was only smaller.

I flipped one coin. Tails. I flipped the other. Heads. I still didn't have an answer. I picked up both coins and did what I'd sworn never to do again.

A woman answered. She sounded sleepy. "Hello?"

"Could I please speak to Luke?"

"He isn't home. Look, it's very late. Who did you say you were?"

"I didn't. It's Jack."

"You really shouldn't be calling at this hour. Why don't you try again tomorrow?"

"I'm sorry."

"Well, I'll tell him you called."

"No, please . . . ," I started, but she'd already hung up.

I'd crossed a line. Luke would be furious with me; I was furious with *him* for not being there and for leaving me to imagine a thousand places he shouldn't be. Was this love I felt? I still didn't know. I had nothing to compare it with. If being in love meant being obsessed and irresponsible and desperate and ridiculous all at the same time, then it was love.

I rode back on the road. It was safer, quicker, and I was past caring about being caught. You couldn't even scream in Mobius—the bugs would fly into your mouth.

Trudy was home, wiping dishes that had been air-drying on the rack for days. Her expression was so carefully blank she must have been practicing.

"Where've you been?"

"Phone booth. You haven't paid the bill. *Again*." I wanted a fight.

But all she said was, "I was worried about you."

"You don't need to be." I stomped off to my room.

I was lying on my side with my eyes squeezed shut. I sensed she was there, standing in the doorway.

"Jack, I want to tell you . . ."

"Go away," I hissed, but I didn't mean it.

"You know when I left? Do you remember the fight I had with Ma?"

I opened my eyes and shook my head. "I only remember you driving away."

"I kept looking in my rearview mirror and waiting for one of you to come after me."

"I didn't know you weren't coming back. Not right away."

"When did you realize?" she asked.

I tried to remember. "A few days, I think. Nobody said it out loud. I was standing in the hallway and I just knew. It seemed like every time there was a fight, Ma took another picture down."

Trudy sighed. She looked around my spartan room. "You need something on the walls in here."

I sat up and pulled my knees to my chest. "I'm starting over. You know what Ma's like. I wasn't allowed to change anything . . ."

". . . couldn't pick your own colors . . ."

"...leave the furniture where it is ..."

"... Blu Tack marks the walls!"

We laughed.

Trudy picked at her fingernail. "So. What's happening with ... him?"

"I don't want to talk about it if you're going to tell me I'm stupid."

"I won't. I won't say that."

"You don't know him."

She folded her arms. "Jack, it took me a long time to figure this out, and I'm giving it to you for free: It never works if you love him more. It just won't. And if it happens that you do love him more, and he knows it, it's over. The beginning is as good as it will ever be. The rest is trying to avoid the end."

I smiled, but I wanted to burst into tears. "That's some speech, Gertrude," I said. "So, what do I do now?"

"If it doesn't make you feel good, don't do it. It's as simple as that."

"It all feels good, even the stuff that hurts."

"Yeah," she snorted. "That's one of life's great mysteries. Night." She turned to leave.

"Trudy?"

"Yeah."

"I missed you. I'm glad you came back." I turned on my side again and rested my head on my hand. "You've never told me much about your trip. Tell me the best thing and the worst thing." It was the question Ma used to ask us both after school. She didn't allow shortcuts or general answers, like "good" or "terrible." She always wanted to know why, and she never gave up until we told her everything.

Trudy's gaze flickered. "Not that stupid game. I wouldn't know where to start."

"Start at the beginning."

"It's a long story and not much happens." She moved her hand as if to brush me away. "And Jack? Next time, leave me a note."

"I can take care of myself," I said, flopping onto my other side.

"That's exactly what I said." She closed the door.

4

The new supermarket in Burt, a twenty-minute drive away, was bigger, cleaner, and they discounted dented cans and threw out soft fruit. In the roadhouse, Alby left everything on the shelf until it either sold or rotted away; he relied on customers who only ever bought enough goods to fill a handbasket, or locals who didn't drive, or old people who had never shopped anywhere else. The population of Mobius was about six hundred and falling, so that amounted to an average of nineteen customers per day, which meant I had to serve approximately one person every thirty-six minutes. And that was only if Astrid called in sick, which she did that Tuesday and Wednesday.

It gave me plenty of time to think about things I didn't want to think about.

Alby popped in and out. The rattling of the metal staircase always told me he was coming well before I saw his tired gnome face. Upstairs, Mr. Broadbent would occasionally shriek, and Alby's soothing tone would follow. Through the pipes and cracks in the ceiling, their sounds were as clear as if I had my ear pressed to the door.

Nothing much happened until just after two; then three things happened.

I had just finished polishing the floor with the dry mop. The bells above the shop door jangled, signaling, in the same second, the arrival of a customer and my discovery of the 417th black diamond. I leaned the mop against the shelving and took a measured breath.

"Ahem."

"Be right there."

I must have miscounted, or counted out of sync. But no, the aisles were five black diamonds across, and the middle and out-side diamonds counted as odds, the two inside rows as evens. . . .

"Excuse me?"

"Just a *minute!*"

Alby might have moved something. The diamonds I couldn't see I didn't count. And if I'd counted out of sync, I would have noticed sooner, plus there would be an even number at the end instead of one stray. . . .

"Can I have . . . ?"

I whacked the mop handle with the flat of my hand. It fell to the floor, twanging. I walked up the aisle to the checkout. Bradley Creech: local, nice-looking, a little intense. We had done it, twice, in the backseat of his car. I hadn't seen him around in a while, not since soon after I'd left school.

"Hey, Brad," I said. "What can I do for you?"

He cocked his head and gave an apologetic shrug, like he was still trying to place my face.

Maybe it was the juggling act my brain was trying to perform—either a new black tile had materialized, or I had been counting wrong for *seven years*—but I had the sudden urge to make him remember.

The bells jangled again.

"About a year ago. You and me."

"Sorry." He shifted uncomfortably. "I just want to know if you have any masking tape."

"We have Scotch tape. Here." I reached behind me and slapped a roll onto the counter. "It was right after you broke it off with Tegan. We were drinking, and you had to leave your car at the—"

"I'll just go to the hardware store." He left.

My vision narrowed to a pinprick of light. I started at the beginning, counting slowly, stepping into each diamond as I worked my way down aisle one. If I could just get to 416, I would go back to the counter, serve my eleventh customer with a smile on my face, and everything would go back to the way it was.

"Have you lost something?" said a deep voice.

Yeah. I'd lost count. "No, I've found it, but I need to make sure."

"Can I help?"

The third thing: Jeremiah Jolley counted diamonds with me in Bent Bowl Spoon.

"Where would you like me to begin?"

I asked him to start at the end, to only count the whole ones. We passed each other at the halfway point in aisle two; he didn't look up, but I stopped counting and watched him right to the end. He gave every diamond grave attention, like he might be graded on his final answer.

It would have been a couple of years since I'd last seen him—I guessed he would be eighteen now. Jeremiah wore loose jeans and a sloppy black T-shirt that looked two sizes too big. His hair was the same: dark, shaggy, down to his shoulders. His voice was familiar but much deeper, his words still precise, as if he'd written them down earlier and knew them by heart. He walked the same way, as if he was being shoved along from behind by an invisible pair of hands, and he kept his head down the way I remembered, although that was probably because he was counting. But there was a startling difference: He'd grown so tall and broad it was a wonder he hadn't split through his skin. Jeremiah was never present enough in my life for me to notice exactly when he left. He was always odd and kind of cold. I'd hoped life would work out for him, in the same way I hoped an unwanted puppy would be adopted from a shelter—I cared, but he wasn't the one I'd pick.

I continued, though I'd lost count. We met back at the front counter.

"How is your mum?" It seemed like the right question, though I had a dozen others I would rather have asked. *You look different; do you feel different? Are you still the same scared, weird little kid on the inside? Did the bullying stop when you went away, or are people cruel wherever you go?*

"Certifiable. I came to sign the papers," he said.

Rumor had it he knew all the answers and then some, but Jeremiah's gaze was a steady, dark-edged gray that revealed nothing.

"Oh. Sorry." I looked away, embarrassed.

"I'm joking. They're trying to get her medication right."

"Well, I hope she's better soon. She's really proud of you. She talks about you all the time when she comes in."

He seemed alarmed at that.

Roland Bone slammed his way through the door. "How long does it take you to get my smokes, J?"

Jeremiah shrugged. "Roly's driving me around until I can fix Mum's car."

"It's great you guys are still friends," I said. Roly pointed, and I reached for the packet of cigarettes. "I hardly see anyone from school."

"We're not friends. We're cosurvivors," Roly said, and looked up at Jeremiah. "He got big, didn't he? I'll tell you, though, he could have bloomed earlier and saved us a whole lot of walking the long way home." He peered down at his own scrawny frame and flexed a bicep. "I tried protein shakes but nothing happened. Those guys on the label are probably on the juice—knowing my luck I'd just grow another head."

"Well, if you're going to have two heads, Mobius is the right place for you." I passed him the packet. "Anyway, you look all right to me, Roly."

He checked his watch. "I'll be a man in sixty-five days, three hours, and nine minutes. Will you wait for me, Jack?"

"Not in your best sweaty dream, Roland Bone."

Jeremiah handed me a twenty-dollar note.

Roly laughed. "Erin Morgan had six toes on each foot, remember? Geez, is there even a name for that?"

"Polydactyly," said Jeremiah.

"Ever met a chick with a third nipple?" Roly unwrapped the packet, tapped out a cigarette, and wedged it behind his ear.

Jeremiah didn't blink. "It's more common than you might think."

Roly gave me a look loaded with apology. "He still thinks he's smarter than the rest of us. I thought that might change once he discovered vaginas and marijuana. See ya, Jack."

Jeremiah followed. When he reached the door, he turned and mumbled, "It was before he broke it off with Tegan. And I counted four hundred and seventeen."

• • •

That afternoon Ma strolled past the roadhouse again, dragging her shopping cart behind her. It sagged, nothing inside it. She wore her town clothes, a white blouse and navy pants—she never left the house in a dress—and her hair was pulled into a tight bun that pulled the wrinkles from her face and squeezed them into her chin. She held her spine too straight; she walked like royalty in cheap shoes.

"Mum" was too soft for somebody like Ma. She was all acute angles and short sentences and sharp slaps, if we asked for it, and we often did. Trudy had worn the edges off Ma's temper by the time she left, and I got off lightly. I wondered if Dad was catching it now. Still, I felt a surge of affection for her swollen ankles and sensible shoes.

I'd ignored the diamonds successfully for a couple of hours. Instead I focused on unpacking Alby's botched order of forty cartons of toilet paper. I began building a display, hoping to shift as many rolls as I could before they ended up in our spare room. I stacked two solid piers on either side of aisle two and tried to join them with an arch in the middle, but the arch collapsed. I settled for using a bridge of cardboard, and the thing ended up looking like a doorway.

Upstairs, the old man moaned and shrieked. I thought of Gypsy, going quietly. Mr. Broadbent, not so.

Alby called me. "Latch the shop door, Jack. It will only take a few minutes, if you don't mind."

I went up. Alby, still wearing pajamas, was trying to open his father's mouth.

I picked up two yellow pills. "Won't he take them?"

Alby shook his head. He wiped his hands on his pajama bottoms. "He wants his whisky, and I'm not giving it to him."

"What do you want me to do?"

"Ask him," he whispered. "He might do it for you. Otherwise we'll have to hold him down."

Mr. Broadbent tapped his foot and whistled through his false teeth.

Me, half the size of them both, trying to hold a grown man down while Alby forced pills down his throat? Not likely.

"Please, will you . . . ?" I leaned across suddenly and pinched Mr. Broadbent's nostrils. His mouth opened and in went the pills, far enough down his throat that he either had to swallow or choke. I pulled my fingers back before he bit. He swallowed. And shrieked.

"Now why didn't I think of that?" Alby sighed. "Can you watch him while I take a quick shower? Shop'll be all right."

"Of course."

I sat on the windowsill next to Mr. Broadbent's recliner, reading aloud from the newspaper, one eye on the street in case a customer came by. I'd done the same thing dozens of times before. Alby always took ages. I would too, if I had to put up with all that shrieking. As long as he was done by half past four, I didn't mind. Alby had hidden the clocks, but somehow Mr. Broadbent knew—in the same way Gypsy knew we were going for a walk before I picked up her leash. I could handle most things, but not his four-thirty routine.

I fed him small pieces of a corned-beef sandwich and half filled a glass from the whisky bottle hidden up high on the kitchen cupboard.

I found a box of Jenga blocks under the coffee table and started building a tower. Mr. Broadbent's foot stopped tapping. He watched. His eyes shifted from my face to my hands, back again. He let me put the last block in place, waited until I turned back to the window, stretched out a shaky finger, and knocked the tower down.

"Alby, look," I said when he came out, dressed and shaven. "Watch this."

I built the tower again, and Mr. Broadbent did the same thing.

Alby only flinched at the clatter. "Gettin' him to stack it would be real progress. But you're—"

"A good girl. Yeah. I know," I grumbled.

I don't know what made me think I could bring him back. He would respond to certain things, like food, open doors, loud noises, but he reminded me of a windup toy: *bam*, then nothing. Maybe it was only one way from wherever he was— one foot in another world and no crossing back.

I packed the blocks away. Mr. Broadbent fell asleep with his mouth open. I hoped Alby wouldn't smell the whisky on his breath.

• • •

I walked my bike to Astrid's after I finished work. The fuel tank was almost empty—the fumes would just about get me home. Astrid lived in a saggy two-bedroom house at the edge of an empty field, half hidden by thigh-high weeds and an abandoned tractor. She adored company. I'd sit at her kitchen table while she smoked and paced and made plates of finger food out of whatever she could find in her cupboards.

It took three knocks before she answered. Her eyes were streaming, and she had a twisted piece of tissue sticking out of one nostril. Behind her, the TV blared. Adam was sitting cross-legged on the floor, still wearing pajamas, hypnotized by a cartoon. His dark hair was a static mess, and the carpet was littered with candy wrappers.

"Oh, you're really sick."

"It's worse than it looks." She sniffed and removed the tissue. "And what do you mean, *really*? You mean *very* sick, or *actually* sick?"

"Actually."

"Nice."

"Can I come in?"

"Did we get paid?" Astrid asked.

"No. Not yet."

"Mother*fuck*. Sorry, hon," she called to Adam.

"Alby said tomorrow. He has to liquidate some assets."

"Which is code for?"

"I wouldn't count on it."

"*Mother*fuck."

"So, can I come in?"

"Look at me," she wailed. "I'm Typhoid Tess."

"I won't breathe in."

"It's not a good time," she said. "You should go home."

"I think I might be going mad."

"Are you kidding me? You're the most together person I know."

"I spent the afternoon looking after Mr. Broadbent. Come on, let me in. What's wrong with you?"

"Go home, Jack," Astrid repeated with a sigh. "I'm going back to bed." She closed the door.

I wasn't used to being left standing on her verandah. I wondered what I'd done wrong. I can't read subtext—I never could. It seemed to me that if people would just say what they meant, we'd all get back half our lives in wasted time.

I rode the last stretch home and dropped my bike on the front lawn. Trudy's friend Madison was over, and I couldn't wheel past her car. Inside, they were drinking wine at the kitchen table and listening to the Cranberries; in another hour or two they would both be drunk, and one of them would be wailing. I could never pick who it would be: Trudy, who got as far as Europe, or Mads, who never left Mobius and still lived with her parents.

"Jack's home," Trudy said.

"Hey!" Mads squealed. "We're drinking." She was dark-haired, bird-boned, and small-chested, with a pale, pinched complexion. Compared to Mads, Trudy and I looked as if we were born chewing cornstalks and hauling milk pails.

"I can see that."

"What are you doing home? You're early," Trudy said.

"I'm late and I live here." I grabbed a bag of popcorn from the pantry, threw my bag on the couch, and heaved my body after it. My bones were beginning to ache.

Trudy started chattering about work in the high-pitched voice of a fresh-picked conversation. She closed the bifold door between the kitchen and the living room. I took that to mean I wasn't invited to the party and turned on the television. It was a documentary about cheetahs. For once I didn't look away when it got to the killing scene. The cheetahs singled out a young antelope and separated it from the pack—got it running in ever-smaller circles until its legs gave out.

People do that too. *Sisters* do that. I glared at the closed door and pitched popcorn at a hole in the veneer.

Through the door, I could hear Mads telling her story about the time she and Trudy had caught the bus out to a music festival, fallen asleep, and woken up in the wrong town. It was a funny story. I'd heard it before and laughed so hard I had to cross my legs, but that day it made me sad.

It was her best story and probably always would be.

Long after I'd gone to bed, I heard Mads leave and, not much later, Trudy in the bathroom, heaving. I padded in, handed her a cool washcloth, and held back her hair.

Sunday. *Sundaysundaysunday,* my heart sang, but there was something wrong with my body.

While I slept, my muscles had been shot full of lead. The sheets were soaked, and I could only breathe through my mouth. I rolled onto the dry side (a queen-size bed and I still slept on one side) and dangled one leg to cool off. Two minutes later I was freezing again. I called for Ma, and my voice sounded like someone else's; then I remembered Ma wasn't there.

An hour later I stumbled into the hallway and made it to the bathroom. There was not much better than cold floor tiles on a hot cheek. I located my missing hairbrush underneath the cabinet but didn't have the strength to hook it out, and saw daylight through an open-ended copper pipe that fed through the wall. I spotted a lone, shriveled raisin, too, and I'm pretty sure we had a conversation. I was still lying there when Trudy got up.

"I'm sick," I moaned.

"What the hell is wrong with you? You sick?"

"I just said that."

"So go back to bed. Quit drooling on the bathroom floor."

She took a step back. "Come on, I need to take a shower."

I hauled myself upright using the side of the bathtub. "Can you drop me off at the reservoir in a couple of hours? I can't ride and, anyway, I've got no fuel."

"How will you get home?"

"Walk." I sneezed and wiped my nose on the back of my hand. "Crawl."

"Fine."

I staggered back to my room and put my head on the pillow for just a few minutes, or so it seemed. When I woke, the house was quiet. Trudy had gone without me.

I whistled to Gypsy and hauled her onto the bed. The soft white patch on her chest was the shape of an upside-down heart; I pressed my face into it and I bawled. I'd got so used to slogging through the days with Sunday in plain sight—now I was sick, and there was nothing to look forward to.

Luke would think I wasn't coming. Or maybe he wasn't going to turn up anyway after the night I called his mother. It was so hard for us to be together.

I jumped between both scenarios and decided I liked the one where he showed. To pass more time, I dozed and daydreamed. I counted the pounding pulse in my temple, per minute, the beats between Gypsy's snores. It was bad enough being stuck in Mobius—now my world had shrunk to the area of my bedroom and the bathroom.

That night I gave Trudy my coldest stare, plus another seventy-five dollars out of my savings under the mattress. I asked her to let Alby know I was taking a few days off and to please, *please* pay the phone bill. I slept again, and the next time I woke it was past midnight, the horrible day over.

5

Three days passed before I felt human again. The flu had apparently ripped through most of the town. Alby had been sick too, and since Astrid had recovered she'd been running the roadhouse singlehandedly. Trudy avoided me way more successfully than I thought possible, considering we shared a bathroom and I kept falling asleep on the floor. If we met in the hallway, she sidestepped me, holding a can of disinfectant in her outstretched hand like a bottle of holy water.

On Thursday morning I woke before six, temperature normal, legs weak, the skin around my nose red and chapped. I stripped my bed, washed my sheets, and hung them outside. A warm, whippy breeze whistled down through the trees and tied the sheets in knots. Before Trudy got up, I'd showered, slipped on shorts and an old Joy Division T-shirt of hers that got mixed up with my washing, and siphoned a few liters of fuel from her tank.

I wasn't due back for a shift at Bent Bowl Spoon until the next day. I rode into town anyway and listened to the dial tone at the phone booth for a few minutes, before deciding Luke would be at work. I pocketed the coins and pushed my bike down Main Street. Mobius was deserted, and it was still half dark.

I leaned my bike up against the stair railing and peered through the front windows of the roadhouse. Astrid wasn't there as far as I could tell, but she'd been busy over the last few days. Nothing much had changed for decades until I'd come along; now the displays I'd set up at the end of each aisle were different. The two checkouts had been shifted, leaving clean patches on the floor where the tiles hadn't seen the sun. I had a moment of unreasonable panic. I could move the checkouts back. The diamond puzzle could still be deciphered. *Please don't let anything else be different.*

The upstairs flat was closed and silent. If Alby was feeling as deathly as I had felt, Mr. Broadbent could be a spreading stain on the carpet and he wouldn't have noticed. I lingered at the bottom of the stairs. After a few minutes Mr. Broadbent took up his place at the window, staring longingly down the street. I waved. His gaze shifted but settled on the middle distance.

What are you looking at, Mr. Broadbent? What do you see?

A little after ten it was starting to get light. I wandered along Shirley Street. The smell of waffle cones was thick, but the kiosk blinds were down, and the parking spots around the man-made lake were empty. Mobius's World Famous Homemade Ice Cream Shoppe wasn't homemade at all, just Häagen-Dazs masquerading in Mobius's World Famous Homemade Ice Cream Shoppe tubs. The waffle-cone stink never really went away, though the tourists had stopped coming.

I was struck by how green the valley was, even in summer. I turned onto my old street. Ma and Dad lived in the middle of town, across from a playground that nobody seemed to use except me, on aimless days when I came to stare at the house.

I sat in one of the old tire swings and toed the dirt.

"Hello, house," I said.

It was different. The front fence had been repainted a deep evergreen, and the sand-colored house bricks were white. The only things that hadn't changed were the things Dad was supposed to fix—the broken gate, the cracked tiles on the roof, the mailbox with a missing number five. Ma's car wasn't there, but loud music was pumping from Dad's shed at the side of the house.

It had been nearly five months since I'd been home to visit—well, five months since I'd gone inside. It was easier to avoid Ma and whatever confrontation she had brewing, her forced silences, the way she got busy dusting knickknacks as if they had genies inside them, while I sat there feeling like a stranger who was wasting her time. She would carry on cleaning as I sipped water from an old plastic cup that bore my own teeth marks around the rim, resisting the urge to find out if my room had been preserved or desecrated, trying not to provoke her.

It was my fault she was angry. I'd picked Trudy. Things were bad before, but now they were worse. Dad said to give her time.

I was so busy cataloguing the changes to the house and theorizing about the rap music coming from the shed, I didn't notice Jeremiah Jolley until he squeezed into the tire next to me.

"So, when did you get home?" I asked.

"Home," Jeremiah said flatly.

"Yeah, home. Here."

"A week ago," he said. "I don't miss it."

"This place?"

"This noise. Like too many voices inside your head, all gibbering at once."

The steady hum of insects, the whooping birdcalls, the heavy jungle heat—they were so familiar, sometimes I forgot how constant everything was, the way you stop smelling your own perfume.

"That would be the sound of Mobiites, cloning and feeding," I said. "How long will you stay?"

For the billionth time I thought how monumentally stupid it was to build a town between two immense slabs of rock. It's like they found the arse-crack of two tectonic plates and figured the scenery outweighed the risk. The epicenter was right there, in my old backyard. The Bradley house, separating our place from Meredith Jolley's, had stood empty since Mrs. Bradley died six years ago. Even from across the street, I could see the giant crack dividing the house in two.

"Five, maybe six weeks." He tilted his head. "Run DMC."

"Pardon?"

"The music. Coming from your shed. 'Walk This Way.'"

"Technically, it's Aerosmith, and it's not my shed," I corrected, but he had left his tire swinging and crossed the street.

If you didn't lift our broken front gate as you opened it, the hinges shuddered and gave an unholy screech. Jeremiah lifted the gate. He walked right up to the house and ran his hand over the bricks.

When he came back, he said, "You painted over the bricks."

"Well, *I* didn't. I don't live here anymore. I live with my sister." I angled my body away from him. He'd always been a strange kid. Now he was a strange *man* who took up way too much space. "What is it with our house bricks, anyway?"

Jeremiah shrugged.

"You don't say much, do you?"

He shook his head.

"I assumed you'd gone to live with your dad, wherever he is. After the way you were treated here . . . I mean, I wouldn't blame you. Your mum was so lost after you went. My mum used to take her food, but she put the untouched plates back on our doorstep. Eventually, Ma was like, well, she's obviously not going to kill herself or anything, and . . ." I stopped my babbling too late. "Sorry. I bet she's glad you're home to take care of her." I got up and steadied the swing. To hide the heat in my face I said, nastily, "Nice chatting with you."

Jeremiah took the longest breath. I started walking as he began talking, fast, like he couldn't stop.

"Home," he repeated. "I kicked dirt into that hole two years two hundred and twelve days ago. Yes, I'm counting. Did you have Mrs. Denton at school? I liked her. When I was ten, she told the class to write three hundred words about Mobius. Easy enough. At that time, our population was nine hundred and seventy-two. Also, a week before that, Mrs. Denton put her hand on my shoulder. I shrugged her off because I can't stand people touching me, and since then she'd been giving me these wounded looks. I felt bad. She was nice."

"She was nice," I murmured, but he kept on, drawling, staring ahead like he was reading from a teleprompter.

"I wrote three whole pages, which was above and beyond the requirement, except I never mentioned our town's name. I wrote a lot about sheep tails . . . well, lamb tails, because sheep don't have them. When the lambs are a few days old, the farmer puts a small rubbery band around the tail, about four or five centimeters from its base. A few minutes later, the lambs take off on a crazy lap around the field trying to shake this thing off. Eventually, the tail goes numb, and after about ten days it dies. The tail, not the lamb. It sounds barbaric, but if you don't dock them, they get flyblown, which is— apparently—infinitely more distressing than having your tail drop off in a field. I wrote about Mercy Loop, except—and again, maybe I was *too* obtuse here—I didn't mention the name. I wrote about how Mercy Loop folds back onto itself, so you come and go the same way, and then it diverts back onto the main highway. I detailed the impact the bypass road had on Mobius, but I may have veered into even deeper allegorical territory by likening it to a drip-feeding tube that keeps a brain-dead person alive. I even drew pictures."

I slid back into the tire swing and nodded politely, wanting it to be over, wishing I could end a conversation abruptly the way Trudy could. Or Astrid. Jeremiah had a mind like the White Rabbit—I couldn't keep up.

"You know, I still remember the look on Mrs. Denton's face when she read it. I knew I'd done something that couldn't be undone. Mrs. Denton called my mother, and we waited for her on those sticky vinyl chairs outside Principal O'Malley's office. I was terrified—it was the first time I'd ever been in there. Mrs. Denton kept letting out these shaky sighs and shuffling the pages. Eventually, she said, "So, the part when you . . . you're saying . . . cut off the road and the town will die and . . . ?" I was so proud. She'd got it. My stupid ten-year-old self beamed at her and said, 'Yes! It would be kinder to the sheep!'"

"I don't get it," I said.

"I was skipped ahead a year at school. Then another. I was unable to say or write anything without scrutiny. My mother had been told that something wondrous—not plain old weird, as she suspected—had sprung from the murky Jolley gene pool, and so began my re-education. Expensive, fruitless music lessons, summer school, extra math classes, tutoring, even way-out-of-town appointments with a psychiatrist who slurped Cup-a-Soup between puerile questions and licked his beard like a cat.

"When I was twelve, I had a continuing bout of diarrhea and stomach cramps accompanied by fatigue and weight loss. Dr. Ames said my symptoms were typical of a child with a nervous disposition. He told me it was all in my head. That afternoon I stole a toaster from his clinic's staff room and turned it into a defibrillator. I didn't allow for the probability that his receptionist would be the toast eater. She was okay, just shaken. I never claimed responsibility but somehow my mother knew, so she made plans to ship me out to my uncle's place in Melbourne. By the way, I self-diagnosed. A slide, an electron microscope, and a smear will do it. It turns out eating pizza without washing your hands after playing cow-shit Frisbee with Roland Bone can result in an explosive case of giardiasis."

I laughed. "That's pretty detailed."

"Anyway, I was happy to leave. Better to go elsewhere,

someplace people haven't already made up their minds."

"If it helps, I never did make my mind up about you."

He gave me a twitchy smile. "So." He nodded at the house. "You're visiting?"

"Yeah, but I don't go inside."

Ask me why, I thought. *Ask me.*

He didn't. "Your house is the only building in the whole of Mobius with limestone bricks."

"I'm sure you're going to tell me why this is relevant."

"It isn't relevant; it's just interesting. Have you ever looked at them?"

"I've been really busy."

"They're layers and layers of history. I used to go over them with a magnifying glass, trying to identify the fossils inside."

"Uninvited, I might add," I said. "At least now I know why you were lurking in our yard."

He stood. "I've got to go."

"Me too," I said, but I didn't get out of the tire.

"Promise me you'll tell me if I look ridiculous driving my mother's car." He reached into his jeans pocket, jangled some keys, and crossed the road. He folded himself into a tiny hatchback.

From where I was sitting, it looked like he couldn't sit upright. He did look ridiculous.

I left the tire swing and trudged along our driveway. Music

was still coming from Dad's shed. As I moved closer, I could see him through the dirty window, bobbing his head like a maniac. Dad was short and bald; I couldn't remember a time when he'd had hair. Sometimes, when I looked at him, it took me by surprise to see my own blue eyes staring back. Trudy and I were so like Ma, it was as if she'd created us all by herself, and Dad had wandered into our lives when the first part was over.

My father was headbanging. Dad being in the shed was normal—whenever he'd got a whiff of tension or pending calamity, he'd be out there, bowed over his bench, making his wood carvings—but this was out of character. Another omen, more proof of change. What next: a convertible and a toupee?

Jeremiah Jolley chose that moment to reverse out of his driveway, tooting the horn. Dad froze and looked up. I ducked behind the corner of the house. A few seconds later the music shut off, and the shed door creaked open.

I took off, hurdled Mrs. Bradley's dividing fence, and kept running until I was out of sight. Some revelations I wasn't quite ready for.

6

I could spend hours rearranging the furniture in my room. That night I moved my bed four times, although it could only really go one way without blocking the door or barring the window.

I liked small spaces. The forest—I didn't see it as a vast and frightening void, but as a chain of a million contained spaces linked by trees. I liked my small town the way it was, with only one way in and out. Moving furniture was one way to stop feeling like scattered confetti.

My furniture: bed, mattress, side table, bookcase, rug. I owned the video recorder but not the television, the cushions but not the couch, a set of hanging cutlery, the hammock on the front deck. Only five white plates remained from the set of eight I'd had when I moved in, and three of my crystal water glasses were chipped but still usable. I had brought brand-new belongings for my spanking-new life, nothing borrowed, gifted, or stolen. Four hundred and sixteen dollars hidden in an envelope under the mattress, plus the loose change in my money box, and roughly ninety cans of tuna: mine.

It pleased me that the number of dollars under my bed matched the number of diamonds in Bent Bowl Spoon—until I remembered I'd found a new diamond. I stole one dollar from Trudy's purse to make up the difference, then put it back because it would mean I owned everything in my room except that dollar. Every one of my actions had an equal and opposite effect; everything I did threw out the balance. I was sure there was some kind of theory that rationalized my thinking, but I hadn't stuck around in school long enough to find out. It scared me that I was starting to believe I might have to stand completely still—with my eyes closed and my fingers in my ears—and let the universe go on without me in order not to screw things up. Still, I didn't *feel* crazy, just desperate for my feet to find the bottom.

The bed ended up back where it started.

"Are you done making that god-awful racket?" Trudy whined. She was lying on the couch reading a magazine, slapping one sandal against the heel of her foot. She looked like she was still wearing yesterday's makeup.

"Did you get the phone reconnected?" I asked.

She hesitated for a beat. "Nope."

"Why not?"

"Could've, would've, should've. Didn't."

"So, what did you do with the money I gave you for the phone bill?"

Trudy waved her free hand. "You know, food. Cleaning products."

"*Cleaning* products?"

"Incidentals."

"The *fuck*, Gertrude."

"We needed bleach and mouthwash because, incidentally, you have a dirty mouth. *Jacklin.*"

I picked up the wall-phone receiver. "Hello? Hello? Is that you, life? We must have a bad connection. Are you there?" I held it out to Trudy. "There's nobody there. Here, you try. No?" I pressed it back to my ear. "Sorry, I'd love to be with you, life. I hope you'll still be there, life, when this phone is reconnected. Hello?" I sighed and replaced the receiver. "She hung up."

"Who did?"

"My *life!*" I yelled. I made a noise like a strangled parrot and flounced off to my bedroom. After a few minutes of pacing, I strolled back out, calmer, ready for round two.

"We need to talk, *Jam Stain*," I said.

"Ready when you are, *Maximus Tittimus*," Trudy answered. She folded her magazine and tucked it down the side of the couch.

"Who told you that?"

"Ma."

"How does she know?"

"Apparently they called her that in high school too."

So now my nickname was borrowed. Secondhand. When I'd first noticed boys staring at my boobs, I'd believed, *One part of me is beautiful.* It was enough for me back then. I folded my arms over my chest.

"When did you talk to Ma?"

"We didn't talk. We shouted."

"I asked you when."

"I don't know . . . two, three days ago. Why do you care?"

"I don't. I just didn't think you two were speaking."

"Sometimes she calls into the pub to ask me about you," Trudy said flatly. "And, more often than not, she takes the opportunity to remind me that I screwed up my own life and that there's a special place in hell for me if I drag you down to my level."

"I'm sorry," I said. I didn't know what I was apologizing for. "We both know Ma has never forgiven you for leaving."

"You don't get it, do you?" Trudy spat. "I didn't *leave.* Anyway, she's not mad at me. She doesn't care about me. She's mad at you—you weren't supposed to turn out like this!"

Like what? All I did was work and save and feed a starving cat and hold back my sister's hair while she threw up, and stare at my old house because I didn't feel I could knock on the door, and wait, wait, wait as my world kept shrinking.

"How did we get from me asking what you did with my money to you lecturing me? You're turning into Ma!"

"And you're turning into me!" Trudy fired back. "If I don't call you on your bullshit, Jack, who will?"

"Thank you for being honest," I said.

"My pleasure."

"And fuck you for being mean."

She gave me the finger and picked up her magazine.

The next morning I skipped breakfast, slung my satchel over my shoulder, and went to the forest. I couldn't call Alby from home to tell him I was taking an extra day, and I didn't bother with the phone booth. I liked the aimlessness of these days off. Maybe I wouldn't go back.

Gypsy followed me until the blacktop ended. I could have sworn there was an apology in her expression. The road started to wind, and the gravel was slippery; her old joints couldn't take it. I slapped her rump and she turned back. I told her to stay off the road; she'd take her usual shortcut home, through the trees.

When I reached the gate and the NULA STATE FOREST sign, I was breathing hard and sweating.

Nula: It meant here, there, and everywhere. The sign said the forest started here, but there was no edge to something that big; it didn't even stop when it reached our backyard, not quite two kilometers away. Like our neighbors, we'd just carved out a space in the thick of it. The forest was in my blood. I knew its paths like the lines on my palms; I knew where not to tread, where the mine shafts were hidden. Most people thought the place was evil, but they were wrong—people did this to the forest, not the other way around.

There were four cars in the parking lot. The air was still, but distant voices were coming from the main track—probably bushwalkers. Near the beginning of the track there was a map on a board, a donation box, and a unisex pit toilet. The map showed the walking trails, but over the years new paths had been worn into the forest floor. Visitors were supposed to sign in to the guestbook, but they rarely did—they wrote creepy comments or drew hangmen instead.

I touched each car's hood with my hand. Three were new-looking four-wheel drives, the engines still warm. The fourth was a low, white Subaru with a large dent in the rear passenger door. The metal was cool, and leaves were piling up in the grille. I peered through the dirty windows—empty.

As I headed up the main track, a red wattlebird hopped along in front of me, barking calls, and I could make out the hulking shadow of Pryor Ridge through the trees up ahead. We locals knew that most of the people who'd never come out had been found there. The maps and walking trails led away from the ridge, but it was as if they were drawn to the darkest place, dark like their minds, and risked getting hopelessly lost or falling down a mine shaft to find it. I knew that made no sense. I had lived with the legacy of the suicide forest for most of my life, but I was no closer to understanding. Maybe, once you were committed to giving up on life, risk was nothing. I wondered if, once they got there, they were disappointed. Up close, the ridge was bare and exposed—not such a private place to die.

I could never settle on a single emotion when I thought about it.

I veered off the track and kept walking for another few hundred meters until I reached the bottle tree. Out of habit, I paused to listen.

The bottle tree was a large spreading gum, split through the middle, growing out in opposite directions. It wasn't marked on the map. When the wind blew from the west, the bottles played like panpipes, or like wailing ghosts, depending on what you believed. The bottles and notes were left behind, like the padlocks on bridges but secretive, furtive, and when the tree was too burdened, they were posted into the cracks in the side of the mountain. Over fifty years of communication between the living and the dead—suicide notes, love notes, confessions—all crumbling to dust.

I wanted it to stop; I also felt a responsibility to preserve what was there. Sometimes I would read them and wonder how things might have been different if the words inside had ever been spoken.

The bottles weren't singing today. For a second the first

rays of sun broke through the canopy, and a taut strand of what I thought was a spider's web glistened. It was knotted around the base of the tree, and when I touched it, it didn't give. Fishing line. It led deeper into the trees, away from the ridge.

I followed, occasionally touching the line. It was stretched to breaking in places and hummed a faint vibration. I didn't wonder why the line was there, only what might be at the end. Sometimes they would use string or wool, sometimes ribbons tied in bows, or chalk marks on branches, or even stick arrows on the path—all signs to mark the way back out, or to guide the stretcher in.

Looking the other way wasn't a crime, Ma would say. It wasn't that nobody cared, but what could you do? There was no changing a mind that far gone, and it wasn't the business of strangers. The forest was public property—it couldn't be fenced off and guarded twenty-four-seven. The last town meeting had been over four years ago, and again nothing had come of it; the last person they'd cut down had been almost a year ago.

The sweat went cold on my skin, and my pulse surged all over, like hundreds of tiny heartbeats. Ahead, scratched into the wormy bark of a tree, a crude arrow pointed up. It was bleeding sap, still fresh. I didn't look straightaway; I focused on an army of inch ants trailing along a twisted vine and started counting under my breath. My shoes sank into the damp path as if the forest was trying to swallow me, feetfirst.

I looked up. Swinging from a thick, horizontal branch about four meters above my head was a glass bottle. Inside it, a roll of paper. The bottle seemed to hover, suspended by the same transparent fishing line I'd traced to the spot.

I let my breath go and stumbled back. Weak legs, tingling fingers, thumping heart. Trudy said I couldn't change anything; she'd warned me about what I might see. Climbing that tree would have taken agility and strength—but it was only a bottle.

The anger bubbled up, as it always did. *This is my home.*

I sensed movement—nothing I could see or hear but real enough. I listened, picking through the shadows layer by layer, searching for a source. Beyond a cluster of feral blackberry, I saw it: an unnatural shape amongst the vertical lines of the trees. I took a few slow steps to my right to get a better look. I could make out the shape of a two-man tent—and one man, thin and messy-looking with a goatee and a ponytail, staring straight at me. I jumped, but I wasn't scared. He appeared so slight, so *beaten*, the wind could have carried him away.

"I'm Jacklin. I live here," I said fiercely, marching toward him.

He seemed to consider whether or not he'd answer. "Pope," he said, after a long pause. "Just passing through." He turned his back and busied himself, using a branch to sweep the patch of dirt around the tent. "You can follow the line back out. You know where it is."

"I know my way out."

How long had he known I was there?

He ignored me.

"Why are you here?"

He shook his head and paused with a hand on his hip. "Camping. Not that it's any of your business." His gaze swung my way again.

"There are better facilities down that way." I pointed. "No power or showers, but there's water and a toilet block."

"I don't need any facilities."

"You're not allowed to camp this far up. I'll have to tell the ranger, and he'll give you a fine."

He smiled then. It made him seem gentle and very sad. "I'd appreciate it if you didn't. I'll be gone soon. I'll leave everything the way I found it, promise. Nobody will even know I was here." He gave an awkward scout's honor–style salute.

"I'll know. Please." I knew I sounded desperate. "I'll show you where the campsite is. I'll help you pack up."

This was too big for me.

I could have passed for twenty-one, but I felt twelve again. I guessed he was about ten years older, closer to Trudy's age than mine. I should have headed back the way I came and taken him at his word; Ma was right about not getting involved. The last thing I needed was more responsibility.

"Is that your car? The white one, down in the parking lot?" I babbled.

He nodded.

"If it's there much longer, they'll start looking for you." I glanced behind me to where the bottle hung, swinging ever so slightly. "Why are you doing this?"

Something seemed to click. His thoughtful expression turned sharp. "Are you trying to save me, Jacklin?"

"Yes," I blurted. "I would like that very much."

"I'll tell you what. You can come back every day to check on me if it makes you feel better. I'll be here—not hurting anybody, not lighting fires or skinning rabbits or trampling the flora—just here, quietly sweeping my patch and reading my book. Is that okay with you? And one day I won't be here anymore and you can stop worrying. Sound okay?"

The urge to get out of there was too strong. I backed up, tripping over the fishing line, which was tethered to his tent pole. The tent sagged, and he rushed to re-peg it.

"There are mine shafts everywhere," I called, treading backward along the track.

"I've seen the signs."

"Mudslides, sometimes, if we get a lot of rain."

He glanced up. "Blue skies, Miss Jacklin. Blue skies."

My last glimpse, before I rounded a bend and the shadows took him, was of his face, lifted to catch the weak shafts of light breaking over Pryor Ridge, and his hand, reaching to touch the beams.

That night I thought about him, and it rained a steady, drumming rain.

7

On Saturday morning I woke to a strange, violet sky with mottled clouds. The forest was pink and streaky from rain. As always, I arrived early to open up the roadhouse. My key didn't fit the lock. Astrid was already there, and she took her sweet time letting me in, holding up one finger in the air to signal that she was busy, she'd be there in a minute.

So I waited and waited, and I got angry. I stepped back into the street so I could look up at the windows of the flat, but the blinds were still closed. Alby could barely change his own mind let alone a set of locks. It was Astrid's fault—first she left me on her verandah and closed the door in my face, and now she was leaving me standing on the street while she took over my life. She was probably stealing from the register. How many changes could one person make in five days? I'd never taken sick leave before, and I vowed I'd never do it again. I ran my fingernails through the white letters of the weekly specials chalked on the window.

Everybody did it—those special signs never lasted a week.

Screeeeech. Toilet paper, five bucks for a twenty-four pack. *Screeeeech.* Twenty cents a roll. Four packs in a carton. Forty cartons, ninety-six rolls per pack, three thousand, eight hundred and something rolls in . . .

"Astrid, open the door!" I yelled, and smacked the glass with the flat of my hand.

Astrid jumped and scurried over, fumbling with her keys—*her* keys, with a grinning picture of her Cabbage Patch Kid hanging from them. She got the door open, dragged me inside by the elbow, then stepped outside to look up and down the street.

"Jesus, keep your pants on!" she snarled.

Bent Bowl Spoon smelled different, like rancid coconut oil, instead of its familiar odor of putrid fruit. I didn't like it. I couldn't even tell where the smell was coming from—I imagined it steaming up from some foul entity summoned by the rotten aura I was emanating. To top it off, at that moment I remembered I'd forgotten to feed the cat the night before. It was probably because I'd been picturing the guy in the forest, sandwiched between layers of mud, like one of Jeremiah's fossils.

"Why'd you change the locks?"

"Alby couldn't find his set, so that only left yours. We couldn't get in, so we called a locksmith. The locks were over thirty years old—it was easier to replace them."

"Why'd you move the checkouts?"

"Alby did it for me," she said.

"Why?"

"I keep telling you. I always whack my hip trying to squeeze into mine. Yours has more space, so we moved it over." She pulled down the waistband of her skirt. "Bruises, see?"

I eyed her suspiciously.

"It's good to have you back." She tried to smile and stood too close. "This place isn't the same without you."

Why did that sound so ominous? She was just Astrid, my friend.

"Where'd my toilet paper display go?"

Astrid shrugged an apology. "It fell down. You nearly killed a customer. They're stacked along the back wall."

I wandered along aisle two to the rear of the roadhouse. Where the racks of empty cartons used to be stood a wall of white. At a rough guess, there were at least thirty diamonds hidden under there.

"You've been busy," I said, but Astrid was gone. Why was she being like this? Why did she have to change everything?

Somewhere upstairs, her new keys jangled. I hated the sound, like a cheese grater on my nerves. Next to my checkout, taped to the column, there was a carefully typed list of procedures I'd been carrying out successfully since I'd worked there without a fucking list—at the bottom, Alby's scrawled initials and a smiley face, presumably Astrid's.

I spent the next two hours moving every single packet of toilet paper back to the front of the roadhouse. It had to be done—only the everyday things in my life were holding it together.

I started rebuilding my display. Astrid said nothing, but her sighs came at a rate of about one every two minutes. This time I went one better, spanning two aisles with an arch of epic proportions, supported by two flimsy bridges of flattened cardboard. The arches sagged in the middle, but held.

When I had finished, I sat on top of the stepladder and counted the packets to make sure they were equal on both sides. I became aware that I had an audience.

"Twice in a week," I said without taking my eyes from the display. "You never used to shop here, Roly."

"Ode *de toilette*," Jeremiah mused in his deep, deep voice.

"Jeremiah needed a laxative suppository," Roly stated, staring at my great white behemoth in awe. "It's a portent. You're uncanny, Jack."

"Roly needed a packet of cancer," Jeremiah said. "You know, if you interlocked the packets, the whole structure would be more stable." He scratched at his chin. "That cardboard will weaken through the creases. A buttress could work."

I came down from the ladder backward, missed the bottom step, and landed in Jeremiah's arms. He set me upright like I was a saltshaker.

Astrid appeared, carrying two more packets of toilet paper. "You missed a couple," she said, and laughed, but I could tell the difference between her plastic laugh and her real one.

"A buttress will transfer the downward force of the arch into the column. Like this." Jeremiah took a pen and notepad from behind my checkout and started sketching. "It's rudimentary, but you get the idea."

"Silence, wretch! The flapping of your gums wearies me," Roly interrupted, holding up a hand.

"Go on," I said.

Roly snapped his fingers. "Let's go, J. *Yoo-hoo*."

Jeremiah only frowned and kept writing his notes.

"Help. J's fallen down the well again."

"Jack, we really should be getting back to work," Astrid warned. "I'll just add these."

She went up the ladder before I could stop her, placed the last two packets and all of her weight (I could swear) onto the fragile bridge above aisle two. As the display came down, she teetered on the top step and dived elegantly into the carnage.

Jeremiah stopped drawing.

Roly had a nice view of Astrid's underwear and took his time hauling her out.

"Are you okay?" I asked.

"I told you! It won't work. You nearly killed me!" Her face was flushed and pretty. Her expression was mean.

"I'm sorry."

Jeremiah said, "Toilet paper isn't hazardous . . . statistically speaking."

If I so much as twitched my bottom lip in the hint of a smile, she would scratch my eyes out. I bit it instead.

Astrid backed up and regarded me from a safe distance. "Alby says he has to let one of us go. But don't tell him I told you. He'll want to say something to you himself."

So that was it: She was worried about losing her job. I wouldn't be the one to go—I was indispensable. I minded the shop, and the old man. I was a good girl. These changes had been sneaky acts of sabotage; I had to mark and defend my territory, like the time Trudy and I had to share her room for two months, and Trudy divided the room using a strip of tape. The battle lines were drawn. Astrid was flaky, disorganized, and occasionally dishonest, with legs up to her armpits and a knack for divining truth, and now I didn't like her. I didn't like her at all.

Jeremiah was still waiting, his pencil poised above the paper.

"I was here first," I said. "Show me that buttress thing again."

After Roly and Jeremiah had gone, Astrid just about took the skin off the floor tiles, scrubbing them with bleach. Big mistake—only the dirt was holding them in place. I watched but didn't comment. It was the kind of job that only got bigger once you'd started, and it kept her busy while I served the odd customer and catalogued all the things she'd messed with.

She had hung a male nude calendar in the ladies' toilet; I gave the boys some dignity by using a permanent marker to draw them tuxedos. I nudged my checkout a few inches closer to its original position. Astrid's, too. I ripped up the new procedure list and tossed it into the trash where she'd see it. I ate her yoghurt from the staff fridge. We worked without speaking for nearly four hours, and neither of us acknowledged the mess of toilet paper, still lying where it had fallen. The stench of bleach had almost covered up the new coconut smell, but I found myself inhaling over a crate of oozing peaches.

In the afternoon, Alby came down and asked me to look after Mr. Broadbent while he ran some errands. I didn't mention what Astrid had said. I didn't ask for the last week's pay, either, although I'd noticed Astrid had paid off her staff account in full.

Alby stared at the toilet paper. "You need to clean that up. It's not safe."

Astrid threw me the darkest look but nodded sweetly. "I told her, but there's no telling some people. I'll do it. *Again.*" She walked off, hips swaying, skirt short.

Alby watched. "You're a good girl, Astrid."

A full-body tremble started somewhere in my knees.

"I have a boyfriend," I told Mr. Broadbent.

He was wearing loose cotton pajamas, worn through at

the elbows, and sat slumped in an armchair that looked like a distended organ growing out of his bony back. I'd played classical music on the radio for a while, but he didn't seem to be listening. I switched the channel back to rock.

"He's older. Not old-old, but, you know. I'll be eighteen in less than a year and then it won't matter."

He didn't blink. I pushed pieces of sandwich between his lips, and he gummed them, slowly and carefully.

"Astrid is swinging her hips for Alby so she can stay. That's so cheap, don't you think? Trudy was right about her—she's only out for herself."

His expression didn't change. He didn't understand what I was saying anyway—even better, he didn't talk back. I had a lot to say and no one to tell, so it was perfect.

"Trudy treats me like a child when it suits her and a grown-up when she needs money. I'm too young to drink with her and Mads and I can't have my boyfriend stay over, but I'm old enough to split rent. Double standards, hey?"

He must have stopped chewing some time ago, but I hadn't been paying attention. One of his cheeks ballooned. I held the plate up to his mouth, and he obligingly spat out a wad of soggy bread.

I lowered my voice. "There's a man up in the forest. His name is Pope. I don't know why he's there and it's probably none of my business, but . . . what if it's happening again?"

He was interested now. His legs started jiggling, and his

eyes darted around the room. I held a glass of juice to his lips. Mr. Broadbent's arm shot up and knocked it away. I yelped. Orange juice pooled in my lap and soaked through my jeans. I squeezed my legs together and waddled into the kitchenette.

"What did you do that for?" I dabbed at the stickiness with a tea towel. My back was turned, and I could only sense his movement, but it must have been quick. When I spun around, he was standing at the window, parting the blinds, scratching at the glass with his fingernails.

Oh, God. Four thirty. I peeked through the battered blinds. The sun had nearly disappeared behind Mount Moon. The sky was a bedazzled pink, the last rays as white-bright as a star. Already, Main Street was empty: no cars or people.

Mr. Broadbent launched into a series of waist-high movements so intricate they seemed automated. His knotty fingers plucked and folded, twisted and pressed, wound and shuffled things I couldn't see, with tiny, precise movements like a watchmaker's, all with absolute concentration.

I sidled away with my back to the wall.

As far as I could tell, his pupils were focused on the emptiness directly in front of him. How could a void be something a person could see? The hairs on my neck and my arms stood up. I kept still. Could I hear noise, deep in his throat, like humming? His usually creased face was curiously serene. Whatever he was doing in his mind, it was joyful. I'd seen it before, but for me—inside that stark, sad room—it was always terrifying.

I unlocked the door and squeezed through the gap, easing it shut behind me. A few minutes later, I heard his slippers scuffing on the carpet, moving toward the door. I sat on the stoop outside and held the handle.

Inside, Mr. Broadbent raged, all the more unsettling because he didn't utter a word.

At quarter past five, Alby returned. It was nearly dark. My hand was cramped onto the door handle, and it had been quiet inside the flat for about ten minutes.

"Do you think he's dead?" I said.

"God, I'm sorry, Jack. I got held up." Alby peeled my numb fingers away. "It's okay. He'll be asleep now. He would never want to hurt you, you know. He can't help it. He's just lost somewhere, in here." He tapped his skull. "I won't let it happen again. I forget—you're young. Maybe Astrid could help out more often."

"I'm fine," I reassured him. Give Alby a reason to keep her on? Not likely. "He likes me better."

"That he does." Alby smiled. "Business had better pick up soon. I've decided to close the Laundromat. You know where the keys are if anyone asks, but it's a waste of time opening." He rubbed his red eyes. "It's amazing what you find in the dryers." He turned out his pockets and offered me a single pearl earring, a metal cigarette case, and a cheap plastic watch.

I shook my head.

"Oh, here," Alby said, reaching into his back pocket. He

handed me several folded fifty-dollar notes. "Tell me if it's still short. Take some more stock, whatever you need."

I stuffed the money in my pocket. "Thanks. We don't need anything."

"Marie Gates said Trudy said you saw a car go up."

My heart skittered. "I did."

"Anything we should worry about?"

I pictured the locals, streaming up the mountainside with their torches and pitchforks. I wasn't sure it was the kind of saving this guy, Pope, needed. To someone who didn't know better, their fear might look like anger.

"I don't think so."

"It's black tonight. You okay to get home?"

I started down the steps. "I'll be fine. You know I do it all the time. I'll see you Monday?"

"Monday," Alby said. "Monday's a new day, right?"

And Sunday comes first, I thought.

8

Trudy got home late from her Saturday night shift at the pub. I was already in bed, pretending to be asleep. Not that she would have known—she didn't bother to check. In the morning I found that she'd never made it into her bed; passed out on the couch, she slept through my hair-drying routine, the rattling pipes, the screaming kettle, and the clink of my spoon in the cereal bowl.

I was having a good hair day. My skin was clear, and my jeans fitted like another skin. I left 270 dollars on the kitchen table for my half of the food, rent, and electricity bill, the last two due on Tuesday. Alby had shortchanged me again. The only reason I cared was that the number of dollars hidden under my bed was still decreasing.

If only to have a conversation, I willed Trudy to wake up and try to talk me out of going to the reservoir. But she only stirred, rolled onto her back, and threw an arm over her face.

I slammed the door behind me.

Outside, I caught a glimpse of Ringworm, just a bent twitching tail in the tallest grass. It was a clear, cool morning. The ranger's car cruised past the beginning of the dirt road to the forest. It slowed at the end of our driveway but kept going.

My bike started the first time. It was never that smooth.

I rode the long way to kill some time—past Ma and Dad's house, Astrid's, past my ex-best-friends' houses from grades four, seven, and nine. Nobody was around.

All anyone did in Mobius was sleep.

I thought about letting myself into the roadhouse to grab some supplies for a picnic, but then I remembered I didn't have a key. Hatred pooled in my stomach. Add to that a mix of nervous energy and some maybe-out-of-date milk and I had to pull over twice to swallow heartburn and suck air. I put off arriving at the reservoir for as long as I could before the thought of missing Luke altogether was too much.

The surface of the dirt road was churned up, either from the rain or from too many tires. As I passed, clouds of midges swarmed and settled in the weeds by the side of the road. I rounded the last corner, and the reservoir appeared, glinting green, flat as glass, and the burning sun was straight ahead, full in my face. For a few blinks I couldn't see. I over-revved where gravel had spilled onto the asphalt, and the back end of the bike slid out. I overcorrected, wobbled, and stalled.

There was applause. Laughter. The parking lot was full of

vehicles, the kind handed down by older brothers and sisters or bought from dodgy, cheap-car dealers—first cars, the kind I wanted but couldn't afford, or legally drive.

Over the last year I'd tried not to think about school, or the people there. There was nothing I missed. Not the teachers, who weren't impressed with my frequent absences or my mediocrity; not the awful mingled odor of pharmacy-brand body spray and desperation in the halls; not my near-constant state of hypervigilance from the minute I walked through the gates. I never could prove I was smart on paper, and I remember thinking from about thirteen that I wished I could skip this part altogether. Crawling out of bed for work wasn't as hard as getting up for class—the days passed more quickly. Over time I had begun to care less about details: how I looked, who noticed me, and who didn't. As I pushed my bike into one of the few empty spaces, I cared all over again.

"Helloo!" I called, too brightly, like a desperate salesperson. Nobody answered. I made a show of knocking the gears into neutral and kicked the bike stand down, scouting the crowd through my hair.

There were about ten of them, the usual people: Jenna Briggs, Cass Johnston, Will Opie and Becca Farmer, plus a few guys I hadn't seen before. Only Will and the girls were from Mobius—the rest were from bigger towns, but we'd all been at the Burt Area School. Already, they'd all gone back to whatever they were doing before I made my entrance.

I recognized Elise Markham and zoned in on her—like me, a year ago she wasn't anyone special. But she'd changed a lot. Her dark hair was short and styled, and she was pretty now, by anyone's standards. She wore a disdainful expression, but at least she was looking at me. I figured she'd developed more than a few airs and no graces since I'd last seen her. Dressed in a bikini top and denim shorts, she was draped over the hood of somebody's car, one cheek packed with a lollipop and the other cheek sucked in.

"Hey," I said.

Elise stared and sucked. After a long wait, she pulled the lollipop out and spoke. "Didn't you leave last year? I haven't seen you around."

"Yeah, I left. Got a job and moved into my own place." Not the perfect truth, but close enough. "I couldn't stand being there anymore."

"What's it like?"

"What's what like?"

"Having your own place."

The others were setting up deck chairs and laying towels on the flat rocks near the edge of the reservoir. Elliot something was chasing Tara somebody with the skeleton of a dead crayfish. Two guys ran and bombed into the reservoir—the upside-down sky on the surface shattered.

It's lonely. "It's great," I said.

"Did Cass and Jenna invite you?"

"Oh, I'm not here for this." I waved my hand. "My boy-friend's coming. We meet here every Sunday."

"Anyone I know?" She stuck the lollipop back in and lifted an eyebrow.

"Luke Cavanaugh." I said it too loudly and with a note of smugness.

Elise shrugged. The name meant nothing to her. I felt foolish again.

"He's older," I added. "He's not small town." *Shut up, Jack.*

"Don't know him." She pointed to a guy who was taking his shirt off. "Me and Aaron have been together six months."

"Aaron *Mackenzie*?" Another unexpected metamorphosis from zitty boy to a guy I didn't mind watching while he took off his shirt.

Elise said defensively, "Yes. *Aaron Mackenzie*." She slid off the hood and threw a towel over her shoulder. "I have to go." She stepped up behind Aaron and slid her arms around his waist. He caught her hands and held them.

I couldn't help watching. They were all so easy: easy in their friendships and their good looks, easy in their bodies. The sun had peaked; they were sparkling and golden, and I hated them. Did I miss something crucial? Would I still be feeling sad and left out? Was I better off gone? If I had stayed, would this have been the year I became a butterfly, too?

I leaned into my bike and drew circles in the dirt with my toes. Occasionally someone would look my way, and there would be a short remark followed by a longer silence.

How hard was it for one of them to ask me to join them? In my best dreams, I would tell them *No, thank you very much.* I didn't need them. But if they had asked, I would always wonder: *Why? Why now? Why not back then?*

I willed Luke to come, right at that moment, to pull up and step out of his car, search the crowd, look for me, find me, slide his arms around my waist so I could catch his hands and hold them there. *Now, Luke. Right now would be good.* He was tall and dark, he moved like an alley cat and played football, and girls wanted him. He drove a serious car, albeit borrowed, but for appearances it didn't matter. I needed him there to prove that if I didn't have what they had, I had something better. I had crossed over.

I unstrapped the bundled blanket from the seat of my bike, tucked it under my arm, and made my way along the hidden path to the other side of the reservoir. Denim squeaked where my thighs rubbed together, and I cursed my tight jeans. They watched me go.

I felt the change the minute I arrived at the clearing. This day had a new beat. Somehow I knew I'd been moving toward it for weeks.

An hour passed. He wasn't coming, and I knew it before that hour had begun. Did he stay away because I wasn't there last week, or did he give up on me before that? I wished I could put my love for Luke away until I knew how to deal with it—preserve it, like the flowers Ma sometimes pressed between the pages of her books. But they got brittle and lost their color. I tried to remember if my relationship with Luke had ever been perfect, but I couldn't.

The sounds of splashing and screaming grew muffled, as if I was underwater. In one patch, the greasy slick on the surface of the reservoir rolled and slid like a living thing. I counted even more crayfish carcasses, picked clean by the birds. Everywhere I looked I saw dead husks—empty, oily things, lying on the bank of Moseley's Reservoir.

The golden people played out their Sunday afternoon across the water, and I played out my final fantasies, lying on our blanket, an empty space where Luke should be. Were we broken up? Were we ever together? If he came, at this exact moment, it would be equivalent to turning up at my high school reunion in a private jet. But it wouldn't change anything. It didn't matter what I imagined—in real life, if they had asked me to join them, I would have smiled and said, *Sure, I'd like that.* And I would have been grateful for the invitation. Real life had a way of calling you on your bullshit.

Trudy and Mads were hard at the cask when I got back to the house. Through the window, I could see Mads was smoking. Trudy usually made her go out onto the deck, which meant they were pretty far gone.

I sat on the hammock, waiting until I felt calm enough to

go inside, but Gypsy started whining at the door. Trudy's face appeared.

"What are you doing out there?"

I slid the door open and let it slam behind me. "Breathing." I fanned the air and coughed. "No shift tonight?"

"Called in sick," Trudy said, and mimicked my dry cough perfectly.

"Let's move," I blurted. "Let's go and live somewhere else."

"Uh-oh," she said, gently tracing the pouches under my eyes. She held her cool palms against my heated cheeks.

My face crumpled, and I thought, *Why can't I control my own face?*

Trudy led me into the dining room and patted a spare chair. "It's time."

"Time for what?" I sniffed and sat.

"Initiation into the Sisterhood of the Cask."

"You sound like you started quite a while ago."

Trudy mock-frowned. "I'm as jober as a sudge. I'm not as thissed as many thinkle peep I am. The drunker I sit here, the longer I get, and get my mords all wuddled up and fool feelish."

"I'm not up to it. I'm going to bed."

"Oh no, you're not! We're going to cheer you up." She squirted wine into a glass, right up to the rim.

I threw it back to keep her happy, but she immediately topped it up from the sweating cask on the table. "This is disgusting."

Mads and Trudy dragged their chairs and boxed me in like two concerned bookends.

"Mother's milk," Mads said. "It'll put hair on your chest."

"What happened?" Trudy asked, and leaned so close I could count her pores. "Maybe we should talk about breakup etiquette before you make a complete fool of yourself."

"I didn't say we broke up. He just didn't turn up."

"Same difference."

"Oh, honey," said Mads, wet-eyed. "Love is a splinter. It'll fester for a while, but eventually it'll work itself out."

"Love is a splinter," I repeated.

"Nice," Trudy said. "But you're wrong. Love is a pie."

"How is love a pie?" Mads scoffed.

Trudy stood up and held her wineglass as if she was making a toast. "It's something you put your whole heart into. You stand on his doorstep and you offer him this pie that you have baked tenderly, and he picks at the crust, maybe takes a bite; then he gives you back the pie and says, 'I don't like this pie. I don't want your pie.' And you're left with a pie that will never be perfect again. The next time you offer your pie to someone, they know someone else has already taken a bite. Maybe all the filling is gone and you only have soggy pastry to offer. In return, all you get is someone else's half-eaten pie because that's all you deserve when that's all you have to trade. Or you get someone else's perfect pie but, by then, you're partial to half-eaten pie, so you fuck up their pie and move on. First love is a show pie. Every love after it is a reheated delicatessen pie, and it tastes like shit, because you remember what first pie tastes like and it'll never be the same again. So, now you've learned to protect your pie and you'll never make the mistake of holding it out with both hands again—now you'll offer your half-eaten pie with one hand, while the other hand will stay behind your back, holding a fork."

"What's the fork for?" Mads asked.

Trudy made a stabbing motion, then slapped her forehead. "My point is, Mads, never ever show both hands."

I laughed. "Love is not a pie. That makes no sense."

"It will someday."

"You're a freak," I said.

"Freaks like us," Trudy said triumphantly, "don't get our hearts broken."

Trudy and Mads got steadily more drunk. I was only a couple of glasses behind. I lit a cigarette and smoked half of it expertly but without enjoyment, before Trudy snatched it away and ground it out. I kept whining. I blamed our possible breakup on distance, then on Luke, and finally on myself for not being older and more . . . just more. Trudy said letting go was classy and hanging on was undignified. Mads confessed she once drove past her ex's house thirty times in one night, and for six months she'd gone to sleep wearing one of his shirts that she'd stolen from his washing line.

"This almost makes up for a very ordinary day. I love you, Gertrude," I said goofily.

Trudy smiled and mock-dabbed the corner of her eye. "Wanna play cards?"

The cask emptied. This was how I had imagined every night would be, plus or minus Mads: our own place, our secrets and dreams spilled across the table. Ma would have loved to see her girls together like this. I'd caught up. My vision blurred and glittered; my elbows got sticky. We ate cheese without crackers and licked onion dip from a spoon.

"I've changed my mind," Trudy announced.

"Oh, God. What is love now?" Mads groaned.

"Not about that. I've been thinking. You're right," she said to me. "You should be able to invite your boyfriend over. Ma doesn't live here and we do. So, it's decided. He can stay over if that's what you want."

Mads nodded and patted Trudy on the back.

Trudy waited, bright-eyed, for my reaction.

The alcoholic daze lifted. I was left with clear, painful perception. Trudy wasn't given to performing random acts of kindness; she wouldn't do anything for anyone if it didn't suit her. "You're seeing somebody."

She drew back as if I'd spat, but Mads's expression gave Trudy away. "What's that got to do with anything?"

"Don't even try to pretend you're doing this for me."

Trudy looked uneasy, angry.

"You are, aren't you? You want to play sleepovers with your new boyfriend, and you don't want to look like a hypocrite."

Gypsy—who could always sense when we were about to boil over—pressed her body against my leg beneath the table. She shook.

"You're only seventeen. You could get me into a whole lot of trouble with Ma," Trudy said. "I thought you'd be happy."

"You went overseas when you weren't much older than I am," I yelled. "I know it's not for me—I'm not stupid. Thanks a lot. You're about two weeks too late. Luke and I never had a chance."

Gypsy moved away, and my leg went cold. I left the table and marched into the living room. Mads was already stuffing her things into her bag.

"Don't leave," Trudy said. "Sleep it off on the couch. *She* can leave. *We* were having a good time." She slammed the dining room door.

A violent draft blew my hair back. I stabbed my middle finger into the hole in the veneer.

I found Gypsy lying on my bed. She huffed and moved over.

"I hate her," I whispered, wiping her chin. "And I'm sick of carrying on better conversations with old people who drool and can't talk back." I stared into her beloved face.

She gazed back quizzically.

"You are my people," I said.

9

On Monday, I went across to Mrs. Gates's salon during my lunch break, but not before I'd eaten Astrid's tuna salad sandwich. She'd brought Adam with her and let him play shopkeeper on my checkout; he'd filled a cart with stock and stacked it all on my counter. Astrid had been scrubbing surfaces so diligently that Bent Bowl Spoon was in danger of coming apart; I had hardly anything to do, apart from cleaning up Adam's mess.

"I don't know. I just need a change," I told Mrs. Gates. I sat in front of one of her mirrors, turning my face from side to side.

"How much of a change?" She parted my long hair and flipped it, feathering out pieces around my chin. "I've been cutting your hair since you were halfway up my shinbone, Jack Bates, and not once have you ever told me anything other than 'Half an inch.'"

"Make it red. And cut it up to my shoulders."

"Red? That's a bit radical for you. And you don't have the complexion for it."

I stared at her black frizz and her white scalp and tried not to laugh. "I want something new."

Not like me. Not like Trudy.

"Your mother will have me strung up." Mrs. Gates shook her head and checked her watch. "She has her appointment in half an hour."

Ma's weekly treatment and blow-dry—in all her years she'd never come out looking much different, just freshly sprayed and stiff with Mrs. Gates's signature hairspray, the Black Death, which gave off an odor that made me worry she'd go off like a firecracker if she strayed too close to fire.

"I forgot about that," I said. "Okay, just the usual. Half an inch."

"I can do you both at the same time," Mrs. Gates said, warming to the idea now that it was hers. "Color's going to take a while. We have to block out this blond with brown, and then put on a tint."

"I've changed my mind." I was not in the mood for Ma. "I have to get back to work."

"Alby won't even notice you're missing. Besides, it seems like Wrong Turn Astrid is looking for things to do." She gestured across the street. Astrid was cleaning the front windows. Adam was with her, whizzing a cart up and down the sidewalk. "She's turned out to be rather . . . industrious after all, hasn't she?"

"Yeah, she's a real treasure." I glared at Astrid through the glass—all legs and ridiculous hair—and the force of it made her turn around. "I really should go. I'll book in another time." I unsnapped the cape.

Mrs. Gates pressed down on my shoulders. "Sit. Now what's that sister of yours up to? Nobody could work out how to change the keg last night."

"She's sick."

Mrs. Gates sighed. "Tell her that ranger guy came in moping after her again."

Less than ten seconds and there it was. I didn't even have to ask. And ten minutes later, there was Ma.

Mrs. Gates had tied my hair in a ponytail and cut it off, just below the band. She jammed me into the torture device at the sink with goo on my head and cucumber slices on my eyelids. I heard the jingle bells over the front door and the *scuff-scuff* of Ma's shoes.

"The usual, Moira? Or will you be wanting a change too?"

The chair next to me squeaked as Ma settled into it.

"Jack's halfway to making the biggest mistake of her life so far. You've got about nine minutes to talk her out of it," Mrs. Gates said.

Silence for the longest moment. For the first time ever, Mrs. Gates had nothing to say. Neither did I. The chair squeaked, and the bells jangled.

"Ma?" I said, and tried to sit up. I peeled off the cucumber slices.

"She's gone," Mrs. Gates said. "Aren't you two getting along?"

"Did that just happen?" I sat forward. Dye ran down my neck.

"It did. Well, you can't live this close without rubbing up some friction, but I won't have you scaring off my regulars," she said. "Let's do this. What's the final decision?"

"Red as you can make it without giving me a whole new head."

"Gotcha."

"It'll grow out if I don't like it, right?"

"Jack, this will be one long, leisurely repentance."

"I've made bigger mistakes, Mrs. Gates."

I left Bent Bowl Spoon early, before it got too dark.

I rode from Main Street to the forest without knowing exactly where I was headed until I steered up the dirt road. I'd skipped through a range of emotions and ended up numb, my face stiff with dried tears. I tried to call Luke from the public phone, but the receiver cord had been hacked off. Vandals for sure—not the first time it had happened, but the worst time. My hair was shocking red, razor cut to just above my chin, shorter than I'd worn it for more than half my life. Astrid had laughed in my face. My belief—that a change was as good as a new personality—dissolved. Mrs. Gates was right to warn me: The color turned my skin yellow. She didn't warn me I'd feel less like a girl.

The forest was steamy after a night of light rain followed by a day of sunshine. The air clotted in my throat. I crept up quietly, tracing the fishing line without touching it. It had become slack in places, but I could see where Pope had been treading a new path as he moved up and down the hillside.

When I saw him, I experienced a blood rush that felt a lot like love. He was sitting on a stump just outside the open flap of his tent. I wondered what was inside.

"I'm still here," he said, glancing up from the book in his lap. "I heard your bike."

"What are you reading?" I asked, stepping out from the shadows.

He closed the cover. "I'm not reading. What did you do to your hair?"

"You're looking at words. If that isn't reading, what do you call it?"

"I'm listening to my thoughts . . . or I was. Now I can't hear them."

He didn't seem angry. Did he have any emotion stronger than sadness? The whites of his eyes were red, as if he'd been rubbing them. His hair was still tied back, matted in places.

"Sorry. I was just checking on you. I'll leave you to it."

"I'd appreciate that."

"It's your life," I snapped, and turned to go.

"Well, it's not really, is it?" he said. "Now you're here, our lives have touched each other's, which goes to show, even if you come to a place to be completely alone, you can't be." He sighed. "This is a world where we can't be alone anymore. There are too many of us."

I snorted. "You don't like people much, do you?"

"I like people fine," he said, and stood up.

"You don't have to be by yourself to feel alone."

"But you do have to be by yourself to *be* alone. I didn't say I wanted to feel alone. They're two distinct states."

"Maybe your misery needs company."

"See, these are the conversations I came here hoping to avoid," he grumbled.

"Jerk," I said, and he choked back a laugh, which made me go one better. "Prick." I started to cry.

"Oh, damn."

He gestured to the stump, and I sat next to him, smearing snot and tears on my T-shirt. "Don't," I said when he offered his own sleeve. "I'm fine. I've just had a very bad day."

"Clearly. It's getting dark. Won't your parents be missing you?" He peered along the path as if somebody might be coming for me. "Look, when you get to my age you'll realize it was nothing. By then you'll have real catastrophes to compare this—whatever this is—with."

"You're right," I said. I took a deep breath, brushed off my backside, and retied a loose shoelace. Once I was composed, I said, "I'd better go. You're absolutely right."

"Oh, you don't mean that."

I started off along the path. "No, I don't. But that's what you wanted to hear, right?"

"I suppose I did. But you can tell me what's wrong," he called. "If you want to talk about it."

"I don't want to talk about it. I just wanted to cry about it." I picked up my pace, moving away from the ridge.

He followed, jogging. "It's a guy, right?"

"What would you know?"

"It's always a guy."

I stopped and turned to face him. "Why? Because I am shallow and predictable and I have *small problems*?" A full-blown tantrum was building, born of embarrassment and frustration, a jumble of feelings I couldn't separate. "I don't even know you. Stop *following* me!" I kept going.

"You came here," he said, falling into step with me. "Look, tomorrow you'll be falling for somebody new or making up. Ten minutes later, you'll be declaring undying love. That's how it goes."

"Why would I give anyone that kind of power over me?" I said, quoting Trudy. "He's got to say it first."

"So it is a guy," he said. "And what kind of screwed-up manifesto do you call that?"

I glanced at him: He was blushing. "I'm going home now.

You should leave too. It's a sacred site—you'll stir up the ghosts."

At that word, he came to a halt and drew back.

"Boo!" I hissed over my shoulder, breaking into a jog.

"What happens if you don't say anything important, out loud, ever—have you considered that?" he called. "Forget it. Go home. Don't come back here. . . . What's your name again?"

"Don't worry. I've already forgotten you, too," I said. I ran.

The storm finally came. It had been hanging in the air the whole day, thick and heavy. Trudy had chosen the television over me for company and banished Gypsy to the hallway. We'd had one brief, wordless interaction when I'd come in from the forest: She'd pointed to a corner where Gypsy had messed on the rug.

Rain pounded the roof, drowning out the television, which Trudy had turned way up. I counted my remaining cash, set aside enough for the next two weeks' rent, and moved my bed into the center of the room, leaving a moat of space around it. I was pleased with myself. I had to change my thinking. There was always another way.

So Ma didn't want to talk. I understood. Her silences were nothing new to me. Trudy, on the other hand, was usually quick to forgive—the last to apologize, but the first to speak. She never lasted long in her own company.

I set out another can of tuna for Ringworm. The stash in the bottom of the pantry was dwindling. I never knew when he came, only that the cans were always spotless by morning.

I tried doing things I used to enjoy, like reading magazines and listening to CDs, but I found myself at the window again, chin in hands. My door stayed closed, and nobody came knocking.

At midnight, the rain eased and the house was quiet. I checked to see if Trudy had fallen asleep on the couch, but she wasn't there. A sliver of light was still showing under her bedroom door. I tiptoed closer—stepping over Gypsy, avoiding the creaks—and heard her talking to somebody, low and . . . sexy.

It was then that I noticed the yellow cord, snaking its way along the hall and disappearing beneath her door.

The phone was back on.

My toilet paper obsession was more a monument than a display by the time I had completed it according to Jeremiah's detailed instructions. He was right: The arch was fully supported by both interlocked columns and surprisingly solid when I leaned up against it.

"You're losing your mind," Astrid said. "I don't know how you expect to sell any of these without pulling it apart."

I stood back to admire my work. She had a point, but I wasn't going to give it to her. "I just wanted to finish it. I don't care what you do with it now."

Astrid put her hands on her hips. I noticed she'd had her nails done. "I'm just saying. What if a customer comes and tries to pull one from"—she leaned over and tugged at a packet in one of the columns—"here? What if the whole thing falls down again?" She gave the packet a good hard yank and it slid out.

I held my breath. The structure didn't budge.

Furious, Astrid eyed the hole.

"Jenga," I said, and cracked up.

The old Astrid would have laughed too. This one yelled, "And stop eating my fucking sandwiches!" She stomped away to the lunchroom.

I caught my own reflection in the drinks fridge door, and I didn't find anything to laugh about. I *was* losing my mind. She watched me from the small window on the mezzanine, jaw working madly, eyes fierce.

Astrid had put aside a carton of "cracked" eggs under her checkout counter. I opened the carton, pressed my thumbnail into the bottom of each egg, and placed them carefully back into their nests to plug up the breaks. With a bit of luck she wouldn't notice until she got home.

"Jack," Alby said.

I jumped and turned around, wiping my thumb on my apron. Alby was studying the counter as if there was something there I should see.

"Jack, I feel sick about it, but I have to let you go. It's not fair to keep you working here when I can't afford to pay you."

Look at me. Look at me. He wouldn't, or couldn't.

"What about Astrid?" I choked out.

Alby shrugged and said, "She has a kid so I'll try to keep her on for as long as I can. I don't know how long that will be."

I looked up at the lunchroom window. Astrid was gone. We had nothing in common; she was a shitty replacement for my sister. Voodoo and unbreakable curses were in order.

"I've spoken to Max, and he says you can clear tables on Friday and Saturday nights, if you want," Alby said. "And I could do with some help with my father, as you know. Three afternoons a week, say, Monday, Wednesday, and Friday? I can afford a few hours, but not thirty."

"I don't know," I said.

"He likes you best." He gave me a hopeful smile.

"Fine. But you still owe me." I started clearing out the cubbyhole underneath my checkout. There were things in there belonging to another life: a name badge I'd never worn—I knew every single person in Mobius, and they all knew me; the leaf I'd found in my underwear after the second time with Luke; a CD Astrid had given me that I'd never played.

"No rush," Alby said, and put his hand on my shoulder. "Finish the day. Finish the week if you want to."

"I'll go now," I said through my teeth. "I have things to

do." *I have to get out of here before Astrid finishes her lunch break.*

"I'm sorry, Jack."

"It's okay. I've kind of been expecting it."

"How could you? I didn't know it myself until yesterday."

He scratched his eyebrows, which had turned almost completely gray.

10

Unemployment seemed like the worst thing that could happen to me, but, given the events of the last few days, I was surprisingly calm. And free. I had the deadness safely tucked away and all of my catastrophes tallied and ticked off, like an anti-bucket list:

No job. Check.

No income. No license. No car. Check.

I'd filled my tank with stolen fuel as I left the roadhouse, so there was that. I took some overripe peaches, too, and a packet of tampons for old times' sake. I didn't pause once to count the diamonds.

Lost love. No friends. Family feud. Bad hair. Incontinent dog. Check.

I was stuck between yesterday and tomorrow. I did have right now—and right now I needed to see Ma. I had no idea what I would do or say when I got there, but I strapped on my backpack and rode sidesaddle to the house, just to see if I could do it. I could.

I noticed a familiar dirty white Subaru, and, just off Main Street, I passed Pope. He was standing outside Alby's Laundromat, holding a bulging plastic bag and staring at the CLOSED sign. I didn't wave—I couldn't, not riding like that—but he did, an accidental reflex that quickly faded.

This time I parked my bike on the front lawn and went straight up to the door. I pressed the doorbell several times. There was still no answer and no music coming from Dad's shed. Ma's car was missing again. Where did she go, all these days?

Across the street, my tire was swinging as if the ghost of me was sitting in it. I folded onto the verandah step and pulled my knees to my chest.

I had not quite two hundred dollars left to my name. Ringworm hadn't keeled over yet, so I figured the tuna was safe to eat as a last resort. Trudy had warned me more than once that if I couldn't pull my own weight, then she wasn't going to do it for me. I stretched out a foot and kicked my bike. At least I had a ride.

"It's still there," Jeremiah said. "I've been keeping an eye on it and it hasn't moved. Not an inch."

"My bike?"

"Your house."

He stood on the sidewalk, just outside the gate. I checked him over: greasy denim overalls, unbrushed hair, and steel-capped boots, like a cross between a biker and a giant. He stared at my hair. His expression gave away more than his manners would let him.

"I told you—it's not my house. I haven't been inside for a long time," I said. "Today I was going to, but there's nobody home."

"You don't have a key?"

"Not anymore." I'd left them on my dresser the day I moved in with Trudy—not because I'd been asked to but because somehow I knew it was expected.

"Your mum has been coming to see mine at the hospital," he said. "It's nice of her. She brings magazines and they chat. Well, your mum does most of the talking."

"What do they talk about?" I asked bitterly.

"I don't know. It's like a shift change—she comes in and I clock out. Look, do you want to wait inside?" He gestured toward his place. "It's starting to rain."

I hadn't been inside that house for a long time either. Not since I was about ten. Ma made me go along to a Tupperware party with her—Jeremiah stayed in his room all night, and I ate so much salami and cheese I went home with a stomach-ache.

"Don't be shocked," Jeremiah warned. He unlocked the front door and held it open.

All along the entrance walls—and in the living room, the kitchen, the dining room as well—there were shelves, many of them crooked. I had the unnerving sensation of being in a fun house. And on those shelves were eggs, hundreds of eggs, all carved and decorated.

"What is this?" I asked. "Is it her hobby?"

Meredith Jolley had lived down the street and worked in the butcher shop for as long as I could remember. She rarely smiled. I always noticed her fingernails, raw, pink, and witchy, packed with meat, like she'd gouged somebody's face. But the butcher had closed, and now I knew what she'd been doing for the last couple of years.

"This"—Jeremiah jabbed his finger at one of the eggs—"is what probably landed her in the psych ward."

"What do you mean? They're just eggs." I picked one up. It was large, gray blue, and gilded with gold leaf, a miniature royal family inside. "They're pretty."

"I don't know. This is all she does. Since she lost her job it's easier for her to focus on intricacies than it is to face the big, ugly world, I guess." He took the egg from me and placed it back on its stand. "It's how she handles disappointment. You know—single mother with an only child and unhealthy expectations."

"Not really." I thumbed my chest. "Two parents, psycho sister, zero expectations."

I touched another one I liked—it was smaller, a duck egg, perhaps. It didn't seem fragile with its thick coat of lacquer, but, as Jeremiah picked it up, there was a crack, like a can opening. His index finger punctured the bedroom ceiling of the Princess and the Pea, just above a stack of miniature mattresses that appeared to be made from sanitary pads.

He looked to me for a reaction, and I looked at him, waiting to decide whether he thought this was comic or tragic. It was the funniest thing that had happened to me all day. I didn't mean to laugh, but all I could think was that I'd done the same thing, twelve times, not an hour before.

Jeremiah made a noise, a cross between a choke and a sigh: He was laughing too. The shattered shell was beyond repair. What he did next proved to me that I was probably evil and beyond hope myself: He sabotaged another three eggs by pressing his thumbnail into them, one by one, and placing them back into their stands.

"*Whoa,*" I said. "Have you done that before?"

He shook his head, but I wasn't sure it was a denial. "I take my acts of petty rebellion where I can," he said. "Maybe that makes me mean, but otherwise I think my head would explode."

"How is she doing?"

"She'll be right to come home soon," he said. "I suppose I'll be heading off once she's settled back in. The doctor says I should try not to upset her. I don't even know what use I am here, apart from paying the bills and feeding her damned cats."

"If it makes you feel better, that's all I do too," I said. "I've been eating Astrid's lunch for days. And I've just lost my job."

"You've said that before: *if it helps, if it makes you feel better.*"
He tilted his head. "Are you in the business of making people feel better?"

Was he making fun of me? As far as I could tell, he was serious.

"I want to learn how to drive." It was out of my mouth before I knew it.

"I'll teach you," he said.

"For real?"

"I'm stuck in Mobius with a miniature car, house-sitting four hundred eggs. What else am I going to do?"

"Thanks. I think."

Ma didn't come home. Eventually the desire to see her wore off. Sitting in Meredith Jolley's dustless living room, I thought of the last real conversation I'd had with Ma—one where I'd whined about the width of my backside, knowing full well hers was almost the same size and shape, hoping for some connection, even if all we could do was lament the size of our arses together. Ma was having none of it. She said that I'd go from chubby to lean to lush to chubby, and, inevitably, I'd end up solid like her and Trudy. It was *our lot*, she said grimly, so I'd better get used to it and enjoy the lush part while it lasted. And all the time she'd flicked and jabbed her feather duster like it was a weapon.

I left Jeremiah's house after two cups of coffee. We didn't make plans. In a small town like Mobius, we didn't need to.

That night the telephone was in Trudy's room again. The cord was carefully and, I believed, deliberately concealed between the carpet and the baseboard. I heard her talking, but I couldn't work out what she was saying. I spread out on my island-bed and waited for her to finish, plucking at a stray thread on the quilt cover, winding it around my finger until it turned blue. I leaned across and slid the window up, but it was airless and hot outside, too.

Maybe I slept. I must have. I stirred to the sensation of weight on my chest, and when I tried to move, I couldn't— the heaviness was my own arms crossed over my heart. My straitjacket was the sheet; the sound of loud breathing was only me. I untangled myself and smoothed the sweaty sheet over my legs. It was pleasantly cool.

For more than an hour I flipped into different positions and counted the seconds on the clock. Nothing changed—I was still wide awake, and there were still precisely sixty seconds in a minute.

I gave up trying to sleep and took up my position at the window, settling my elbows in the grooves worn into the frame. It was a black, empty night. Familiar silhouettes became dangerous and strange. I missed the moon when I couldn't see it.

A dark shape pulled itself from the shadows. I drew back. I called to Gypsy in a low voice and snapped my fingers, but she couldn't hear and didn't come. The shape took a leap and landed gracefully on the deck railing. It picked its way along the beam and stopped in front of my window. It took me a moment to give it a name, and by then I'd already attached the thing to my nightmares: Ringworm, more flesh now and less bone, bigger and more solid than that starving cat in the tall grass, but I still believed that if I reached out to touch him, my hand would pass right through.

Ringworm yowled and hissed. I backed away. He spun to face my window, balancing all four paws on the thin railing as if he might dive through the mesh. The hole was bigger now too. If he wanted, he could easily claw his way inside. I leaned forward and pressed my whole weight onto the window to bring it down. It creaked and jammed.

A few weeks before, I would have shot into Trudy's room and taken her shouts in exchange for company. Instead, I battled the window until it inched down and closed completely. Ringworm held his ground. His yowling sounded like questions.

I climbed back into bed and pulled the sheet over my face. It was my fault. Trudy was right. I would have to stop feeding the damned thing.

At half past three the following afternoon I went up the steps to Alby's flat, stealing around the back like a thief, to avoid the front windows of Bent Bowl Spoon.

Alby opened the door. "I wasn't sure you'd come. I wouldn't blame you if you didn't."

"Beggars can't be choosers," I replied.

I threw my bag on the couch. There was a twenty-dollar note on the table, which would cover the rest of the money I owed Mrs. Gates for my bad hair. Mr. Broadbent was in his armchair, seemingly asleep, except his chest was rising and falling too quickly.

"You're a good girl, Jack," Alby said, then left.

I paced in anticipation of crazy hour, tracking the minute hand on my watch. I closed the blinds and double-checked the locks. I made a delicate cucumber and mayonnaise sandwich and cut off the crusts.

It started with a single, tapping foot. I tried to distract him with loud classical music and food. I built Jenga towers and destroyed them myself when he paid no attention.

At twenty past four his hands started to flap. He got out of his chair and wandered in circles. All the deadbolts and closed blinds and crustless sandwiches in the world wouldn't keep him inside.

Alby's spare set of keys was hanging on a row of hooks near the fridge. I slipped them into my pocket and took the half-empty whisky bottle and the twenty-dollar note.

I unlocked the door. Instead of slipping out and cowering on the doorstep, like every other time, I held out my hand to Mr. Broadbent. "Here," I called. "Come."

He hesitated, not meeting my eyes, shuffling from one foot to the other, like a freed circus elephant that still feels the phantom weight of its hobble.

"Come," I said again, touching his shoulder.

I led him to the door. At the last minute he leaned back on his heels, like he was readying for a trick; it was only when he caught sight of the sky that his whole body relaxed and his eyes crinkled as if I'd pulled on a loose thread. It was a smile, or as close to it as he could summon without regular practice. He took a deep breath like he'd been underwater forever. I half expected him to sprout wings from the bumps of his spine—*pop, pop*—as he tensed for flight.

"Go!" I shouted.

I flung the door open, and he brushed past like the barest breeze, all skin and bone and ridiculous potbelly.

I followed him down the stairs, far enough behind that he had a good head start. The lightness in my chest expanded. Whatever had been in there, tick-ticking away, defused (well, a small piece of it), and I suddenly understood what Jeremiah had meant about petty rebellion. Given the chance, I'd slip my collar and leave it dangling too.

11

At first I thought Mr. Broadbent just needed to feel the warmth on his face, but, by the time I let him out, the sun had almost disappeared. At the far end of Main Street, the lights were already on. Astrid was locking up the roadhouse, her back turned, oblivious.

Mr. Broadbent dashed across the street and set out on his usual route, sticking to the sidewalk. I was glad he was dressed and thankful that Main Street was deserted, apart from a straggler in Mrs. Gates's salon and the usual drunks holed up in the pub. Mr. Broadbent had a fair chance of completing his great escape without being tackled.

I trailed behind him, occasionally waving my arms and calling out, for the sake of appearance. He was quick, but not so quick that he'd be able to outrun me if I put some legs into it. I counted his steps and made mine match; at 114 I felt the first twinge of panic. And a stitch. The farther from Alby's flat we got, the farther I'd have to coax him home with nothing but a bottle of whisky. Past Nicholson's Mowers at number fifty-six and four empty shops in a row from seventy-two. By the time we flew by the ice cream shop, I was all out of breath and rational thought.

At some point I understood that Mr. Broadbent knew exactly where he was going. He couldn't tie his own shoelaces or find his own mouth, but somewhere in his addled mind a compass still pointed true east. He settled into an easy lope, turning sharply onto Third Street. About five hundred meters up, the tarmac and sidewalk ended at the last, unoccupied, house on the street. Here, the road turned to gravel and wound up the hillside. The sidewalk petered out.

Mr. Broadbent kept running.

What if he makes it all the way out of town? What if he doesn't quit running, like those foxhounds that never give up until their hearts stop? And my next sickening thought: *Do old people, like old cats, go away to die?*

I made a real effort to catch up. He heard me coming, skidding on stones, and put in his final sprint.

The road narrowed. I looked back. Below us, Mobius was lighting up, which made it seem darker where we were. The trees were dense and bowed, the road a tunnel to nowhere.

I caught Mr. Broadbent's elbow and gave it a tug. He gasped and wheezed and lunged ahead with me dangling like an anchor, until he gave in. His lungs just couldn't keep up with his ambition anymore. His expression broke my heart.

Even with the death rattle coming from his chest and the cloudy blue film over his eyes, he looked focused and desperate.

"I'm so sorry," I gabbled, and burst into tears. "I shouldn't have done it. I don't know what I was thinking. Please don't die on me."

He put his hands on his knees and lowered his head between them, heaving. We stood together, battling to breathe, and I realized that by the time we got back to the flat Alby might already be there. Somebody, somewhere, would have seen us. I would have some explaining to do. At least it was all downhill on the way home.

"Come on," I said. I tried to turn him around, expecting resistance. "We'll take it slowly." I wondered if I could carry him if I had to. Piggyback, maybe. There wasn't much of him.

Mr. Broadbent leaned into the warm breeze blowing in from the east. Drool strung from his chin. His body stiffened, and he sniffed the air like a dog.

I wiped his chin with his collar and tucked his flapping shirt into his pajama pants. "We have to go."

He slapped my fussing hands away. One quaky finger raised and uncurled. He pointed to the tunnel of trees.

"It's getting dark." I tried again, taking his other hand in mine. "There's nothing up there."

He shook me off. Curiosity got the better of me. By now it was officially dusk—no matter what, I was screwed. I let go of his hand, and he continued, high-stepping, his fingers splayed in front as if he was blindfolded, up the dirt road and toward the blackness.

A reddish moon was rising, not unusual for Mobius in summer. Our shadows stretched long and thin ahead. The insects' chorus grew, changed beat, and merged to become so loud my ears throbbed with it.

Despite the humidity, I shivered.

Near an overgrown trail, Mr. Broadbent took a ninety-degree turn and pushed his way through branches, letting them whip back into my face. I followed, until we reached a high fence with a padlocked gate about the width of the two of us standing side by side. The padlock seemed to confuse him. He stared at it and whimpered.

I gave it a rattle. It was solid brass, quite new. "Locked," I said, wiping grease on my leg.

Mr. Broadbent was motionless, staring into the distance. His windup mechanism had run out. We'd have to go back the way we'd come. As the moon rose, I could make out an object through the trees: a rectangle of light, and darker, silvery shapes in rows.

The old drive-in.

"We can't get in," I said. "It's been closed for years."

I pressed my face against the fence. This wasn't the main entrance, but it was a shorter route if you were coming from our side of town. The drive-in hadn't been used in my lifetime, except as an unofficial dump or somewhere to hang out and burn rubber. Through the diamond-shaped wire, it looked miserable and abandoned: a peeling gray screen on stilts and the speaker stands, an army of robots frozen in time. A couple of burnt-out cars without wheels and a stack of sad mattresses. As in other untended corners of Mobius, the forest was on the march, sending shoots through cracks in the asphalt, curling it up like damp paper.

Mr. Broadbent was still frozen, but his eyes shone.

His hands began to move. He replayed the exact movements I'd seen at four thirty in the flat, only this time he looked up every few seconds to focus on the drive-in screen. With the moon on the rise it had begun to glow, no longer that flat, dirty gray. I saw it then as it might have been: white, majestic, supported by a cast of cords snaking through car windows, the tinny sounds of music, the smell of burgers and hot chips. I imagined a ghostly beam of light cutting the dark—starting small from a gap between bricks and spilling onto the screen.

I had to dangle the bottle in front of his nose to get him started, but he came easily enough once he snapped out of his trance. It took three times as long to get home as it did to get there. Mr. Broadbent smiled the whole way.

Alby was sitting on the top step in the greenish glow of the verandah light. He paid no mind to the moths and flying ants swooping around his head.

"What's happened? Where have you been?" he yelled. He hauled his father up the steps and patted him down, feeling his thin arms. "He's soaked through."

I stammered and apologized, over and over. Mr. Broadbent was floppy with exhaustion. We were both dripping sweat.

"We went for a walk," I said. "We got a bit lost."

"Lost? You've lived here your whole life! He knows every crack in this place. You can't get lost in Mobius."

"It was dark. We wandered too far."

Alby led his father inside and settled him in his chair. He kept checking over Mr. Broadbent as if we might have left some part of him behind.

"You scared the pants off me, Jack. This isn't like you at all."

I sighed. "I've had a shit week."

Alby had the grace to look uncomfortable. "Thank you, Astrid. You should head home now."

I looked up; Astrid was leaning in the doorway to the kitchenette like she belonged there, holding a lipstick-smeared mug in one hand.

"Astrid was worried. She wouldn't go home until we found you."

"I'll bet."

Alby went into the hallway. I heard him rummaging in the linen cupboard.

"I like your hair," Astrid said.

"Then why'd you laugh?"

"It was a shock. You look so different."

"I needed a change."

She cocked her head. "For what it's worth, I'm sorry about the job. I didn't really think Alby would choose me over you. You're always so responsible."

I snorted. "Not anymore." I stopped short of saying *it's okay* because it wasn't, not yet, but I'd get over it. I missed her.

But then she nodded at Mr. Broadbent, who was already drifting off with his eyes half-closed. She kicked his foot lightly with hers and sniggered, "Where'd you take him? Why's he smiling like that? Huh?" She dug into my ribs with her elbow. "Crazy old coot."

Mr. Broadbent flinched and startled awake. He stopped smiling.

"Hey, Astrid?"

"Yeah?"

I handed her the bottle I was still gripping. "Why don't you take this and shove it in your heart-shaped hole."

Trudy was waiting for me when I got home. She still had her bar apron tied around her waist, and her T-shirt was so tight it made her look like a Hooters girl.

"When were you going to tell me you lost your job?"

"Same time as you told me the phone was back on," I said.

"I figured you'd work it out the next time you tried to

call your life," she said. "Seriously, am I supposed to read your mind? Pay your rent? Be the only responsible person in this house?" She had her hands on her hips.

"Responsible?" I said. "I am so sick of that word. Look, if I had caught a fucking jet plane home the day I was fired you still would have found out before I told you myself. You know, the usual telegraph—a series of grunts and clicks carried on the wind." I threw myself onto the couch and flicked the television on. "Anyway, it's not my fault."

Trudy stamped her foot. "It's not a matter of whose fault. It's a matter of who's going to pay the rent."

"I'll get another job."

"Damn right, you will. I asked Max again—"

"I don't want to work at the pub. We can't even live together let alone work together," I snapped. "I'll look in Burt." I settled a cushion under my head and closed my eyes.

"You can't drive. How are you going to get there?"

"I'm working on it. Stop nagging me—you sound like Ma."

I couldn't tell what she threw at me because my eyes were shut.

My bike choked on its last milliliter of fuel a couple of days later. I would have to get used to walking. I already knew where I was going that day. I'd thought about it lying awake at night. Alby's keys were still tucked inside the pocket of my shorts; I pulled them on, tied my now orange hair back, and swiped my face with a wash cloth.

I rummaged for something to eat and found an utterly foreign batch of healthy food in the fridge: yoghurt, tofu, green beans, fancy lettuce, and fat-free milk. Fat-free milk sure didn't come from any of the full-fat cows I'd ever seen in the flesh, so I figured Trudy must be on a new diet.

Trudy and I had taken turns being naughty or nice when we were young, and we were now slipping into the same routine. It was like there was a finite amount of goodness between us, and we could only heave and haul that shared rope, like a game of tug-of-war. I now swore often, avoided chores, and ate junk, lied, stayed up late, and slept until lunchtime; Trudy took on two extra shifts to cover my rent, went to bed early, complained and lectured, started enunciating her *h*s and *t*s in a prissy tone that reminded me more and more of Ma. Every morning, through the fog of sleep, I heard the metallic clunk of the bathroom scales as Trudy stepped up.

I shut the fridge door. I missed routine, contact, conversation—Ma and Dad. I couldn't miss the note Trudy had left on the fridge, written all in red capitals: *COME IN TO THE PUB TODAY*. Normally she would sign off with kisses, but this one ended with a period.

I picked up the phone. The dial tone buzzed pleasantly. I dialed Luke's home number and listened, counting the rings, all the time undecided whether I would speak or hang up. It was the sixth time I'd called in two days and the sixth time it rang out.

I even missed waiting. It might have been often painful and mostly futile, but at least sometimes there was a reward at the end of it. I missed being happy at least half the time. I'd never noticed before, but rage sits just under your ribs.

I hung up.

"Don't you ever get bored?"

"I didn't hear you coming," Pope said. "Are you still spying on me?" He was scooping peas and corn from a can, eating them cold.

"I'm glad you're okay." I shot a look at the bottle, swinging from its branch. "It's not really spying if you know I'm here. Anyway, you never do anything worth reporting."

"*Au contraire,*" he said. "Some nights I howl at the moon and run naked with wolves." He frowned. "What day is it?"

"Wednesday—maybe Friday. I'm not sure." He seemed to think it was an answer. "I brought you something." I dangled Alby's keys. "They're for the Laundromat. I saw you waiting outside."

"I saw you, too. Like Lady Godiva, wearing jeans, on a motorbike." He put the empty can in a plastic bag.

"Who's Lady Godiva?"

He ignored the question. "Why do you have the keys to the Laundromat?"

"I borrowed them. It's okay; Alby won't mind. You can let yourself in. Just make sure you don't use the machine in the middle. It'll shred your delicates."

Pope gestured at his canvas pants and work shirt. "I don't believe that will be a problem. So, if it's Wednesday-maybe-Friday, why are you skulking about and sneaking up on innocent campers?"

"I'm currently seeking employment." I mimicked his posh accent. "Do you know why I think you're here? Do you even know why most people come here?"

"Better than some," he said tightly. "More than most."

"You're very good at not saying what you really mean."

My comment seemed to cause him physical pain. He sat heavily and ran his fingers through his hair. His complexion was raw, like he'd scrubbed it too hard.

"Go ahead. Say something nasty. I'll probably run off again, but in a couple of days I'll be back to make sure you're still here. I am a tenacious blot on your existence."

"Blight," he said. "Why do you keep coming back, Blot?"

I shrugged. "I have no one else to talk to. And your pants are dirty." I was aware that my attempts at humor were starting to sound forced.

A whole minute of silence passed. He seemed to forget I was there.

"Did you know the first one, the very first guy, was a mistake?" I said desperately. "He was some famous naturalist, and there was a sighting of a supposedly extinct reptile, so he comes to the forest in nineteen hundred and whatever and tries to photograph this lizard. Only nobody warned him about the mine shafts. When they find him, the first thing the papers say is that he jumped because his wife had left him. See, it's more likely he just fell, but nobody reads retractions. Then they all start coming. My dad says it's become a religion for lost people. This way, they all become part of a legend, rather than being one lonely body in a rented room or slumped behind a Dumpster. This way, they think they'll have company. And so they keep coming."

My top lip was sweating, and the bottom one wobbled. I didn't want to say the wrong thing. "But he was a mistake, that first guy. If he had watched where he was treading, then none of this would be happening. Can you see? Fifty-three people, all following the wrong guy, and our town has to keep reliving this awful legacy that none of us wants."

Another minute passed.

"I saw your car go up that night. I thought it was happening again and I wanted to stop it."

He shook his head. "Is that really why you think I'm here?"

"You're alone. You're really sad." I looked up at the bottle. "And you've got this thing hanging over your head. What am I supposed to think?"

He didn't seem to know what to say. I watched his mouth working, like he had a wad of gum stuck to his palate. Then it went slack, the way mouths do just before we cry.

"Do you believe in ghosts?" he asked fiercely. "I don't. I think when you're gone, you're gone." He looked surprised, as if this revelation was new and unwelcome. "Sorry. I don't even know why I'm telling you. I must be going jungle-mad up here."

"It's the insects. They never stop. Sometimes the frequency is so high our crime rate triples."

Pope laughed, then caught himself. "I can believe that."

"I used to bring my dog up here a lot, but she's old now and she can't walk properly. If there was anything here, she would have known." I placed the keys on his makeshift stool. "I'll leave these with you. For your undelicates."

"Indelicates," he said. "You didn't answer my question."

"About the ghosts?"

He nodded.

"Everything is changing," I said. "I'm not sure what I believe anymore."

12

The night after I left the Laundromat keys with Pope, I woke suddenly just before midnight. The quaver of a sound was still in the air. Had I screamed? The door creaked open. It was only Gypsy, nosing the gap. I sat up. Gypsy slugged her weight onto the bed; she could no longer jump. Her gray muzzle pushed into my shoulder, and she fell into an immediate, fitful sleep. She could no longer hear—how did she know? I shaped my body to the curve of her spine and lay listening to the beetles butting at the window.

When I was small, Trudy used to kill my monsters. She never told me they weren't real, like Ma, who'd stumble into my bedroom, switch on the light, and revel in my squinting. In the morning there was a punishment for waking her. It was the same, every time: Ma saying, *See? There's nothing here*, her arms wide to show me that there was truth and safety in light.

But Trudy, whose bedroom was next to mine and who

usually heard me first, would never flick the switch. She'd creep in, crouched and ready for combat, because it was entirely possible a monster was eating her sister alive and to hell with it, she was coming in. She collected weapons and lined them up beneath my bed: a smooth, club-ended stick she'd found in the forest, a plastic toy saber, a spray bottle of clear liquid she'd labeled *H_2SO_4 MONSTER ACID!!*, and a homemade garrote she'd fashioned from two sticks and a twisted strand of fencing wire.

The door would open a crack. Her hands always arrived first, haloed by the hallway light, held up in front of her face, poised for a karate chop. She'd press a finger to her lips and nod—*Yes, I see it*—and move stealthily toward my bed, her fierce stare fixed on the corner of the room. She would choose her weapon and arm me with the spray bottle. Our battles were long but mostly silent—we didn't want to wake Ma—and I never had to leave the warmth of my bed. There was just the metallic scrape of the garrote as it cut air, or the whip of the saber when Trudy carved her initials, Zorro style, into a monster's dying flesh.

I got too old for screaming. Later, when I would sneak into Trudy's room, her bed was empty. She didn't lie, she didn't fake her shape under the blankets, and she didn't lock her door to keep us out. She simply stayed out all night and made no excuse or apology for it.

Ma and Trudy yelled at each other when Trudy finally

came home, proving at least half of Ma's theory: There was truth in daylight. It was loud, and ugly. For the first time I noticed that Dad preferred the sawdust stink of the shed. I learned new words for girls who stayed out all night, and I'll never forget the sound Trudy made when Ma pulled her by the hair.

Ma cried when Trudy left, but we swung into an easier rhythm, and, for a while, nobody fought. Years later, on the first night I stayed out way past curfew and came home reeking of beer, I decided I wouldn't stand up to Ma the way Trudy had. I'd take my punishment and wait it out. God knew Trudy's tactics never worked. I'd try something different. But Ma was snoring when I staggered in, and the hallway light was on—her only concession to my childish fears. A day later there was a new, clean space on the wall. She'd taken down the last remaining picture of Trudy and me. That's how I knew she knew.

I don't think Ma cried when I left. She'd gone from yelling to silence, and we all carried on that tradition. When Trudy came back from overseas, Ma was cool, unsurprised, almost civil. She behaved the same way when I blurted that I was moving in with Trudy. By then the hallway wall was bare, apart from my parents' wedding photo. Maybe Dad was the only one who hadn't disappointed her, but . . . in a way, he had left too.

Gypsy groaned and huffed in her sleep. If I didn't get her

out of there, I'd be awake all night. I'd started to be afraid of wakefulness: In the middle of the night, nothing became something, became everything. I sorted and shuffled my worries, fretting. Now there were too many things I couldn't change back.

I got up and went to the bathroom. I brushed my teeth for the second time and hoped that going through my bedtime routine again would reset my clock. But as quiet as I was trying to be, somebody else wasn't bothering.

I listened outside Trudy's door, straining to hear above the cricket song. I slid down the wall and sat with my bare legs against the cool floorboards. It sounded like Trudy was crying in her sleep. I checked the kitchen. The phone was right where it should be. I went back to listen again. Trudy moaned.

I took a spray bottle from the bathroom and an old wire coat hanger from my bedroom. It was entirely possible she needed saving from her own monsters—at the very least she would find it funny. I was so sure.

I practiced swishing my initials in the hall. I was going in. I turned the handle.

If I had to pinpoint the exact moment I went over the edge, I'd say it was this one. Trudy wasn't alone, and she wasn't crying. She didn't need me, and she didn't need saving—she had her ranger, and it was pretty clear they were a good fit. Now I had all the more reason to keep Pope to myself. Trudy was getting some, paying the bills, behaving like a responsible adult for the first time in her life, and, as was tradition in my family, I'd have to pick a corner, any corner, as long as someone wasn't already in it.

"This is the smallest car in the universe. My knees are touching my ears," I whined, inching the car away from the curb. Jeremiah had stuck oversize pink learner's plates on the car because his mother's printer cartridge only had magenta ink. "Will they give me a real license or a Barbie one?" I braked and parked again.

"The manual says it qualifies as a car."

"Does it say anything about codrivers?" I asked, jabbing my thumb at Roly, who was in the backseat. "He's making me nervous."

"That's ripe," Roly said. "I'm shitting my pants back here."

"You mean rich," Jeremiah intoned. "Unless you're talking about your pants. This thing won't go over a hundred, so unless we hit a tree sideways, you're probably going to survive. And they'll turn the plastic surgeon away because the impact will accidentally fix your face."

"*Bwahaha.* What's the last thing to go through a bug's mind when it hits your windshield? Its arse. *Bwahaha,*" Roly snorted.

"Your pants will be the first thing to go through the back of my head when we hit a tree. Stink it up, Roly; you'll have the last laugh."

"Shut up! Everybody just shut up." I tried to concentrate on coordinating my hands and feet. Everything was backward. On my bike, I was used to changing gear with my left foot and accelerating with my right hand. But in Meredith Jolley's car I had to change gears with my left hand and accelerate with my right foot. "I need somewhere to practice without getting in the way of traffic." What I really wanted was to get out of my old street before I ran into Ma or Dad.

"Find a dirt road," Roly suggested.

"They all go uphill. If she drops the clutch, the car will end up in somebody's living room."

"So, you drive it up and she drives down."

"Different action, same result."

"I have an idea," I said. "Here, you drive." I started to climb across to the passenger seat and realized Jeremiah was so tightly packed in he'd have no chance of switching places without peeling back the roof. We got out and changed spots. "Let's go to the old drive-in," I directed. "You remember where it is?"

"That could work." Jeremiah nodded to himself. "Okay." He put the car into gear and drove off.

"Is that still there?" Roly asked. "I thought they were going to bulldoze it."

"It is," I said, without elaborating. When we reached the road Mr. Broadbent had led me to, I pointed. "Turn. Turn here."

"It's not this turnoff; it's the next one." Jeremiah seemed

to know where he was going. He pulled into what looked like an entrance to a farm property—just a cattle guard and a rusted swing gate. "I've always suspected I was conceived here," he said.

"How could you possibly know that?" Roly scoffed. "Were you there? Anyway, I can't imagine Meredith sharing details. Legend has it you were an immaculate conception."

"It's true," I agreed, remembering what Trudy had said about Meredith Jolley never having seen a penis.

"It was my conception. Of course I was there." Jeremiah shrugged. "Mum always cries when she hears 'Arthur's Theme,'" he added mysteriously.

"Do you ever wonder . . . ?" I asked, and stopped. "Sorry. I just can't imagine not knowing who my father is."

"No, it's okay," Jeremiah said calmly. "It's comforting enough that I don't resemble anybody in Mobius, and nobody has come forward to claim paternity. That's all I need to know."

"There's no sign," I said, to change the subject. "Why the cattle guard? This doesn't even look like the right place."

We climbed out and surveyed the padlocked gate. Weeds had woven through the mesh, and the guard was useless, packed with dirt and more weeds. The gate looked as if it hadn't been opened in a long time.

"I assume the cattle guard was to keep the cows out because cow shit would be unwelcome at the drive-in."

Roly and I groaned. Jeremiah took everything so seriously. Even when he was being funny, I wasn't sure whether it was intentional. I certainly didn't expect it when he kicked the gate, violently, explosively. Roly and I took a step back.

"Ease up, J. That's vandalism."

"It's some kind of felony," I agreed.

"It's abandoned," Jeremiah said, panting. "It doesn't count."

"I've got an idea," I offered. "Between us we could probably lift the Barbie car over the gate."

"Or we could go cross-country," Roly said. "Ram the fence."

It took three kicks for Jeremiah to loosen a rotting fence post and pluck it out of the damp soil. He coiled the fence wire around it and set the post aside in a tidy roll. And that's how we ended up driving Meredith Jolley's miniature car down an embankment and up the other side, Jeremiah shoving the rear bumper like a draft horse and Roly steering the car through the gap in the fence. Once we were through, Jeremiah hopped back in and followed the driveway, dodging potholes and fallen branches.

"All we need is beer and popcorn," I said as we caught the first glimpse of the screen. In daylight, it was wide and gray, taller than I'd thought. The asphalt was crumbly, broken into a thousand puzzle pieces. Automatically I began counting the robot speakers, but I had to start over each time somebody spoke.

"I don't think this is a good idea," Jeremiah said, as the

car rocked over the destroyed asphalt. "I mean, in theory it was, but this place is a wreck. We're going to split a tire." He parked next to the decrepit brick building in the middle of the drive-in. "One hundred and twelve."

Roly got out first. "Hey, look at this!"

"One hundred and twelve what?" I asked.

"Speakers." Jeremiah yanked on the hand brake. "I can see your mouth moving. One hundred and twelve speakers, if that's what you're counting. You can double-check, but I already did, twice."

I blushed and bit back something nasty he didn't deserve. It's not like he hadn't witnessed my craziness before, and been a part of it, but acknowledging it so . . . *offhandedly* . . . made me cringe.

"Are you getting out?"

I did, ungracefully, with my chin in the air.

"Check it out. Hey, J, come here." Roly had swept an arc of dirt from a high window. "Boost me," he said, and bent his leg.

Jeremiah lifted him, one-handed.

"You've got to see this!"

Roly had always been excitable. In middle school it was endearing; in high school, not so much. He had no boundaries. In an area school that big—over twelve hundred students—it was dangerous. Nobody could stand his habit of butting into conversations or venturing into areas of the school grounds that had been appropriated by a particular group. Eventually, people turned on him. He started walking behind Jeremiah Jolley, which spared him the brunt since Jeremiah was a far bigger target. He took the seat behind the school bus driver, which amounted to voluntary exile, and Jeremiah went with him. They'd seemed okay to me. They were always together, so it wasn't *dire*. When Jeremiah left, Roly was on his own. He became reserved, but in an odd way, as if somebody had screwed his lid on too tight.

Jeremiah hoisted me up next.

I peered through the grime. I could just make out a few tattered boxes on the floor and a cobwebby contraption with spools and reels and levers.

"You're stuck here for a few more weeks, J," Roly said from below, "until your mum gets her head right. I've got nothing better to do. Jack's been sacked. . . ."

Jeremiah lowered me down.

I dusted off my hands. "I was let go. That's different."

"Whatever you want to call it, you've got some time on your hands. You might as well spend it up here with me and J, watching porn on the big screen."

I didn't answer right away. I was thinking about that screen and how it might look if it was white again.

"Yeah, maybe," I said. "I've got other things I should be doing." I needed another job. I had to figure out a way to pay Trudy back.

Roly squinted through the rectangle he'd shaped with his

fingers. Suddenly he let go and slapped his thigh. "Sorry. I forgot. You've probably got better things to do with the rest of summer than hang out with the bottom-feeders. But then again, maybe things have changed now you need a driving instructor and a *car*."

"Bottom-feeders? What does that even mean?" I turned to Jeremiah for support, but he seemed familiar with the sentiment behind Roly's attack. He looked uncomfortable, not confused. "Tell me. I don't get it." But I did. Kind of. I was starting to. Small towns have long memories, narrow shoulders, and big chips on them. "Oh, wait. What, are we still in high school?"

Roly stood up and shoved his hands deep in his pockets. "What do you think, J? How's the water flowing under *your* bridge?"

Jeremiah wasn't listening. He stared up at the screen.

Roly jabbed a thumb in Jeremiah's direction. "He doesn't want to ruin his chances of spending time with a real live girl, especially one with tight jeans and big . . . *you* know." He stalked off with his hands in his pockets.

"You don't know me by how tight my jeans are!" I yelled. I stopped myself from picking up a clump of asphalt and firing it at him.

It would have been easy enough to walk back home. I didn't need the drama. Roly half turned, his lip curled. Jeremiah was having a staring contest with the screen, and I was suddenly hyperconscious of everything: the monotonous beat of a Mobius summer, a beat I used to know and move to without thinking about the steps, the loneliness, the money worry, the hate, the dragging ache of loving somebody who didn't love me back. I couldn't stop waiting for Luke, because waiting was all I knew. I'd let my world shrink down to that. It was an addiction, and everyone knew the only way to kick a habit was to replace it with something else.

I clapped my hands twice. "So, whoever gets the door open can choose the premiere."

Roly whooped and took a ten-meter run-up to give the door a flying kick, only to land on his back. Jeremiah took two sideways steps and nudged the door with one enormous foot. It disintegrated.

Roly and Jeremiah bumped fists.

"What do you think?" Roly asked.

Jeremiah considered the equipment and shook his head. "I think this could take a while," he said.

13

I flipped over on the couch to let blood flow into my left side, which had gone numb. I wouldn't have been surprised if the sore spot on my hip was the start of a bedsore. Christmas was in two weeks. I couldn't have afforded a tree even if I'd wanted one. Astrid had set up a row of raggedy potted pines along the front of Bent Bowl Spoon. By the next morning they were all gone. Stolen. I could have told her it would happen and saved her the trouble, but it wasn't my problem anymore. I was resigned to letting this Christmas slip away; it was just another day with too many rules and traditions.

We'd spent last Christmas around Ma's table. Trudy's first Christmas home in years, and we marked it as a family—not talking, barely eating, making volcanoes out of lumpy mashed potato and picking strings of pork from our teeth. I remembered Dad reaching for a newspaper and snapping it open. The crack sounded like a starter's gun, except this was a challenge to see how long we could all keep the hair-trigger balance between rudeness and civility.

After the table had been cleared, I helped Ma with the dishes. Trudy was asleep, her feet up on the good couch. Ma slammed plates. She muttered to herself. She beseeched the ceiling and asked God what she had done to deserve such slovenly children, which, unfairly, included me. Ma was absurdly pleased that every complaint she'd ever made about Trudy was justified. Her fury built. The day ended with Trudy throwing the few things she'd unpacked back into her suitcase. This time she only made it down the road, and now here we were, supposedly living the dream.

"*Roll me ooo-ver in the clooo-ver, roll me over, lay me down, and do it again,*" Trudy sang as she wiped dust from the bookshelf.

"Shut. *Up*," I called from the couch. There was a documentary on the TV about the migration of the Christmas Island crabs.

"Nobody's gonna rain on my pa-*raaade*."

"I liked you more when you were mean," I mumbled.

"Have you done anything about getting a job?" she asked, leaning against the door frame. "Because I'm getting *jack* of paying your rent." She smirked. "Get it? But seriously, you might have to move back with Ma."

My heart bottomed out. "Serious?"

"I'm just messing with you. As if I would send you back."

I laughed, but not too hard.

"Max has given me a pay raise. He says I pull more on the OTB than the others combined. I'm a lucky charm. I read the horses' names when they're placing bets and tell them which ones I like. By the way, we got the gas bill. It's on the fridge." She flicked a casual wave behind her. Her hair had fresh blond streaks. "Thom's taking me for Indian tonight. Hey, we should get a tree."

Trudy had started bookending unpleasant news with chit-chat. I knew to look for the sly pinch in the middle, but it was her comment about a tree that stung more than the gas bill. Trees were cheerful. Trees were meant to have gifts put under them. Gifts were meant to be returned. To return a gift I needed money, and to receive one I needed friends. Or family. This was going to be the worst Christmas ever.

"I hope you don't mind Thom staying over so much. It's too hard to spend time together when he has to drive all the way home to Burt. My hours are crazier than usual."

Lucky her, to have and to hold whenever she felt like it. I linked my fingers and twisted them until they hurt. We'd traded places, couldn't she see?

Ranger Thom had stayed over six nights in a row, ever since my forced entry into Trudy's bedroom. He was tall and thin with legs so bowed you could see acres of daylight between them. His fair hair was close-shaved, and he touched his forehead whenever he answered Trudy, as if he was tipping an invisible hat. He reminded me of Goose, from *Top Gun*, minus the shades. I was too embarrassed to get to know him better, though I was well acquainted with his arse.

"You should put some clothes on. It's after four. Thom will be here soon."

I gestured at my drawstring pajama pants and tank top. "I've got clothes on." I tried to run my fingers through my snarly hair, and they got stuck. "The female crabs release their eggs at the turn of high tide during the last quarter of the moon," I pronounced. "They all wait on the beach for just the right conditions."

"Fascinating. Clever crabs."

"The males cut and run after mating."

Trudy gave me a tender look. "I'm going to vacuum. Do you want me to do your room?"

Don't be nice, I thought. "I'll do it later. Stay out of my room." I fixed my stare on the screen. As the crabs crossed a road, a truck ran over them. The documentary makers had set up a camera at ground level to film the carnage; I wondered whether they'd got the footage in one take or asked the driver to back up for a better angle. I tried to calculate how many crabs would be killed in four takes. Four seemed like a reasonable average. Four times several thousand crabs for seven seconds of footage illustrating real-time roadkill. Bastards.

"They close the roads. You know, to protect the crabs during migration," Trudy said. "Oh, Ma wants us around there for Christmas dinner. We have to bring a dessert. So, anyway, they shut down the roads, and the locals have to get around on foot. The crabs get right of way. I don't know why they keep showing this bit," she finished, wrinkling her nose.

I turned away from the screen and buried my face in a pillow. I moaned, "Tell me when it stops," and I didn't mean the crabs.

"Surely you have better things to do than traipse up and down this mountain every day," Pope said. He'd rolled his pants above the knee and torn the sleeves from his shirt. He was starting to bleed into the colors of the forest, or maybe he was disappearing. "You've got so much to look forward to. You're young. And you're pretty when you're not scowling and kicking things."

"I don't. And I am not." I kicked the base of a tree with my toe. "Surely *you* have better things to do?" I countered. "You've been up here for weeks now. Don't you have a real life somewhere?" I dropped a brown paper bag just outside his tent flap. "Tofu salad," I said. "What are you hiding in here, anyway?"

"Salad?" He smiled and grabbed the bag. "You might have saved me from scurvy."

"You look happier," I said, backing away, watching him eat. "That's good." I scowled.

Pope stopped chewing and said, "I'm not gunning for happy. I'll settle for peace."

"Yeah. Me, too." I sat on the ground, mindless of the dampness seeping through my shorts. "Pope?"

"Yeah."

"What if there's only a certain amount of everything—you know, like money, how it changes hands, or like water. There's only so much of it, and if you gain something, it must be taken from someone else, and when you lose something, it means somebody else has gained."

"Forest philosophy," he groaned. "Lord help me."

"I'm serious."

"What are we talking about?"

"I don't know . . . love? Happiness? Good and evil?"

"Well, for one thing, water and money are tangible. I don't believe we can measure those other things."

"It just feels like we can't all be winning at the same time. My sister is happy—and I hate it."

"If your theory is true—and I'm skeptical—it's probably not a proximity thing. She's not taking from your bucket just because she's family."

"It feels like it."

"Maybe that just makes you a shitty person with a hole in your bucket," he said. "You should try being a decent human being sometime."

"Wow," I said. "That's harsh."

"Look, I'm sorry. I'm not even talking about you, really. Forget it." He stood. "Walk?"

"I just walked two kilometers to get here."

"Come on. Clear your head." He set off without me.

I watched him haul his body up the track, toward the ridge, as if his shoes were full of mud.

"Do you like it up here?" I asked, catching up.

"God, no."

"Then why? Why do you stay?"

"It's something I have to do. Haven't you ever done something because there's no way around, so you have to go through?" He looked back at me. "It's awful up here at night. You have no idea—there are so many noises, and bugs, bugs everywhere. It's . . . very unpleasant."

Only Pope would describe fear as "unpleasant."

I wondered where he came from. I imagined he had the kind of parents who lived in a house with hundred-year-old ivy growing on the outside walls and who slurped tea from fourth-generation heirloom teacups. But Pope wouldn't care about those things. He was the rebel of the family—he would have dropped out of university to teach English to refugees or save endangered marsupials, or campaign for human rights. His hoity-toity parents were disappointed in him, but they loved him anyway; they funded his travels on the understanding that he come home for weddings and funerals. He'd loved a girl once, but she'd broken his heart. His beaten-up car had once belonged to a dear friend who'd left it to him in his will, and he was sentimental about things like that. That was as far as I'd got with my theories, and none of them explained why he was in the forest, putting up with bugs in his sleeping bag, and listening to the wind play through that solitary bottle.

"Of course I have an idea. I live here," I said. "I know why I'm here. But what about you?"

"Why *are* you still here, then?" he asked, turning it back on me. "I grew up in a small town like this. I couldn't wait to get out."

The edges of the life I'd dreamed up for him blurred and shifted. Scrap the ivy—the teacups could stay.

"I guess I don't know any different."

"Ignorance is bliss."

"Ignorance is boring," I said. "But I'll find out one day. I have plenty of time." I smiled, but he only turned and started back down the hill.

"I washed my clothes," he called. "You were right about that middle machine. It shredded my jacket."

"I warned you."

"I know. I was in a hurry so I loaded all three at once." He reached into his pocket. "I found this." He handed me a single pearl earring.

"Oh," I said, recognizing it. "I know where the other one is."

He seemed unsurprised. "Well. You'd better be off, then." He surveyed the patch of open sky above us. "It'll be getting dark soon. Gosh, the nights are long here."

I nodded. I'd stopped being offended by him. "It's the ridge. It blocks out the sun. You're camped right in the armpit of hell. My dad says there's nothing else to do but sleep in Mobius, which is why it suits drunks and narcoleptics."

"I think I'd like your dad," he said, chuckling. Then he seemed to remember he wasn't supposed to laugh and asked, "You haven't told anybody about me being up here?"

"No."

"I appreciate it, and the visits. Like I said, you must have better things to do."

I shrugged. "It's no big deal—I come up here all the time anyway. If someone asks, I'll tell them you're communing with the ghosts." His expression changed again, and I was worried I'd upset him. "I don't sleep much these days," I added in a hurry. "And you're my friend."

"I suppose I am," he said.

14

The next time, we took Roly's pickup. In the back we'd stashed some borrowed tools, a couple of paint rollers, and some cleaning supplies, plus a carton of beer. We were only missing white paint from our supply list. Since we couldn't pool enough money or fuel to drive to the paint store, I volunteered to break into my dad's shed.

"Couldn't she just ask?" Roly said.

"She doesn't go in the house," Jeremiah said.

"But it's a shed."

"I don't think that decision is based on an aversion to particular buildings, but you'd have to ask her."

"So how does she know there's any paint in there?"

"It's a shed, Roland. The likelihood of paint is worth investigating."

Roly nodded, as if it all made complete sense. I was getting used to being left out of their conversations, as if I was a coma patient who couldn't hear anything they said.

We waited at Jeremiah's house until both my parents' cars were gone. I couldn't be sure of their routines anymore—I only knew most places were within walking distance, and if Ma had bothered to get into her car at all, it was likely she'd be gone for a while. I didn't mind so much about getting caught by Dad, but the same theory applied.

"What now?" Roly said. "Do we come too?"

"I'll go by myself," I said. "Just in case."

When I told them I'd break in, I may have exaggerated—I knew there was a key in the hanging plant outside the door. The problem was finding the paint. Dad was still hoarding wood for his carvings. It was stacked along the rear wall, and now it had begun to spill into his workshop area. There was an inch of sawdust underfoot. I loved the smell. It reminded me of playing hide-and-seek and winning. Nothing had changed in there, except the wood took up more space, which meant that he was using less or collecting more. On the tool wall behind the bench, he had drawn around the shapes of hammers and chisels and mallets so they each had their own, exact, place to hang. I ran my finger through the dust on the workbench and left a deliberate trail leading to my handprint.

The stereo was new. I'd heard it, but now I could see he'd mounted monstrous speakers in opposite corners. I switched it on, and bass vibrated through the shed, clumps of congealed sawdust swirling and dancing. I jumped.

"Shit!" I fumbled to turn it off.

No paint in the metal cupboard near the door, but I did find a box full of old toys Dad had made: a checkerboard, peg puppets, an abacus, and a bag full of miniature wooden doll furniture that had belonged to Trudy first, then me. I pushed my hand deep into the bag and searched until my hand closed around the familiar shape of the doll's toilet; I drew it out and opened the hinged lid. It was faded and crumbly but still there—Trudy's brown Play-Doh, which she had rolled into a coil and pressed into the bottom of the bowl. I didn't know whether to laugh or cry, faced with proof of a memory that was so acute, yet so far away that I wasn't sure if it had been real.

I rummaged for more treasures, losing time as each wave of remembering hit. I found a battered suitcase with *Jack* written on the handle and snapped open the catches. Stuffed inside were dozens of small, wrapped bundles. Inside those were old drawings, macaroni necklaces, and bits of clay figurines I'd made at school.

Eventually, I found the paint inside the broken freezer, the last place I thought to look.

"Got it," I said, panting.

Jeremiah and Roly were sitting on Meredith Jolley's front verandah, not moving, not speaking.

I reckoned there were about ten liters of white paint left—probably not enough, but it was a start. My hand was indented with a purple crease from the metal handle of the paint tin. I'd heaved it back to Jeremiah's house, along with the bag of doll's furniture, three of Dad's wooden sculptures, the abacus, and, in my pocket, Trudy's cat's-eye marble I'd coveted since I was three.

I'd got rid of all the reminders of my life before—now I was stealing them back.

Jeremiah saw me coming and jumped up. He took the bucket and nodded at the bag. "What's the other stuff?"

I massaged the blood back into my fingers. "Just some things that belong to me."

"Huh."

Roly yawned and stretched. "Somewhere, people are leading productive, meaningful lives. Have we even considered if this is legal?"

"I've considered it," Jeremiah said. "Worst-case scenario—we could be prosecuted for improvement of public property." He lifted the bucket into the back of Roly's pickup and stowed my loot behind the passenger seat. "Beer's getting warm. Ready?"

Jeremiah drove, Roly surfing in the back, holding on to the roll bar. I rode in the back too, with the bucket pinned between my knees and the roller held aloft like a triton. We passed Astrid, who was writing specials on the front window of Bent Bowl Spoon, and Ma, who drove by in the opposite direction, upright and joyless. I waved at Ma. I waved at the closed blinds in Alby's flat and felt guilty that I had shirked even the minor responsibility of three afternoons a week—but in a moment the guilt was gone. I even waved at Astrid, who put her hands on her hips. I was young and free, and nothing could stick.

"You crazy kids!" yelled Mrs. Gates, smiling.

We cruised down Main Street. As we passed the pub, Roly let go of the roll bar. "We're crazy kids!" he shouted, and held his arms above his head.

The sun, high overhead, looked like it would never sink. The three of us, unlikely friends, were on our way to snatch back a wasted summer; nothing could touch us, not even me, who had a gift for ruining everything. This new Mobius was a copy of the original, only better.

Warm beer hits twice as hard as cold, especially on an empty stomach. A couple of hours later, our productivity had slowed. Jeremiah had become obsessed with the equipment, and he hadn't emerged from the projector room. Roly and I painted the screen. So far we'd finished most of the bottom section, except for one corner. We sat on the platform, legs swinging, drinking the last few beers.

"It's looking good," Roly said.

I disagreed. "Its glory days are over. Some things you can't bring back." I thought of Mr. Broadbent. "The past is the past is the past. God, I'm smashed."

"It's a long way down," Roly said. He kicked off one shoe and watched, fascinated, as it fell. "This doesn't look very safe." He wobbled the railing in front of us. It groaned, and rusted chunks broke away, dropping into the weeds below.

"Don't!" I felt woozy. I scooted backward, leaned up against the dry corner of the screen, and closed my eyes.

"I won't know if I can get it to work until we have power," Jeremiah called up to us. "Why have you stopped?"

My eyes creaked open. He had finally come out of the room, coated with dirt and sweat. He frowned at the top of the screen. For a smart guy he couldn't see the obvious.

"We can't reach," I called back. "We're too short."

"We're too wasted," Roly said, and flopped onto his side.

Jeremiah climbed the ladder and inspected our work, and us. From his sour expression, both were way below standard. "Don't roll off and die," he said, nudging Roly with his foot.

"That would be very inconsiderate," I agreed. I figured Jeremiah had thirty kilos on Roly and me—that was the only possible explanation for him being able to stand, let alone pick up the roller and carry on painting after all that warm beer.

I closed my eyes again and kept them shut even when I heard the whisper of a wet brush, slopping paint into my dry corner. "Do you want me to move?" I mumbled.

"No," he said. "Stay there."

The brush kept moving. Lulled by the hum of insect

song and by the booze in my blood, I let myself go limp. I dreamed we were all asleep on the platform, curled up on our sides, while the forest grew tentacles that wrapped around us, scooping us up into hammocks.

I could have stayed in the fantasy hammock forever, but I leaned forward just in time to throw up over the edge of the platform.

Roly stirred and sat up. "Are you okay?" Half his face was sunburnt, the other half patterned by the knots in the wood.

I laughed and coughed and threw up again. "Sorry."

"Don't be. I may join you. Where's J?"

I levered myself into a half-standing position and hung on to the wobbly rail. "I think I need to go home." It was getting dark, which shouldn't have surprised me, but given the time I'd lost, passed out, it was unexpected.

Headlights came on. The pickup moved and came to a stop near the bottom of the ladder. Roly skidded down on his backside. Jeremiah offered to carry me, but I made it down by myself.

"Are you okay to drive?" I asked him.

"I only had three. You two knocked off most of the carton," he said.

"That explains a lot," I moaned. My temples throbbed.

Roly got in the back and lay flat like a starfish. "I want my mother."

"I want my mother too," I said.

Jeremiah passed me a bottle of tepid water and helped me into the front seat. "I'll go slowly," he said. "Tell me if you need me to stop." He drove with one hand, pinning my forehead against the headrest with a huge palm to keep me upright.

"It's okay. I can do it," I told him, but when he let go, my head hit the passenger-side window, and my cheek slid down the glass. I saw the screen, much brighter than it had been when we started, with about a meter from the top still unpainted, and one dirty patch in the bottom right-hand corner left behind, a rough outline of a gray girl, her arms draped over her knees and her head slipping to one side.

"How did I get home?"

Trudy and Thom looked up from where they were cuddling on the banana lounge in front of a movie.

"What time is it?"

"It's almost midnight," Trudy said, wearing her neutral expression. "You've been asleep for about seven hours." She paused the movie and disentangled herself from Thom.

"How do you feel?" Thom asked. "That must be some hangover."

I blushed. With some effort, I focused on his face and blushed again. He was nice-looking, with kind eyes and blondish stubble on his chin, a nice mouth, and a nice nose square in the middle: nice, nice, nice. I went into the kitchen and poured myself a glass of water. I sipped it slowly in case it came back up.

Trudy followed. "You don't have to be rude," she hissed. "He asked you a question."

My brain felt as if it was rattling in my skull. My mouth tasted of beer and vomit. When I commanded my body to move, it did what I asked, but grudgingly and three seconds later. I sipped another mouthful and paused to see what would happen. So far, so good.

"You don't remember anything, do you?"

"Leave me alone," I said. I remembered leaving the drive-in earlier. Nothing after that.

"You stink. Have a shower. And warn me next time if some weird biker person is likely to turn up on my doorstep carrying my wasted sister. I nearly attacked him with a pair of scissors." She pressed a cool hand to my cheek. "You could have been dead for all I knew. That's what I thought at first— you were dead."

"He would hardly have brought me home if I was dead," I said. "So how did I end up in my room?" *Please don't tell me ranger Thom put me there.* At this rate I would never make eye contact again.

"Him. He carried you in there—the biker. What are you doing hanging around people like that? What are you getting into?"

I stepped back. "Can you not yell at me? My head hurts.

And you mean Jeremiah. He's our neighbor, remember?" I refilled the glass and made moves to crawl back into bed. "I can't face a shower right now." I stumbled along the hallway with Trudy close behind.

"*Who?*" she said.

"It was Jeremiah and Roland Bone, so you don't have to worry. Out of the three of us, I'm by *far* the worst influence."

I threw my body onto the bed, which was a mistake—by now my brain was a walnut. I felt it bash around in there as if the fluid had all dried up. I put the pillow over my head. Muffled silence, except for Trudy's breathing, like a birthing cow.

I lifted my head. "God, are you still here? Go be with Thom. I'm fine."

Trudy lunged. She grabbed my arm and dragged me off the bed. I hit the floor, bellowing. Trudy hauled me up from behind, digging her fingers into my armpits and shoving me along in front of her like a sack of manure. At the bathroom door she gave me one hard shove. While I leaned over the sink, she ran the shower.

She elbowed me in, fully clothed, without waiting for the water to run hot.

15

Six days before Christmas, I handed over the last of my money to Trudy. We weren't speaking much, other than to snap at each other about Christmas dinner, which was suddenly a big deal—to her, anyway.

"I'm going to make profiteroles. You know, like cream puffs."

"Knock yourself out," I said.

"I won't be eating any, though," she added, and patted her stomach, as if I needed reminding that I had an incredible disappearing sister. "I'm on a roll." She stared pointedly at me, lying on the couch in my pajamas. "Maybe we should just take a fruit plate."

I turned away. "I don't care. Do whatever you want."

"You should try caring sometime. Like, about how you look, how you speak, and about that permanent arse-shaped dent you've made in the couch."

"I'm getting an education."

"Watching B-grade documentaries?"

"Did you know, seahorses are monogamous and mate for life?"

"Whoopee-doo."

"A blue whale's tongue can weigh more than an elephant."

"Fascinating. And pointless."

"Just putting my arse-shaped dent into perspective for you."

"I give up." Trudy shook her head.

I stopped feeding Ringworm. I hoped he would just fade away, or at least start turning up at somebody else's window. I stopped counting because there was so little left *to* count. I set up the abacus on my windowsill to keep me from sitting there, and one night I put the doll's toilet on Trudy's pillow to remind her that things didn't cease to exist just because you outgrew them, packed them in a cupboard, or found something new.

Four days before Christmas, Trudy told me that Mads was moving in with us. Trudy couldn't afford the rent and bills without help, and, since she and Mads worked together, they could carpool to save fuel—oh, and would I mind moving into the junk room, since I was freeloading?

"It's tiny. It doesn't count as a bedroom," I moaned.

"It will have to do."

"Are you asking me, or telling me?"

"We don't have a choice," she said.

"You mean *I* don't have a choice."

"Shift your stuff, Jacklin."

Thom was kind enough to help me move my furniture. He was *always* nice, even when Trudy and I were spitting and tearing tufts out of each other. He never took her side, and he even threw the odd sympathetic smile my way.

"There's not going to be much room for anything other than your bed in here," he said.

"I know. It's a cell with a window."

"I've got a little sister," he confided as we slid my mattress along the hallway. "We get along much better now that we live apart."

"Trudy wasn't here for half my life," I exaggerated. "We hardly know each other. I was basically an only child."

"Where was she?" he asked.

He really didn't know.

"Traveling," I said. "Backpacking." At that moment Trudy came out of the kitchen, and I followed through with some of Ma's choice descriptions. "Gallivanting. Shirking responsibility. Slack-arsing around." I waited until she tuned in, then I added, "Whoring around Europe."

Trudy gasped and hit me on the arm.

"Ow!"

I punched her back. It must have hurt, because my fist throbbed and her eyes welled up.

"Separate corners, ladies," Thom said.

He didn't need to tell me. We were already there.

Mads moved in the next day. She turned out to be an unexpected ally—she was a fan of my all-day pajamas and agreed with me that being with Thom was making Trudy lose her edge. And she watched documentaries with me for hours.

"So what's a group of porcupines?" Mads asked.

"A prickle. But the best one is—get this—a *flamboyance of flamingos*. There's also a murder of crows, a bale of turtles, a knot of frogs, a wisdom of wombats, and a shiver of sharks."

"No way."

"Yes way. And let's not forget a fever of stingrays, a memory of elephants, and a tower of giraffes."

"Where do you get all this stuff?"

I tapped my skull.

"You are a bloat of hippopotamuses!" Trudy called from the kitchen.

Mads got up reluctantly. "I have to get ready for work. It's my turn to drive. Will you record that one about the lemurs for me?"

"Of course. I've seen it twice, but I could watch it again."

Trudy threw Mads's car keys at her head. "Pull your finger out. You're going to make me late."

"Scientists have discovered that rats laugh."

"No way."

• • •

We were late for Christmas lunch. Trudy nagged me to help her make the pro ... prof ... cream puffs. She'd fussed for ages, but they deflated as soon as she took them out of the oven. We tried to puff them back up by injecting extra cream, but they fell apart before we'd even left the house.

Of course, it was my fault we were late. My fault that the cream puffs exploded.

Ma opened the door looking harried. "Girls," she said. She wore a yellow apron, and her gray-blond hair was parted in the middle, braided, and coiled at the nape of her neck.

"*Fräulein,*" I said.

Trudy jerked her elbow into my ribs. "*Frau,*" she hissed.

Ma patted her hair. She looked nervous. I caught the scent of her hairspray, mixed in with the familiar smells of Christmas: spice, doughy Yorkshire puddings, the meaty odor of the perennial pork that Trudy and I both hated but Ma had insisted on serving up, every year, for as long as I could remember. I prayed there was applesauce.

"Merry Christmas," Trudy said, and held out her bowl of limp salad.

"Merry Christmas," I echoed, offering my tray of cream shrapnel.

Ma recovered and examined Trudy: thinner, dressed conservatively in three-quarter pants and a white shirt, her makeup just a dab of color here and there. Then me: My hair had grown out to a jagged mess, and the color was a startling orange. Nothing I owned complemented my hair, or vice versa, so I opted for a green dress over torn black tights. At the very least, I looked festive in a Halloweenish way. My outfit, my expression, those oozing cream puffs—it all added up to a sight so offensive Ma took a step back.

I showed my teeth.

"Your friend Thom is already here," Ma said, and held the door open to let us in. "He was early," she said witheringly.

Trudy, to her credit, didn't bite. She breezed past Ma, gripping her salad. I thrust my tray into Ma's hands and followed. I counted nine ghostly rectangles on the wall just inside the door.

"Little stranger." Dad told me off with a smile and drew me in for a hug. He paid no attention to how I looked, but then he never had. He grabbed Trudy, too, but she was halfway through an apology to Thom, and she pulled out of Dad's embrace.

Thom had a plateful of Ma's mince pies in front of him. I knew from experience that they smelled heavenly and tasted mostly like orange peel once you got past the sugar and the pretty crust. He caught my eye and made a face. I put my fingers down my throat just as Ma was checking me over again.

I slumped into a chair and popped a bonbon with myself.

Dad smacked my hand. "You're not a kid anymore. Your mother will want you to leave them until after we've eaten." He poured wine for everybody except me.

Once again, I was too old for some things and not old enough for others.

I expected the next half hour or so would be barely tolerable—Ma would get busy in the kitchen, and Dad would make dad jokes. Trudy and Thom would play footsies under the table until the food was served and the real fun could begin. But my theory was blown when the doorbell rang.

Nobody seemed surprised. I heard Ma open the front door and speak quietly. Seconds later, Meredith Jolley was standing uncertainly in the doorway with Jeremiah behind her. One of his big hands rested on her frail shoulder.

"Merry Christmas," Jeremiah said. "Thank you for having us."

Meredith slid into the closest empty chair as if her legs were about to give way. Her long fingernails bit into the edge of Ma's table. She wore an oversize shift dress, a hospital band around her wrist, and rabbit slippers on her feet.

Jeremiah took the seat next to me. The last time I'd seen him, he'd lugged my passed-out body home, and I hadn't bothered to call and thank him. In fact, I'd gone out of my way to avoid him.

"Got plans for New Year's Eve?" he asked.

I shook my head. No Luke—no plans. No life.

"Roly and I are going to camp out and watch the fireworks at Burt's Football Field," he said. "Do you want to come?"

"Okay," I said. "I haven't been for a couple of years."

"Hey, I didn't recognize you when you brought Jack home," Trudy told Jeremiah. "Sorry if I was rude. I thought—"

"No problem," he cut her off. "Understandable."

"Who's for champagne?" Dad asked, and uncorked a bottle.

I pushed a champagne glass in his direction, but he skimmed over the top of it and poured for the others.

Meredith Jolley eyed me steadily, obviously under the influence of some heavy medication. She seemed mesmerized by my green dress and orange hair. I gave her a theatrical twitch in return, and her expression softened. *Oh, hello, other crazy person,* her eyes seemed to say, which left me feeling uncomfortable and ashamed.

Trudy said, "I'll see if Ma needs help in the kitchen."

Dad jerked his head in my direction, which I took to mean that I should offer too. I shredded my bonbon instead, half listening to the drone of conversation.

"How are you, Meredith?" Dad.

". . . better." Meredith.

"I like your slippers." Thom.

"Sorry, her feet are swollen from . . ." Jeremiah.

". . . home for good?" Dad, changing the subject.

"Not yet. Just a day pass. She needs more rest." Valiant Jeremiah.

All the time I was attuned to Ma—flitting in and out of the corner of my vision—the way you can be acutely aware of a spider on the wall. She passed trays of steaming food to Trudy, who brought them to the table. Thom's hand reached out to touch Trudy each time she passed.

"...Jack?"

"Sorry? I wasn't listening."

"What have you been up to?" Dad.

The room fell quiet. Everybody looked at me.

I lost my job. I lie on the couch all day. Turns out I'm not much of a drinker.

"Trudy and I brought prophylactics," I said.

Blank stares.

"They exploded."

"What?" Thom said, laughing.

"They should be okay, though, they're just a bit oozy."

A dazzle of zebras, a wake of buzzards, a bevy of swans—there was probably a collective noun for just about anything, but I couldn't think of one for a group of hostile humans. A fury of . . . something? I squirmed. Under Ma's heritage table, my leg caught on a splinter—it pierced my skin like a hot needle.

"Oh, just . . . *fuck* it!" I said.

Ma slammed down a plate of pork crackling. I couldn't tell if the spitting sound was Ma or the pork. "Out!" she said in a cold and furious voice. "Just . . . out!"

"Ma, calm down, please. It's Christmas." Trudy's new soothing tone was so out of character it made my skin crawl.

I left the table and went outside to sit on the verandah. I

blamed the insects—they were humming at screaming pitch. I blamed Trudy—she had taken my corner in a decisive coup. I blamed Thom for being nice. I blamed Dad for asking stupid questions and Jeremiah for just being there and Meredith Jolley for bringing more crazy into a house that was already way overstocked. I blamed Ma for being unreachable.

The front door opened and closed quietly behind me.

Without turning around, my first guess: Trudy, the new peacekeeper. Second guess: Dad. Third: Jeremiah, for reasons I can't even begin to rationalize, except that he was eminently sensible and kind. Thom: no, he wouldn't pick a side. Ma: no way, not unless she planned to sweep me off the verandah with her broomstick.

"Go away," I said, which covered all guesses.

Meredith Jolley sat down next to me. She kicked off her rabbit slippers and flung them onto the lawn. The elastic had left marks on her swollen feet. She pulled out a packet of cigarettes from the pocket of her dress and offered me one.

I shook my head. "No, thanks."

"You're missing out on your presents. This one is from your mum and dad." She handed me a rectangular package wrapped in silver paper.

"I have no presents for anyone," I said. I slid my finger under the tape and opened one end of the present. Turquoise leather. A purse. I tore off the rest of the paper. It looked classy and smelled expensive—the last thing I wanted or needed. Ma had put a ten-cent piece in the coin compartment—she'd always told me it was bad luck to gift an empty purse. I laughed.

Meredith leaned across and squeezed the splinter out from my thigh with her sharp fingernails. "That must have hurt," she said, wiping the splinter—and a drop of my blood—onto her dress. "I'm not a big fan of pork," she continued. She lit a cigarette and dragged on it. "Do you think we should go back inside and keep pretending?"

I didn't reply, so she answered her own question.

"Fuck it," she said. Barefooted, she crossed the street and sat in the tire swing.

After a minute I joined her, and together we stared at our houses.

"I'm thinking of becoming a vegetarian," Pope said when I handed him a foil-wrapped package of leftover pork.

"How about some soggy roast vegetables?" I offered a second package.

He unwrapped it and sniffed. "That smells like duck fat."

"It is. Okay, then." I tore open the foil and flung the contents of both into the scrub. The pieces scattered, hitting the trees with wet slaps.

"Great."

"The feral pigs will get to it before it stinks up the place," I said. "It's Christmas day. Did you even know that?"

"You don't find the idea of a starving wild pig eating the dead flesh of its obese, corn-fed, caged brethren offensive?" He smiled. "Of course I know it's Christmas. I haven't thought about anything else for days."

"We had lunch at our parents' house," I told him. "It was a disaster. You're probably better off up here by yourself—all this peace and quiet and nobody to tell you what to do."

"That's dumb," he said. "That's not even close to the truth."

"You're not the first person to call me dumb."

He roughed up his hair in frustration. "I'm sorry. I didn't say that. I like the peace and quiet, but I would happily trade both for somebody to tell me what to do."

"I don't understand."

"Forget it." He put up his elbow as if to fend me off.

"How long are you going to stay up here?"

"As long as it takes," he said resolutely. "Not a day more or less."

"Why are you doing this?"

"Penance."

"For what?"

"For being alive." He sighed. "There—now you have it. You can start your countdown."

"I'm done counting," I said. "I've given up trying to control things. I can't change anything, and I can't stop everything from changing."

"That's life," he said. "Counting change."

I chose my next words carefully. "Sometimes I think you're not real. I wonder if I'm going mad like Ebenezer and you're just a ghost. Every time I walk up that path, I think about the time my goldfish died and I wouldn't go near the tank for two days. He was lying on his side on top of the water and his eyes were bulging and he was covered in whitish slime—I could see that from a distance. But as long as I didn't go near the tank, he wasn't really dead."

"What happened?"

"On the third day he was gone. Ma probably flushed him."

"Why am I like your undead goldfish?" He laughed.

I looked at him square on. "Because I wonder if I would do the same thing if I found your tent zipped up one day and you were nowhere to be found? Would I look inside? Or would I keep on walking?"

Pope slowly stretched out a hand. He grabbed one of mine. His was cool and rough. "Am I real enough for you?"

He let go.

16

"You guys are early," I said through the door crack. "It's only four. You told me half past." My hair was dripping. I had dressed for the dust in old denim cutoffs and a black tank top, but I hadn't put on any makeup or packed an overnight bag.

Jeremiah and Roly were on the doorstep, grinning. Gypsy snuffled happily at their feet.

Roly groaned. "You don't need much. We've got two tents and a full cooler. If we don't get there early, we won't get a good spot."

"Come in," I said, and slid the door open. "There's nobody else here. Have a seat." I gestured at the couch.

I hauled Gypsy away by her collar and grabbed some female flotsam from the couch and the floor. I threw it in the laundry sink without bothering to check whose it was. Trudy and I used to borrow each other's clothing, but, now that she was shrinking, she was inching closer to Mads's size ten than my fourteen. Between the three of us, all messy, the house constantly looked like we were having a tag sale.

Jeremiah went straight over to the movies on the bookshelf. Roly spotted a photo album, sat down, and spread it out on his lap.

"Help yourself," I said.

I did my hair and makeup as quickly as I could. It was humid already—the field would be packed and steamy. I threw some track pants and a thin jacket into a bag and took the pillow and quilt from my bed. The moment the bed was stripped, Gypsy began nesting on the mattress. The older she got the more she behaved like a human. I laid some newspaper down in the laundry and filled her food and water bowls. She wouldn't miss me at all.

"I was hoping for some bikini shots," Roly said, flipping through pages of photos. "But these are cool."

I leaned over his shoulder. "These are old," I said. "Nobody in my family takes photos anymore."

I squinted at a blurred shot of Trudy and me, aged around five and eleven, frozen in the middle of star jumps on the trampoline; the two of us, skating on a homemade waterslide in the backyard; sticky fingers in a bowl of chocolate cake batter; Princess Leia bun-heads.

I snapped the album shut and put it back on the shelf.

I knew the photo on the last page of the album had a picture of us both, eleven and seventeen, scowling, turning away from each other. It was fitting: After that was "the Gap." After that was "Trudy's Adventures in Europe" and "Jack-Missing-Trudy Years" closely followed by "Jack Flying under Ma's Radar" and "Riding in Cars with Boys."

Jeremiah had only reached the *L* section of our vast movie collection.

"Shall we go?" I grabbed my keys and stood by the door. Resentment made my throat tighten.

Jeremiah took the pillow and quilt from me and carried them to the car. He had to stoop to get through the doorway. Roly jiggled around like a five-year-old.

"Can I drive?" I asked.

"No!" they answered at the same time.

"Shouldn't you leave a note?" Roly asked.

"I don't answer to anybody," I said. Why bother? Trudy didn't care. I hadn't forgiven her at all. I knew those years would still be missing even if we had pictures.

Burt was a sprawling town built on the flat—a dust bowl in summer, more civilized but less pretty than Mobius. It was where we got our fix of fast food, mall shops, and out-of-town bands at the Crypt, a dingy club in the basement of the old bank. We passed right by the area school on the way in, and I felt strangely nostalgic for a place I never wanted to see again. Jeremiah had been subdued on the ride, leaving it to Roly and me to pick music and chatter. I wondered if he regretted inviting me along. If that was the case, he didn't have to worry—I wouldn't be cramping his style, whatever style that was.

We parked a few streets away and lugged our gear under a row of pine trees outside the perimeter fence, a long way from the action but quieter if we did eventually try to sleep.

Burt's Football Field was already becoming a tent city. The grass was flattened, and the center looked like a giant patchwork quilt, almost completely covered with blankets. Most were unoccupied, set up early to reserve the spot. A two-person band played country twang on the main stage, but nobody was paying much attention—the real band and the real party wouldn't start until eight. Until then it was a case of holding on to our spot, finding food, and pacing the alcohol intake.

"Need help? Jeremiah asked.

"I'm good, thanks." I set up the tent I'd borrowed from Roly and stuffed my bag inside.

"I never get used to this—it's past six and still light," Jeremiah said.

Roly said, "How many people do you think there are? Two thousand?"

"Thereabouts," Jeremiah said. "And more to come. Shall we stake out a spot in the middle, then get something to eat?"

We squeezed into a space and Roly agreed to guard our two and a half meters. We left him sitting cross-legged on a tartan blanket. An evening westerly blew in, stirring up more dust but taking the heat with it. Jeremiah and I lined up for half an hour for lukewarm hot dogs and burnt chips from a van. Jeremiah offered to pay, and I was secretly relieved to put my last ten dollars back into my pocket.

"Do you have a job back in Melbourne?" I asked.

We zigzagged back across the field, juggling food, trying to spot Roly through the growing crowd. I jogged two steps to Jeremiah's one.

"Yeah. I study full-time but I work four nights for a guy's computer business. I just revamp computers from leftover parts."

"Is that what you want to do?"

"No. God, no," he said. "Engineering is my thing. I'll graduate in two more years, but I want to get some practical experience in steel fabrication. So I'll finish my degree and then do a trade as well."

"Engineering. Is that like bridges and stuff? More study, ugh," I said. "I gave up. I couldn't wait for my life to start."

He laughed. "I won't be building any bridges." He stared at me seriously. "And did it?" he asked, but he didn't seem to expect an answer.

I fell in behind him. He parted the crowd easily with his sheer bulk, and clearly he had a better view from up there, because we found Roly, lying on his back, napping. Somebody had built a castle of empty plastic cups next to him.

"Thank God," he said when Jeremiah nudged him with his foot. "I don't think I could have held off a hostile takeover for much longer."

People had begun to squeeze into the gaps, and fights were breaking out over territory. Even the roped-off family-friendly zone had been infiltrated. Onstage, the main act ran a sound check; above, the blue sky faded to black. Roly sat on top of the cooler and chewed his cold hot dog.

Mine was churning in my stomach already. I sipped cautiously on my second beer and found myself watching Jeremiah watching other people. He had a stillness to him that made him stand out even more in such a writhing mass. I used to think it was a protective "freeze and they won't see me" animal instinct, but I saw now that it was an economy of movement—he only moved or spoke if it was necessary—whereas Roly and I couldn't keep still.

Roly handed out cone-shaped party hats. We put ours on, but Jeremiah tossed his aside. The band started to play. We all swung our bodies around to face the stage—Roly alongside me and Jeremiah behind. A group of drunk adults in front of us stood up to dance, and the rest of the crowd followed in one smooth wave. Roly got up and pressed forward, waving his beer around.

I stayed sitting down. I couldn't be bothered fighting for a vantage point, so I shuffled backward to avoid being trampled. Jeremiah moved the cooler to one side as a barrier and pulled me back farther—he just gathered me into him, and I sat between his knees, my back resting against his hard chest. He put one arm across the front of me like a seat belt and took my whole weight. I could tell he was thinking the same thing: If either of us moved, it would become seriously awkward. We stayed in that position for eight songs. By intermission I could tell the difference in timing between the vibration of the bass and the steady bump of his heart.

Roly belched and turned around. His eyebrows pulled up and his mouth turned down. He was deeply unhappy about our entanglement. "Cozy," he said, and snatched another beer from the ice.

Jeremiah took his arm away. My skin went cold. We peeled away from each other.

"I'm going to find the toilets," I said, and stood up. "There's probably a huge line. I might be a while."

I stumbled through the crowd and joined a swarm of people. Hundreds of cans clattered under my feet, and I couldn't see where I was headed. The band had started their second set by the time I reached the front of the line at the Portaloos, so I took my time, washing my hands and splashing my face to cool off. I caught my reflection in the mirror and took the party hat off, stuffing it into my handbag. Outside, I stood on the back of a trailer to get my bearings. *Where are they? How can I push my way back through the crowd? What is this thing with Jeremiah?* Somebody pulled me down from the trailer. Warm hands clapped over my eyes.

"Guess who?"

My heart beat with panicky wings, and I spun around, unable to wipe the stupid look off my face.

Luke. Smiling, wearing a ridiculous green feather boa, jeans, and no shirt. Like no time had passed, like things hadn't changed. *How can he do that?*

"It's me."

I reacted the only way I knew how. My body knew exactly what to do when Luke touched me—it was only my heart that remained clueless. I kissed him, hard. It was that or cry. People moved around us like we were in a bubble.

I pulled away. "It's so good to see you!" I yelled in his ear.

"I know! I was just thinking about you and now you're here. I've missed you. I've been wanting to get up to the reservoir, but . . . you know. Busy, busy. But hey, here you are, right?" He ran his hands down my shoulders and settled them on my waist.

"Here I am."

I smelled bourbon on his breath, and his eyes were fever bright. Maybe he was on something; I couldn't tell for sure.

"Come on!" He grabbed my hand. "Come meet the guys. Hey, so how have you been?" He pulled me after him, parting the crowd. He headed for a spot almost parallel to where Roly and Jeremiah were sitting, but on the other side of the field. "Has your sister lightened up yet?"

"Good," I yelled. "I've been good." This was the kind of

normal I'd craved all those times we met. I tried to peer over the crowd for a glimpse of Jeremiah and Roly, but it was too packed. They wouldn't miss me for half an hour.

"Here. Hey, guys, look who I found. This is Cheever. Rob. Mossy and Jodes." He pointed to the other occupants of the rug, one by one. "This is Jack, my mate from Mobius. Remember? I told you about her." Jodes, the only other girl, checked me over, waved, and went back to measuring her pour.

Rob said, "Hey, Jack."

Cheever kissed my hand.

Mossy stared at my boobs.

His *mate*?

"Have you been up to the reservoir at all?" I had to know.

He handed me a can and pretended to think, but I knew the answer already. He caught my expression. "Why? Have you? Oh shit, you haven't been waiting up there for me, have you? I've been stuck without a car for a few weeks."

"Don't flatter yourself," I snorted. "What, you don't think I have a life?" I opened the can, took a brave slug, and choked down a mouthful of bourbon.

"Phew," he breathed. "Talk about scaring a guy. You're the only one I can count on not to give me a hard time. Don't go breaking my heart."

Trudy was right. I could never tell him how I felt.

"It's so good to see you," he said, and kissed my nose.

He seemed so genuine. He *was* genuine. He was a nice guy, just not a guy who was ready for flowers and matching plates. He twisted a piece of my hair around his finger and tickled my cheek with the end of it. "I like your hair," he said. "It suits you."

"Liar," I said.

He chuckled. "You look like a hot groupie."

"Are you high?"

"Isn't she hot, Cheever?"

Cheever gave him a dirty look and said, "Too good for you, Cavanaugh."

The music stopped, and the crowd started chanting for more. I hated the bourbon and cola but I drank it because the acid sweetness was all part of it. I was *happy*. I would forever associate the taste with the feeling of him, tight against me.

Luke flopped onto his side and pulled me down. "Let's fall asleep here. Let's spend the night together."

"You *are* high." I remembered Jeremiah and Roly. The cartoonish clock above the stage ticked. It was only half an hour until midnight. "I have to go. I'm here with some other people."

"Don't," he said. "Stay."

One of the usual New Year's tracks started booming from the speakers. Luke slid his hand down the front of my jeans.

I slapped it away. "Not here." I checked, but nobody was looking.

"Car?" he asked lazily.

I took a deep breath. "I have an idea." The moment I said it, I felt like I should take it back, but I couldn't.

"Do you want to wait for the fireworks?" he said.

He kissed my neck and pressed closer from behind. All the time his hand was still on pause at my belly button, and all I could think was that I wanted it lower, but not here in plain sight, even though there were plenty of other couples getting it on nearby.

"I don't want to wait."

My conscience deserted. I forgot about Jeremiah and Roly and led Luke to my two-person tent under the row of pine trees outside the perimeter fence. Inside the tent, we took off our clothes and wrapped ourselves in my quilt. Luke pulled a condom from the back pocket of his jeans, and two more fell out. I was just grateful he had one, and I was too far gone to wonder.

Luke fell asleep next to me. I stayed awake, listening to the fireworks fizzle, trying to figure out which of all my emotions was strongest. Even when I heard Roly and Jeremiah later outside the tent, whispering, arguing about whether to check that I was in there, I still didn't wake Luke because I didn't want him to leave.

"I'm here," I called out softly. "Bad hot dog. I wasn't feeling well."

Luke sighed in his sleep and rolled over. I felt his breath on the back of my neck; his stomach flattened into the small of my back, and his knees pressed into the back of mine. He threw a heavy arm across my chest and pulled me in.

I wondered how we could fit in so many ways, but not the one that counted.

17

By morning, there was no evidence that anybody could see. Luke had left sometime in the night—I didn't know exactly when. The two unused condoms were still lying on the floor. I slipped them into my bag. I noticed a love bite on my collarbone, or its less romantic version, the hickey, since there was no love. I buttoned my shirt up to my neck. I ached in places, and the ache was usually something real I could take home, but that morning I wished I could unzip my skin and leave it behind in a puddle on the ground.

I folded and refolded my tent three times before I could fit it back into its sleeve. Jeremiah had gone for coffee, and Roly was struggling with their tent too. The field was trashed: cans, paper, bottles, charred firework canisters, and sleeping bodies everywhere.

"You're quiet," Roly observed. "You missed the fireworks."

"I'm fine," I replied vaguely. "I heard them."

"You did the right thing."

"What are you talking about?" I said. "What did I do?"

He looked sheepish. "You know—not letting things go any further with J."

"Nothing happened," I said. "You saw. You were there."

"He won't think it was nothing," he said. "I assumed you were playing sick on purpose."

"I wasn't playing," I lied. "The hot—"

"The hot dogs were fine," he butted in. His glance flicked over my left shoulder. "Coffee has arrived."

We drove home in silence. Wind whistled a tune through a stone chip in the windshield as we passed silos of wheat and acres of flat, dry fields; it wasn't until we began the steady climb through the hills and turned onto Mercy Loop that there was a hint of green. At the far end of town, Pryor Ridge loomed like a hideous, craggy face above the tree line.

Pope had now spent Christmas and New Year's alone.

"Looks like we missed the real party," Roly said.

Somebody had gone to town on Main Street with a can of spray paint. The jacarandas outside Bent Bowl Spoon were strung with toilet paper and Silly String. Roly snaked the car deliberately through the still-wet paint. I stared out the rear window to see white tire tracks following behind us.

"I'll drop J first," Roly said. "If that's okay with you?"

Jeremiah turned his head sharply at Roly's tone. "I can wait. Take Jack."

The morning-after grunge had well and truly set in. I could still taste bourbon on the back of my tongue.

"Take Jeremiah," I said, my eyes squeezed shut to dull the glare.

"Suit yourself." Roly turned at the last minute and snickered when I was flung sideways. He pulled up at the front of Meredith Jolley's house.

Jeremiah got out and slammed the door.

I got out too. "I'll just walk from here. Thanks."

"It's too far," Jeremiah said. "Roly will take you." He leaned into the car and said something under his breath. They argued.

Roly drove forward several feet with Jeremiah still hanging on to the window. He had to let go, or lose the upper half of his body. Roly tooted the horn, a cheerful sound, at odds with his sour expression.

"I'm sorry," Jeremiah said. "I don't know what's got into him. Just let me get my keys. I'll drive you."

"It's okay." Whatever was going on between them, I didn't want a part of it. I started walking toward Ma's house. "Happy New Year."

Ma opened the door wearing her town clothes, a set of keys in her hand. "Jack?" She looked at me, at my quilt and pillow, blinked a few times, and hid the keys behind her back. "What's wrong?"

"Nothing's wrong. Are you on your way out?" I said. "I

can come back another time." I was the evil nobody wanted to invite inside.

"I was heading out." She sighed and slapped the keys down on the hall table. "But it can wait."

"I just . . ."

"Come on. Out with it."

"I'm really tired." My stomach growled loud enough for us both to hear. "And I'm really hungry."

I craved a big plate of everything I'd ever complained about, or scraped into the trash when she wasn't looking, or secretly fed to the dog.

"This isn't a soup kitchen," she said, but her hard expression was slipping. She stood aside to let me in.

If there was one place that never changed, it was here, in Ma's kitchen, where everything was chipped and faded but so clean the bacteria didn't stand a chance. There were spots under the kitchen table where Trudy and I had stuck enough chewing gum to hold the thing together for another century; Ma's bad knees meant it had gone undiscovered. Whenever she knelt down, you could hear the cartilage squelch.

"Sit."

I sat down at the table. Out of habit, I tucked in my elbows and folded my hands in my lap.

"Tea?"

Ma made us both a cup of tea and set one plain cookie on the side of my saucer. I didn't tell her that I preferred coffee now—I just sipped at the cup and dunked the cookie and pretended to swallow. The cookie broke away and sank to the bottom of the cup.

Ma stayed standing on the other side of the breakfast bar. "So . . ."

"I just wanted to see you." I put my elbows on the table, deliberately, to see if she'd react.

"Do you need money? Is that it? Trudy says you're not handling this business of losing your job very well." She picked up a tea towel and wiped over the spotless counter.

"I don't want money."

I wanted to grab the tea towel, give it the old twist and whip, and knock down the useless knickknacks she had lined up on the shelf. They were all store bought. Not a single piece of the ugly pottery I'd made had ever been put on that shelf; not one drawing had ever been stuck on the fridge. Ma loved me. I never doubted it. But why act like my stuff wasn't precious enough to display? Why wrap it in tissue paper and keep it in the shed? What kind of love was that?

"How's Dad?"

"Fine."

"Is he home?"

"Out the back," she said, and jerked her head.

"How do you stand it?"

"You'll have to be more specific." She gave one last bored

wipe with the tea towel, then folded it into a tight, precise rectangle.

I ground my eye teeth. My head was beginning to ache. "Do you and Dad even talk anymore?"

Two hot spots flared on her cheeks. "Your father is a good man. Find a nice boy, Jack," Ma said. "I know what you've been up to. People talk. I hope you're using protection."

Protection. The kind I needed didn't come in a little foil packet.

"So, if your behavior at Christmas is anything to go by—"

"I had a two-inch splinter stuck in my fucking leg!" I erupted.

"Jacklin!"

"What? It's not like I haven't heard you use that word. Monkey see, monkey do."

"Not my circus, not my monkey." She slammed her empty cup into the sink. "You are supposedly an adult, Jack. Start behaving like one."

There we were again, saying words but talking about nothing, both in the same room but on a different planet.

"Is that it? That's all you've got?" I stood up.

"Where are you going?"

I strode down the hallway. "My room. I left some things behind." I reached the door and threw it open. The single bed was still in the same place, but there was nothing else that belonged to me.

Ma was right behind. "I cleaned it out," she said.

I noticed Dad's jacket hanging from a knob on the wardrobe. "Dad's sleeping in here now, isn't he?" I turned on her. "Are you taking it out on him because you're angry I'm living with Trudy? God, you won't be happy until you drive all of us out of this house!"

She let out a slow hiss. "You dropped out of school. You chose to leave. I never tried to stop you, but it isn't what I wanted for you."

"Where's my stuff?"

"In the shed. This isn't a halfway house, Jack." She sat on the edge of the bed and reached down to smooth the tasseled fringe on the comforter. "You can't just come and go until you find a better place."

"I did find a better place."

"You think I was always this old," she said. She stood, opened the wardrobe, and started refolding Dad's shirts.

On my way out, I drew a childish scribble on a Post-it and stuck it on Ma's fridge. I screwed up the tea towel and took a china bird from her shelf. The empty space would drive her nuts.

Mads picked me up halfway home. I'd wrapped my quilt around my shoulders like a cape and unwittingly dropped my pillow somewhere between Ma's house and the phone booth. I was too tired and pissed off to turn back and look for it.

"Trudy's half-crazy with worry," she said when I got in. "We didn't know where you'd gone last night." She turned the car around and headed back to Trudy's.

"I went to watch the New Year's fireworks at Burt. Were you on your way to work now? Won't you be late?"

"I'm running early anyway. Who'd you go with?"

"Jeremiah Jolley and Roland Bone."

Mads raised her eyebrows. "I didn't know you guys hung out."

"We don't. Much." I wound my window down. "What did you do?"

She shrugged. "Trudy and Thom went out somewhere. I pulled a late shift—I was home and in bed by two. Not my idea of fun. My partner in crime has been kind of busy lately." She gave me a rueful smile. "She's obsessed."

"She's in love."

"I doubt that," Mads said. "Nobody defends the heart quite so fiercely as your sister." She pulled into the driveway. "A word of warning: She's been waiting up for you."

My stomach twisted. I might have missed the fireworks last night, but this would make up for it.

Gypsy met me at the door for the first time in ages, trembling all over. She leaned against me and catalogued every scent. I rubbed her ears and mumbled words she couldn't hear.

"When you have a minute," Trudy said. I could only see her feet hanging over the end of the banana lounge.

I went straight to my room and threw my stuff onto the bed. I put Ma's china bird on the windowsill. My mood plummeted further. The room was basically a coffin with graying paint and a stained ceiling. There was a foul smell in there, like something had died in the walls; it just needed shutters on the window and a plague of blowflies to make it the attic room from the *The Amityville Horror*. I opened the window. The smell followed me back into the hall.

"I can't live like this," I said. "My room is possessed."

"It's quite possibly your own questionable hygiene," Trudy said, and swung her legs off the couch.

"Speaking of which, I need a shower. Like, yesterday."

"It can wait."

"It really can't." I peeled off my shirt and dropped it. Trudy watched as I stepped out of my jeans right where I was standing. "What is it? You said a minute."

Trudy's eyes bugged. "What the hell is *that*?"

"What?" I looked down. My legs were covered in pale, purplish bruises, but I always marked easily. It was nothing out of the ordinary.

"That thing on your shoulder. That's a last-night hickey." She got up and pressed her finger into my collarbone.

I flinched and stepped back. "So?"

"So who gave it to you? Where were you last night?"

"How is that any of your business?"

"It is my business. I'm your legal guardian."

"You are not, and why do you even care?" I scooped up my clothes and went to the bathroom.

Trudy followed, her lips pressed so tight they'd disappeared. "I don't want to send you back to Ma, but I don't see any other way. You're not the easiest person to get along with. You're self-destructing."

"You're such a hypocrite!" I yelled. "What is *wrong* with you people?" I turned on the hot tap and let it run. "Can I have some privacy, please?"

"Just listen for once," she pleaded. I was taken aback by her abrupt change of tone. "I wanted to protect you from all the shit I had to go through. I couldn't stand the thought of her chipping away at your self-esteem like she did mine—but if you keep carrying on like this, I'll have no choice."

"Is that a threat?" I said. "How do you know most of the shit didn't already happen while you were away? What if you were too late?"

"It's not too late. Think about it, Jack." She hovered in the doorway. The phone rang, and she glanced over her shoulder. "It might be better for us both if you went back to Ma's. I didn't come home to find myself in the middle of another war." She waited.

"I can't change who I am."

"You can and you should," Trudy said.

"Get the phone," I muttered. "It'll be for you anyway." Steam clouded the mirror and Trudy's face. I stepped into the shower, and she was gone.

18

The drive-in became our secret project. It was something to do—with my mind, with my hands, and with other people who had nothing to do but kill time. But today Roly wasn't there, and I knew it was somehow my fault.

Jeremiah was still waiting for Meredith to come home from hospital. I decided I was done waiting for Luke: I wouldn't meet him or call him again, not even to say good-bye. There was no point trying to end something that had never really begun.

For now there was the gray shadow in the corner of the screen to paint and, according to Jeremiah, the power to connect, the speakers to test, and the projector to service. It was my job to check the bulbs inside the mushroom lights too. We broke for a late lunch of sandwiches and cold thermos coffee at half past two.

"So, what now?"

"We have to turn on the electricity somehow," Jeremiah said.

"What if it's disconnected?"

"It is, obviously, but I should be able to hook something up if it's still on the grid."

"Don't we need an electrician for that?"

He just grinned around the screwdriver he had clenched between his teeth.

"What if you blow yourself up?"

"Ah 'on't," he said.

Summer beat on around us. Jeremiah worked steadily, trying to decipher the maze of wiring in the meter box. I stayed out of the way, in the shade inside the old kiosk and the projector room. I was useless for the technical stuff and the heavy lifting, so I cleaned and fetched drinks.

Jeremiah pulled up an old three-legged stool and bent over to poke around inside the projection equipment.

"Stupid question," I said, "but won't we need a film to get it running?"

"It's not stupid," he answered. "But I'm more worried about broken parts. I mean, if there's something missing, I won't know what it is. It's like trying to complete a puzzle without a picture." His voice echoed inside the contraption.

"We could ask Alby. He's a walking history book. Maybe there's an archive at the library or something."

"Then people will find out what we're doing up here." He

poked his head out. Spider webs had turned his hair gray. "If nobody but you, me, and Roly knows, then we're not likely to run into any opposition. I'll work it out."

I hoisted myself onto the bench. "Why didn't Roly come?"

Jeremiah shrugged. "He said he was busy." He brushed himself off. "I'm going to see if I can find the connection out on the road. Wait here and don't touch anything."

"Roger." I gave him a salute. "But shouldn't we have a distress signal?"

"I'd say the smell of burning flesh would be unmistakable."

"Don't say that!" I reached out and put my hand on his forearm. The cords of muscle underneath jumped. "Be careful." I squeezed.

Jeremiah reacted as if I'd stubbed a lit cigarette out on his skin: He snatched his arm back and muttered something about it getting dark soon. I watched him make his way down to the road and nursed my hurt.

Don't touch anything, he'd said.

I stared at my hands. They were just ordinary hands—they didn't seem capable of provoking such a strong reaction.

He was gone for a long time.

I climbed up to the platform and started painting over the shadow in the corner. The areas we'd already painted were beginning to peel, and millions of tiny bugs had stuck to the wet paint and died. I gave it two coats, but a hard, pelting rain came from nowhere, and I ran back to the kiosk for cover.

From the shelter of the doorway I watched the paint wash away in streaks. The now-familiar shadow appeared again.

It was useless, like trying to give mouth-to-mouth to someone long dead.

I chucked the paintbrush into a bush. Jeremiah was out there standing in a puddle, playing with electricity. My nerves were completely shot.

Something whirred in the far corner of the room. I lifted a piece of sacking; beneath it, a fan inside a metal cage was spinning fast. It took a few seconds to sink in. The power was on. I flicked a light switch, but nothing happened. I tried a different one, and the lightbulb outside the door popped and blew.

The rain came down in buckets. The gutters groaned and overflowed. I ran outside, jumping the white river that had sprung from underneath the bush. Wet, broken chunks of asphalt winked like fool's gold, and I counted nine out of thirty-four mushroom lights glowing in the dusk. I fiddled with the dial on the nearest speaker. It crackled and spat static. Elated, I punched the air and searched the haze obscuring the driveway out to the main road.

After a few minutes, Jeremiah appeared, hunched against needles of rain.

"You did it!" I raised the crackling speaker as a boom of thunder rolled over the top of the ridge.

"You'll be Frankenstein's bride if you don't put that thing down." He took it from me and set it back in its cradle.

We ran, jumping puddles and leapfrogging speaker posts. We sat up on the platform, admiring our wonderland, uncaring that we were soaked through. A broad patch of shadowy forest separated us from the lights of Mobius, spread out like a circuit board below; a spectacular storm passed right overhead with sheet lightning and bursts of rain that sounded like applause.

"Look at it." I pointed across the valley to the black hole of Pryor Ridge. The rain had become a mist. Our skin steamed. "Why do you think they go there?"

"Who? The doers or the watchers?"

"The watchers, I guess." Again I thought of Pope, but I kept it to myself. Which was he?

"I don't know—maybe it's as close as they can get without stepping off the ledge themselves. Death is life-affirming for some people."

"That's horrible."

Jeremiah shrugged. "It's nothing new. In the eighteenth century, the Georgians used to pay entry to asylums so they could ogle the insane. Public hangings drew packed crowds. Do people stand on the Golden Gate Bridge and wonder at the brilliance of its engineering? No, they peer over the edge. This whole area is so rich in gold-mining history. We should wonder at the tenacity of humans who had no business being that far underground with fuck-all else but a shovel, a pick, and a dream. But no, instead people come to see where other people came to die." He threw up his hands. "It's such a waste of curiosity."

"Have you ever been down a mine shaft?"

"Of course. You think I stopped at licking bricks?" He laughed, then turned serious. "Have you ever thought about getting out of this town? New horizons and all that?"

"Nope," I said. "My horizon is right there. Same place it's always been." I pointed to the thin wash of pink in the sky, to the west.

"Well, that's only because you're sitting still." Jeremiah swayed and inhaled, close to my ear.

"Are you sniffing my hair?" I teased.

"What? No!" He shook his head, shuffled farther away.

"What does it smell like?" I pressed. "Apples and cinnamon? Vanilla? Does it smell like raspberries?"

"I was *not* smelling your hair."

"I used a bath bomb this morning," I said. "It was called Tutti Frutti, but I thought it smelled more like bubble gum."

"Did you wash your hair with it?"

"Of course not. It was a bath bomb."

"Then why would your hair smell like bubble gum?"

"I'm just saying. So, you didn't get a whiff of blood orange, or grapefruit? I know . . . sandalwood. And lilacs. Frankincense and myrrh."

"I don't even know what those things smell like. Olfactory sense is linked to—"

"I must say, I'm disappointed." I sighed theatrically. "You're supposed to notice these things. "Oh, she smells of pine needles and fresh air, sunshine and bliss, musk and debauchery." You don't have to say it aloud, but you can think it." I sniffed the skin inside my forearm. "What's the point of all our lotions and potions?"

Jeremiah squirmed. "Roses?"

"Roses are common. Roses are granny's house and big panties on the washing line."

"How about frangipani?"

I made a face. "I smell like frangipani?"

"Well, no, not really. But at least I know what it smells like."

"Oh never mind." I leaned closer to Jeremiah and looked down. The ground was blurred and far away. I refocused on his face. He wore a baffled expression. "I'm just teasing you," I said. "I fully expected you'd say my hair smelled like hair."

"This is all incredibly complicated," he said quietly, and screwed up his nose. "I suppose I would rather tell her how she makes me feel."

"How does she make you feel? You can practice on me." I laughed and folded my hands in my lap.

Jeremiah looked away. "I would tell her that I like her hands," he began. "I would tell her that I don't like to be touched, but her hands are the exception. I don't like to be made fun of— and she's done that, many times, either implicitly or overtly—

but I would take her ridicule over her not knowing I existed, any day. I'd confess I don't like being wrong about anything, but I hope I'm wrong about her—she's not right for me, I know that, but I want her anyway. I would tell her that being back here is only bearable because she's here too, and, for the first time ever, I don't want to leave. I wish I knew how to tell her how I feel without bringing on an ending of some kind, but I know it's inevitable. And I would tell her I understood if she told me she didn't feel the same way." He folded his hands in his lap too, but he stared at mine. "That's how she makes me feel."

I looked over my shoulder. Our shadow-selves were merged on the screen, though we were more than two feet apart. I understood what he was asking. I had an out: I could go on, pretending "she" was not me—make fun of him, as he'd pointed out so gently, and leave things the way they were.

He wasn't the one I'd pick. But I wanted so, so badly to be adored. To patch up the hurt with something new.

"This is going to make things incredibly complicated," I said primly.

"You're telling me," he replied.

We bumped teeth and my lip bled. It wasn't great, not the first time. But we didn't have to make it perfect. We just had to make it work.

19

I saw Pope in town a few days later. I was going to look after Mr. Broadbent—I felt guilty about letting Alby down, and I needed the money, although it wasn't much. Mads dropped me off on her way to an afternoon shift at the pub.

Pope was standing by his car outside the bakery, looking bewildered, as if Main Street was far too much civilization for him. At least he'd survived the storm.

"How are you?" I said. "Tried the Bushman's pie? The apricot strudel is pretty good too. Avoid the Cornish pasty—it tastes like parsnip and toenails."

"You haven't been up for a while," he said. "I find myself looking forward to our odd conversations. I was craving human contact of the deranged variety, but then some old guy in a bathrobe flashed me and ran off down the street." He patted his pockets, looking for something. "So, yeah, I'm good."

I laughed before I realized what he meant. "Which way did he go?"

He jabbed a thumb east, which I suspected already. "Another guy's gone after him—and a woman, brandishing a broom."

I nodded.

"None of this is surprising to you, is it?"

"Not really, no."

He smiled. "Excellent."

"Why is that excellent?"

"It means I haven't gone completely mad."

"Oh contrary," I said. "It just means you're becoming a local."

"*Contraire,*" he said.

Astrid came out the front of Bent Bowl Spoon and rubbed out the old specials on the sandwich board. It was bad timing. Pope saw her too, and of course she looked like an album cover with her windblown hair and hitched-up skirt and her battered cowboy boots.

"Your friend's waving," Pope said, raising his own hand.

I scowled and kicked a tire. "We're not friends."

"There you go again," he said. "Look, I've got to go." He slid into the front seat and turned the engine over. It sputtered and caught, belching a cloud of black smoke.

Astrid stared at us, shielding her eyes from the sun.

I lingered, waving at the car until it disappeared. Astrid didn't know everything about me anymore.

• • •

I waited at the top of the steps. Alby and Mrs. Gates hauled Mr. Broadbent back home between them, their elbows locked with his. He looked like a prisoner.

"How far did he get?" I asked.

"Pretty far," Alby puffed. "He's had some training lately." He glared at me.

Mrs. Gates offered Mr. Broadbent's elbow.

I took hold of him. "What if we take him for a walk every now and then? Maybe he needs more fresh air."

Mrs. Gates snorted. "He needs more trousers. I have to be off. I've got a client over the sink." She nodded at me. "We need to freshen up that color before somebody shoots you for a fox."

"Thanks, Marie," Alby said.

"Anytime, Albert."

A wheezing sound came from Mr. Broadbent's throat.

"Is he choking?" I said, trying to pinch his mouth open.

"He's laughing," Alby said. "He's got a taste for it now, no thanks to you."

We wrestled Mr. Broadbent inside and settled him in his chair. He dropped into it like a fallen kite. I draped a blanket over his knees and turned on the TV.

Alby gathered his wallet and keys. "He's eaten. I should only be a couple of hours. Think you can handle it this time?"

"I'm a good girl," I reminded him.

Mr. Broadbent watched him leave, eyelids drooping.

I opened up the blinds and let the late-afternoon sunlight pour in. The only place open was the salon—no wonder he was always searching for a way out.

A small sound. I turned around. So much for sleeping. Mr. Broadbent reached under the table, pulled out the Jenga box, and set it on his lap. He shook it.

"Faker," I said.

He gurgled. His eyes crinkled at the corners.

I set up the tower four times. Four times he knocked it over. But on the fifth, he carefully pinched one piece at the bottom and slid it out, leaving the tower standing.

I clapped.

He stuck the piece between his lips, like a cigar.

"Now you're going backward," I said. "Come on, we were making progress."

I took the piece away. He flapped his hands, so I gave it back. This time he held the piece differently, as if it was a pencil; he drew shapes in the air, withdrew another three pieces, and lined them up on the table, slowly pushing them around with his forefinger as if they were planchettes on a Ouija board. I watched, fascinated, waiting for a pattern to emerge. He did the same thing for forty minutes—there was no pattern, just an obsession with pushing the blocks around.

Fed up, I went to the kitchen to make myself a mug of coffee. It was almost five, well past crazy hour. Alby's kettle was old and shrill; clouds of steam misted the glass. I wrote

Luke's name in the condensation—then crossed it out and wrote a looping *J* instead. I rubbed that out too, as if someone was looking over my shoulder. Over the last two days Jeremiah had called twice and left messages, one on the machine and another with Trudy. I couldn't help feeling as if I needed to stop thinking about Luke before I called him back. And I couldn't stop.

The kettle screeched. I switched it off at the wall. As the whistle faded, I heard another noise, like streamers flapping in a breeze. Mr. Broadbent wasn't in his chair; the front door was still closed and latched.

"Where are you?" I called. "What are you up to now?"

The sound stopped.

I checked the bedrooms: both empty, beds made, matching sets of striped pajamas folded on the pillows. On the other side of the flat, a long hallway led to the bathroom and toilet. The toilet door was closed, but he wasn't there. I whipped back the shower curtain in the bathroom. Not there, either.

I was frantic—I'd only left him for a few minutes. I rattled the living room windows and checked the pavement below, looked under the beds and the kitchen table, behind the couch, the bedroom curtains, and doors.

On my second lap I heard the flapping again.

"Ready or not, here I come!" I called.

A throaty gurgle came from behind the door to the linen cupboard.

I'd passed it before, assuming the space behind was too small for a grown person. Inside, it was the size of a large walk-in pantry.

"Gotcha!"

Mr. Broadbent was sitting on the floor, a plucked and withered bird in a nest of empty reels and black film tape. He met my eyes for a split second and went on with his ritual; his fingers found the end of a fresh spool and pulled, feeding the tape through his hands, adding another layer to his nest.

"Stop," I said. I squatted down and held his hands until they were still. "Alby's going to freak."

I let go of his hands. He immediately picked up another black case and struggled to open it. When I tried to take it away, he flapped and bit my arm.

"Shit."

I left him there, unraveling tape. In the hallway, I slid my back down the wall and sat with my arms around my knees. How many had he unwound? It would take me ages to clean up the mess. The films were probably ruined forever, but he was having such a fine time. I'd never seen his hands move so smoothly, so delicately and knowingly and lovingly—no, I *had* seen it before.

I showed Alby the mess Mr. Broadbent had made, and he just shrugged—it happened all the time, he said. He usually rewound the same few ruined tapes. It kept his father busy, and it spared the other tapes, the ones stacked along the top shelf, from destruction. *The other films.* When Alby ushered Mr. Broadbent back into the lounge room, I climbed the shelves and grabbed the four nearest tapes. I wrapped them in my jacket, smuggled them out of the flat, and ran to Jeremiah's house.

"Where's the fire?" he said, rubbing his eyes as if he'd just woken up.

I smiled and opened my jacket. He let me in, and we sat at the breakfast bar in Meredith's kitchen, examining the tapes.

"What, you just took them?" Jeremiah said.

"There were hundreds. Four won't be missed."

"Why didn't you ask Alby about them?" Worry lines creased his forehead.

"You're the one who said this was a covert operation."

"These are all Japanese monster movies," he said, turning the cases over in his hands. "They're really old."

"Will they work?"

He pinched the end of a tape and held it up to the light. "We won't know until we try."

"We could steal Mr. Broadbent," I said. "He knows how."

"Stealing tapes is one thing," Jeremiah said, frowning. "You're nuts, but I admire your enthusiasm."

"I'm serious."

"He's senile, isn't he?"

"His hands know what to do."

"I like your dress," he said, and glanced at my bare legs. "I think this is only the second time I've seen you wear one."

Caught off guard, I smoothed the blue strappy dress to cover my knees. "I borrowed it from Trudy."

Jeremiah backed his chair away. "I called you," he said. "Your sister said she'd pass on the message. Did you get it?"

"No," I answered instinctively. Then I confessed. "Yes. She told me." I grappled with several excuses and discarded all of them.

Jeremiah monitored my expression. "You don't have to lie," he said. "I called. You got the message. You didn't call back. You've filled the gap in my logic." He got up and pushed his chair under the counter. "Look, I'm no good at trying to read body language and subtext or between the lines—all that guff. Just tell me up front, okay? Now, do you want a drink? Would you like something to eat?"

"I'm sorry . . . I would have . . ."

"I changed the subject. It's terribly rude to change it back." He flashed a smile that let me off the hook. "Shall I put the kettle on, or do you want something else?"

We sat in the living room, and he turned on the television. He made us both coffee, but we let the cups go cold on the table. It seemed as if we'd slipped down a gear, and that was fine by me; we were back to easy silence and respectable space. We watched *Dune* followed by *Alien* and ate a packet of chips. I spouted animal trivia, none of which was news to him. Part of me wanted to kiss him again without thinking too hard about it, but another part told me to hold back.

"It doesn't have to be anything," he said out of the blue. "We can just hang out."

"I didn't . . ."

"I wish I could take back what I said at the drive-in. I don't want things to get weird."

"It's not weird," I said. "I'm just not sure where we go from here."

He took my hand and held it. Nothing else. No pressure, no slinky finger on my palm. I waited and waited, and he seemed content to wait longer.

I lasted twelve minutes.

It was clear that he wanted me to make the first move. I knew that part by heart. Courtship was like combat—might as well go straight to the victory lap. It was only sex. If Luke could make that distinction, so could I.

I straddled his legs and lowered myself onto his lap, facing him. His big, warm hands slid up my back and settled on my shoulder blades. He wouldn't touch anything out front without a clear invitation; I gripped both of his hands and made them move.

"Jack?"

I tugged at his T-shirt. "Take this off," I said.

He gave me such a delighted smile there was nowhere to go but forward.

He took the T-shirt off, but not in one clean move. It got stuck on his head, and the whole thing became an awkward dance.

I laughed then, worried that would make him feel self-conscious, but he laughed too. No part of him was fine-tuned; he was big, rangy, and clumsy. Unfamiliar. He wasn't Luke. It wasn't fair to Jeremiah, but I couldn't switch it off. The ghost of one got caught up with the other until I couldn't tell them apart.

We kissed, and this time it was better.

When we came up for air, he said, "What do we do now?"

"Do you have sheets?" I said, and picked up my bag. Inside it, I remembered, were two condoms, courtesy of Luke Cavanaugh. The thought of what I was about to do with them made me feel triumphant, and a tiny bit sad.

His room was plain, just a double bed, white sheets, and puffy curtains. A tallboy dresser stood in one corner. The top was bare. I looked for pictures, but there were none anywhere. There was nothing of him in there apart from two pairs of shoes lined up neatly on the floor. Maybe Meredith had cleaned out his room when he left too.

I unzipped Trudy's dress and stepped out of it. I dropped it next to my bag and Jeremiah's shoes.

We fell together. It didn't matter that everything was different; when you got down to body parts and sensation, it *felt* the same. Finally, there was a switch and I could turn Luke off. Jeremiah held his breath until I chose to move and let him in. Girl on top. It didn't happen for me, but it was fine. The first time was always like being in a new place with the wrong map.

I tried to gauge how he was feeling by his expression, but he turned his face away. I pressed my lips to the hollow of his throat. He flinched.

"What's wrong?" I said, and rolled off him. I was angry. And hurt. This awful disconnection *again*, as if there was nothing left. "What did I do?"

Jeremiah stared up at the ceiling. "I've never done that before," he said.

"Oh Jesus," I groaned. I felt the weight of it, like a secret I wished I'd never been told. "I don't know what to say."

"Why should you say anything?"

"I don't know. It feels like . . . a responsibility." I turned over to face the wall.

"Everybody has to do it the first time, sometime," he said flatly. "Things just got weird, didn't they?"

"A bit," I agreed. I pulled the sheet up and crossed my arms over my chest. I felt like crying, but that would bruise him more. I coughed self-consciously.

He leaned across to pass me a glass of water.

"Thank you." I sat up and took a sip.

"You're welcome."

"Do we really have to be so polite? After what we just

did?" I set the glass down and put my head back on the pillow, my hands pinned under my cheek.

"You're right. Sorry."

I watched the digital clock next to the bed. I would count thirty minutes—then it would be okay to leave.

Jeremiah was quiet. His breaths were deep and even. After twenty-eight minutes, he turned over and rested his hand on my hip. Not asking for anything, just there.

I gave in to it and moved to fill the space. His breath on my neck, his hard stomach in the small of my back, and his knees pressed in behind mine.

Not Luke, but we were a fit.

To fall asleep like that—it was everything.

20

I woke to the sound of a phone ringing. The other side of the bed was smooth and tucked. It took a few minutes to comprehend that the smell of coffee and toast meant Jeremiah hadn't left in the night, and a good while longer to make sense of the facts: I was in his room, in his house. Somehow, I was far less curious about whether I wanted to wake up next to him than I was about whether he wanted to wake up next to me.

I put my dress on, found the bathroom, and brushed my teeth with my finger. My reflection was half-demented, far less flattering than in my mind's eye. No wonder he didn't hang around. I had my bag and sandals in my hands, and I was tiptoeing to the front door when the doorbell rang.

I froze. For some reason, my first thought was: Ma. Ma had come to haul me home by the earlobe. She would give me hell with a side of shame and ground me.

Jeremiah came through the kitchen door and spotted me. "I made breakfast," he said.

"There's someone at the door." I wished I hadn't looked in the mirror. I'd worked up a guilty blush as well as my half-demented look.

"I know," he said. "I came to answer it."

I put my bag and shoes back in his room and slunk to the kitchen. He had set the table for two. I sat down and buttered a slice of toast that might as well have been cardboard and spooned a lump of brown sugar into my coffee.

"Did you miss the last train, Jack?" Roly asked.

Oh shit. "It's eleven o'clock," I said, shrugging. "It's almost afternoon."

"But you're eating a breakfastlike meal. And your hair is sticking up all over the place." Roly sat across from me and helped himself to Jeremiah's coffee. "Hey, did you guys have a sleepover?" he said, as if it was a revelation.

I took a bite so I wouldn't have to answer.

"Jack stayed over." Jeremiah yawned. "Do you want some toast?"

"No, I don't want toast. I came to tell you, I got free passes for a band tonight at the Crypt. Do you want to go?" He flashed a couple of tickets.

Jeremiah shook his head. "You know I can't stand those crowds. It's too loud. There's a four in five probability I'll run into someone I never wanted to see again. Why don't you take Jack?" He made himself a fresh coffee.

I stuffed the food down as quickly as I could without gagging and left the coffee half-finished.

"I'd better go," I said, my mouth still full. "You guys have a good night." I stood and pushed my chair in.

"No, wait," Roly said. He pointed his finger at Jeremiah. "Democracy rules. Ip, dip, dog shit. You. Are. Not. It," he said, and landed on me.

"You rigged that," I blurted.

"What, you want eeny meeny?"

"I'm not stupid," I said, and felt my face go red again.

"If she's it, then she gets the ticket," Jeremiah argued, chewing, completely missing the point.

"No," Roly said with exaggerated patience. "She's not it. *You* get the ticket."

"I don't want to go. And she's it."

"Oh for fuck's sake! I don't want to be it!" I strode to Jeremiah's room and grabbed my things.

Roly came after me and barred my exit.

"What is your problem?" I yelled.

He smirked. "Gee, I wonder. I wonder what my problem could be?" He stuck his index finger into the dimple of his chin.

"I don't know, Roland. Why don't you tell me?"

I would never find out: Roly was taken by the shoulders and steered down the hallway, to the entrance, and out the front door. I heard them arguing. The door slammed.

After a minute, Jeremiah came back to the bedroom. He lounged in the doorway with his arms crossed. "I'm sorry."

"Great." I perched on the edge of the bed. "Now he's going to think you picked me over him."

"I asked him to leave because he was rude," Jeremiah said. "Not because I picked anyone."

I put my face in my hands.

"Don't cry," he said. "I don't know what to do with crying people."

"I'm not." I showed him my eyes. "See? I just don't understand why I piss so many people off these days."

"I'm not pissed off."

"Your judgment is probably skewed," I said. "On account of getting laid and all."

He was quiet for a moment. Finally, he said, "Don't do that," and walked away.

I didn't have to ask what he meant.

Jeremiah dropped me home, and I was relieved to find the driveway empty. Somebody had moved my bike out of the carport, and it had fallen onto its side on the back lawn. Two-stroke fuel pooled in a dirty circle underneath.

I let myself into the house. Gypsy stayed asleep until I got about three feet from her bed, when she jumped, gave me an "oh, it's only you" look, and tucked her nose between her paws. I opened the door to my room. A foul blast of trapped air escaped into the hallway. I pushed the window up and tied back the curtain. It was another hot, airless day. I sensed a presence behind me, but it was only Gypsy. She sniffed, looking disgusted.

"It's not me," I said. "I'll take you for a walk when I've had a shower. I promise."

She sauntered back out. I noticed she was walking funny, swinging her rump sideways, feeling her way by dragging it along the wall. Sadness knocked me off-balance, like a wave I didn't see coming. I sat down. I called her, but she was done with me, and I didn't blame her. I would walk away from me, if I could.

Trudy had left a piece of paper on my bed. It was a list of everything I owed: upcoming rent, bills, my share of communal food, plus a letter of demand from the video store for two movies I had forgotten to return. I was officially in the red. I would have to work full time in a job that actually paid to catch up, and by then I would have accrued more debt. I emptied my money box onto the floor and stacked the loose change into piles. These coins had once seemed like leftovers—now they were all I had.

Thirty-nine dollars and sixty-five cents. I counted again to be sure, and it came to a dollar less.

I tried to get control of my breath. Faster, faster, I sucked in the rank air until I was dizzy with it. I stumbled into the living room and checked between the couch cushions for enough forgotten coins to make the number to a round forty. At that moment it was the most important thing in the world. Somebody, probably Trudy, had vacuumed under the cushions, leaving tracks on the surface of the fabric. Not a single coin, not even a stray chip.

I found a dollar coin in the pen cup near the telephone. I searched my jean pockets and my jacket pockets and down the back of the hallway cabinet. I discovered twenty cents on the laundry windowsill and another five cents in the bottom of the washing machine. I only needed another ten cents to restore order. I remembered my Christmas present, but I couldn't find where I'd put the purse. I tipped the couch over. When I found nothing underneath, I went into Trudy's room.

She'd left the bed unmade. Thom had slept over: His shoes were on the floor, and one of his khaki shirts was hanging on the back of the door. There were two one-dollar coins in his top pocket. I took one and left ninety cents change.

I scooped up my pile of coins and dumped them onto the kitchen table. I sorted and counted them again, but this time the missing dollar coin had rematerialized, and now I was a dollar over. I could have screamed at the injustice of it. I put Thom's dollar back and left him the ninety cents to make up for stealing in the first place. In my mind the crime remained though the evidence was gone.

Slowly the universe leveled out from a full tilt.

Gypsy came into the kitchen and snuffled at her empty bowl.

"I think I had an episode," I told her. "But I'm okay now."

I opened the fridge. It was full of food, but Trudy and Mads had labeled everything, including the soy milk, with sticky notes in escalating warnings—to me. *ACHTUNG!* said the block of cheese and the slab of bacon. *IF YOU TOUCH THIS YOU'RE DEAD,* said the chocolate. They hadn't made a distinction between whose food was whose—so they were sharing now—and there was no sticky note on the shrunken carrots in the crisper.

There was half a bag of dog biscuits left in the bottom of the pantry, next to the almost empty box of tuna cans. I made a mental note to deduct at least fifty dollars from the rent I owed. *Somebody* was eating it, and it was *my* tuna; *I'd* earned it. I wrote *JACK'S TUNA* on the box in thick black lettering and filled Gypsy's bowl with biscuits until they overflowed and scattered across the linoleum. Gypsy followed the trail, butting into the chair legs and cupboards on her way, while I watched and cried.

After a long shower I felt better, but when I reached for my brush, I discovered that my hair products and makeup had been moved to the bottom drawer. I touched the ghost of the hickey on my neck; in daylight it was visible. Had Jeremiah seen it? I used some of Mads's expensive concealer to cover it up and tried on some of her lipsticks.

At two o'clock I took Gypsy for a walk. She balked, like Mr. Broadbent when we tried to take him home. I yanked the leash and dragged her, claws scrabbling, until we got past the mailbox. Once we reached the dirt road, she gave in and followed reluctantly, swinging her head from side to side, breathing in short, panicked snorts.

Nothing was certain in her world anymore. She was afraid of everything. So was I.

It will be okay, I told myself. I knew what was good for her. I would be her guide human, and she would make up for my inability to sense anything coming. Together, we were whole.

Jeremiah called in the afternoon and asked if he could take me somewhere for dinner. I had heeded all the warnings in the fridge, and I was starving, so I said yes.

"What's that?" he asked when I got in the car.

I held up the ziplock bag crammed with coins. "Isn't it obvious? It's money."

"I invited you. I'll be paying for dinner," he said.

"It's not for that." I sat with my knees pressed together, the bag of coins on my lap. "Where are we going? And why are you smiling at me like that?"

He shook his head. "It's just . . . you're hanging on to that bag like it's a rosary."

"I don't even know what that is." I put up my hand. "Stop. Don't tell me."

"I figured you wouldn't want to go to the pub, so I thought we'd go to the Burt Buffet. It's Chinese night."

"Perfect," I said. "Do you mind waiting for a minute?" I ran back inside the house, grabbed some old take-out containers, and swapped my tiny shoulder bag for a bigger one. I climbed back in. "Okay. And would you mind stopping at the supermarket on the way?"

Jeremiah waited patiently in the parking lot while I half filled a cart at the Burt supermarket; he obligingly packed the car's tiny trunk with four bags of premium dog biscuits and eight cans of dog food paid for with forty dollars in coins to a pissed-off checkout operator named Claire.

He hardly touched his own plate at the Burt Buffet. I filled mine three times and went back twice more to fill the containers, which I hid in my giant bag.

On the way home, the car reeked of combination Chinese buffet food. Sweet and sour sauce leaked from the bottom of my bag and seeped into the carpet under my feet.

"Thanks for taking me to dinner," I said.

He nodded, still wearing the same amused expression, the one he'd tried to hide when he first spotted me shoveling food into my bag. I could do anything, I realized, and he would go along with it. I'd wanted to free the turtle in the tank just inside the restaurant foyer, and Jeremiah had rolled up his sleeve.

I watched his hands on the steering wheel. Now that I'd

felt them, I liked them more; I liked him more, now that I'd felt him. It was simple, I thought, to switch from one kind of attraction to another. I didn't know why I hadn't thought of it before: to be wanted was as powerful as wanting—more so, because I could take risks without getting hurt.

Jeremiah hesitated at the turnoff to his house and continued on. It wasn't much, just an easing off on the accelerator, but I noticed.

"Are you taking me straight home?"

"If that's what you want?" he said, not taking his eyes from the road.

"What do you want?" I put my hand on his thigh. "Do you want to go parking?"

He pulled over. The streetlights ended a kilometer behind us. Ahead, the road faded out. I leaned across him and switched off the headlights.

"I parked," he said. "What now?"

"Whatever you want."

"Do you want to just talk?"

"God, no," I said. "Why waste time?"

Jeremiah smiled in the dark.

He was so easy to please it was almost better than pleasing myself.

21

Jeremiah told me that Meredith was coming home on Monday. She was stable, he said. She looked good. She'd asked him to get rid of the eggs.

"Are we going to pack them or destroy them?" I asked.

"We?" he said, smiling.

Over the past week, I'd spent more nights in Jeremiah's room than I had in my own. My bedroom window was left permanently open in the vain hope that the stench would vanish while I was gone; Trudy and Thom had slipped into the comfortable routine of an old married couple, and Thom had taken my corner of the couch. Mads was a floor-sitter and didn't seem to mind.

There was no room for me.

In private, Jeremiah and I had created a space where nothing else mattered. Jeremiah didn't know how to protect his heart, and he handed it to me daily. Nobody had ever looked at me the way he did, like I was something he wasn't allowed to touch, even though I gave him green lights all the way.

Between hanging out with Jeremiah, looking after Mr. Broadbent, and traipsing up to the forest to feed Pope, I was busy and far enough away from my real life not to pick at the fraying edges. Since Jeremiah had few other interests in Mobius, I had him all to myself, in stark contrast to how much of Luke I had been allowed to keep. Jeremiah never asked where I went. He didn't call too often or demand more than I was ready to give, but I knew he was waiting for something—and I knew how that felt.

Together, we wrapped the eggs inside old dusting cloths and entombed them in boxes, which Jeremiah then stacked inside the attic.

"So, four more days," I said. "I guess your mother won't want me hanging around when she comes home."

I hadn't been to visit Meredith. Jeremiah went alone most afternoons, while I sat with Mr. Broadbent, and Alby tried to get his affairs in order.

"She likes you," he said. "She says you remind her of herself." He was taking down some of the shelving from the walls and patching up the holes. "It's a dubious compliment, I know."

"When will you go back to Melbourne?" I hadn't really thought about him leaving. Now that Meredith was being discharged, the day was getting closer, and I needed to analyze why I felt so numb.

"I would say that it depends on you, but that would hardly be fair," he said. "I don't need to be back in class until early February."

"Oh."

"You sound disappointed. Is February too close, or too far away?" He said it lightly, without taking his attention from the screw holes in the wall.

"I don't want to think about it," I said, which was true, but not in the way I think he hoped. "We're out of milk and bread. I'll go and get some."

I hadn't been inside Bent Bowl Spoon since I'd left. Astrid was nowhere to be seen, and the place was a mess: only one cash register standing and piles of stock, still in boxes, stacked up near the door. The fruit and veg crates were mostly empty apart from a few staples with long lives. I shook my head and gave the bells above the door another jangle.

Astrid really sucked at this.

I grabbed a loaf of bread and a two-liter carton of milk from the fridge. Of all the changes, one major difference caught my eye: a patch of bare, dirty floorboards in aisle one. A whole section of diamonds had been ripped up.

"Great," I said. "That's just great."

It was as if all my secrets and obsessions weren't secret at all, but items on the universe's to-do list, written in the sky. Anyone could play. Bonus points for making me swear or cry.

Astrid came up behind me. "What's great? Sorry, I'm on my lunch break." She swallowed her mouthful dramatically.

"I can ring it up if you want," I offered. "Finish your sandwich."

She shook her head. "I don't think it's a good idea. I'm here now, anyway." She followed my stare. "Oh, that. We're pulling them up. They're a hazard, people tripping over them all the time. We're modernizing."

We.

"Will it be just the bread and milk?"

"Yes." I dug into my pockets for money and remembered I didn't have any. And I didn't have a staff tab anymore.

Astrid watched me fumble, clearly enjoying herself.

"Alby still owes me."

She nodded graciously but made me sign a handwritten IOU for four dollars ten. "Just in case," she said, "you know, Alby thinks I'm giving you stuff for free."

"Very responsible," I said. "Hey, I don't suppose there are any cracked eggs?"

She gave me a blank stare.

"Modernizing." I sniffed.

On Saturday morning, Trudy and I had a screaming argument about my absences and my lack of contribution and my general ineptitude as a human being. Mads sat wide-eyed at the kitchen table, gripping her coffee mug with both hands, but stayed out of it. Gypsy huddled under the table with her ears back.

"God, I wish I never bothered coming back here," was Trudy's parting shot. "You are so not worth the grief." Through the window, I saw her kick my bike before getting into her car and reversing out onto the main road without looking.

To make it up to Mads, I did the dishes and threw a load of her washing in with mine. She told me to help myself to cereal, but not to tell Trudy.

"Do you want to sell that thing?" Mads asked, pointing to the bike. "Trent Matthews was asking around for a second-hand bike yesterday."

"Tell him five hundred," I said. "But just quietly, I'd take four." It wouldn't be enough to pay off my debts, but at least I could clear things with the collection agency. The letters were piling up now. I'd stopped opening them.

"Your room stinks," Mads said.

"Tell me about it. Why do you think I don't sleep in there?"

She smirked. "I didn't think it was the smell keeping you away."

"You mean Trudy?"

"No, I mean I thought you'd found somewhere else to sleep."

I didn't feel like going into the details. "Mads? You and Trudy have been friends for a long time, right?"

"Since pigtails. Since forever."

"But what about after . . . She stayed in touch with you while she was away, didn't she?"

"As much as Trudy stayed in touch with anybody, I guess," Mads said warily. "Why?"

"It's just . . . she makes such a point about how she came back for me, but she never kept in touch. It's like she didn't care what happened to me while she was gone, and now she cares too much. We fight all the time. I don't know why she bothered coming back either."

"That's her business." Mads cut me off. "I'm not the one you should ask."

"Did she ever tell you about it? Tell me the truth," I pressed.

"Some truths aren't mine to tell." Mads put her cup in the sink and rinsed it. "You're asking the wrong questions," she said. "When Trudy makes it all about you, it probably isn't."

I rolled my eyes. "God, why can't anyone say what they really mean?"

"Exactly, Jack," Mads said. "You're onto something."

Jeremiah tried for over three hours to make the projector work. The individual parts seemed to be rolling smoothly, but, even in daylight, we could tell there would be no picture on the screen.

"I don't understand," he said, scratching his head. "I've checked everything. This shouldn't be difficult at all."

I sat facing backward on an old kiosk chair, chin on my hands, watching him fiddle. I was tired. Bored.

"I'm telling you," I said, sighing. "He *knows*."

"Give me another few minutes."

"You said that an hour ago," I reminded him.

"You can't kidnap a sick old man. It isn't right." He jammed his finger in a hinge and swore. "I won't be a part of it," he said. "I'll figure this out."

"What about Roly? Has he forgiven you yet?"

"For what?"

"For thinking in your pants," I goaded. He would have to kiss me to shut me up.

Right on cue, he threw down the tool he was holding and brushed off his hands. We were getting very, very good at this.

Mr. Broadbent perched on the backseat, both hands folded in his lap as if he was in church. I sat next to him. Jeremiah, still shocked that he was going along with it, muttered to himself in the driver's seat.

"Alby won't be back until six," I said. "Think of it as community service. Or an excursion."

"Why do I have the feeling I've been manipulated?" He shook his head.

Mr. Broadbent gurgled and drooled. I put my jacket over his face as we drove past the pub. Surprisingly, he left it there.

"You'll have to hurry up. It's quarter past four." The sun

was going down already, but, so far, Mr. Broadbent remained calm. "I took a few more tapes as well. I got *E.T.* and *Close Encounters.*"

Jeremiah smacked his hands on the steering wheel. "But of course! Theft, kidnapping, trespass, and destruction of private property." He counted them off on his fingers. "Have I missed anything?"

"You love it," I said. "Right now you feel more alive than you've ever felt before."

"We're going to need a defibrillator when he"—he jerked his thumb—"keels over. Oh the irony."

Jeremiah parked beside the projector room.

I took the jacket off Mr. Broadbent's head and rummaged in my bag for a tissue to wipe his chin. I found the crumpled party hat from New Year's Eve and slipped it on him, careful not to snap the elastic under his chin. He blinked. His hand curled into a claw, and he pawed at the window.

"See?" I said. "He knows."

I got out and opened the door for him, but he sat staring at his legs as if they wouldn't work.

"You'll have to lift him out," I told Jeremiah.

"I will not," he said. "Jesus, what have you put on him? What's he doing now? What's he doing with his hands?"

"Quick! Before he runs out!"

"Runs out of what?"

"Memory! Hurry up, before he forgets again." I tried to

lift Mr. Broadbent myself, but he lashed out with his feet.

"You're mad," Jeremiah said calmly. "You. Are. Mad."

We squared off.

"What was the point of bringing him here then?" I put my hands on my hips.

"I wasn't thinking," Jeremiah said. "It's not something I'm proud of, and you shouldn't be either. We have to take him home."

Mr. Broadbent had other ideas. Like a sleepwalker, he got out of the car and walked stiffly into the projection room. He negotiated the step without looking, as if he was preprogrammed.

We followed him and stood near the doorway, careful not to make any sound that might snap him out of his trance. He sat down and touched the equipment, and his fingers started dancing, except this time he had all the props. He grunted, discarding the tape Jeremiah had tried to feed into the projector. He chose another tape from the pile, and his hands worked for several minutes without stopping.

The light was fading. Our shadows grew longer; the mushroom lights glowed. Jeremiah's misgivings had vanished.

Suddenly Mr. Broadbent stood and stepped out of the projection room ahead of us. His stare was fixed on the screen as though he could see something we couldn't.

I went back in to see what he'd done differently, but the setup appeared to be exactly the same as Jeremiah's earlier efforts.

I flicked the main switch a couple of times, but nothing happened. Obviously the projector had been damaged somehow.

"No way," Jeremiah said outside the door.

"What is it?"

"He spoke," he whispered. "Come here. Listen."

"He can't speak," I hissed, but I went outside to see for myself. Mr. Broadbent's mouth was moving, soundlessly, like he was chewing gum. "What did he say?"

Jeremiah's eyes were big. "He said . . . he said . . ."

"What did he say?" I leaned closer.

Jeremiah pressed his lips to my ear. His breath made me shiver. "He said, '*Showtime!*'" He gave me jazz hands and danced a jig.

"You *arse!*" I yelled.

Mr. Broadbent jumped and started rocking.

"You complete arse." I put my arm around the old man's narrow shoulders and tried to lead him back to the car. He made it harder by sitting on the ground in protest. I grabbed him under the armpits and tried to haul him up. "*Help* me," I growled at Jeremiah.

Jeremiah folded his arms across his chest. He wasn't smiling, and he wouldn't budge. "We're busted," he said, nodding. "I can see headlights coming up the road. I told you this was a *bad* idea."

Minutes later, a car turned into the drive-in entry. Alby's silver hatchback cruised into view.

"Oh no." I groaned and sank down next to Mr. Broadbent. "I'm done for."

Alby took his time getting out of the car. He left the engine running and the headlights on as he gave Mr. Broadbent a once-over. He grimaced when he saw the party hat, but he ignored me.

"Have you checked the cable?" Alby asked Jeremiah. "It's under the console. Right underneath." He went into the projector room and slid his hand beneath the counter. "Come here and have a look. It's always been a bit dodgy."

I heard a click, and Jeremiah said, "Oh."

The top left corner of the screen flickered and lit up.

Alby came back out. He rubbed his chin and pondered the screen. "It needs calibrating."

"How did you know?" I asked him.

Alby thrust his hands into his pockets and rocked on his heels. "I know because I must have spent a thousand nights here when I was a kid. My father owned it. I still own it. I own half of bloody Mobius, and all of it is worth zilch less unpaid taxes."

"I meant how did you know where we were?" I said, feeling sheepish.

He snorted. "Some of my films are gone. My father was missing. And from down there it looks like a bad trip up here." He waved at the town below us.

"You can see the mushrooms," I said.

"The whole town can see the mushrooms. You only had to ask, Jack," Alby said. "I don't know why you have to do everything the hard way. Now, if you don't mind, I'll drive my father home and thank you not to keep taking him. He's a sick, old man."

Jeremiah sighed. "Do you want us to shut it down?"

I threw him a filthy look.

"Keep it going if you want. It can't hurt," Alby mused, stroking his chin again. "As long as you don't blow the place up—and look after the films. People won't come, though. You know that, don't you?"

"Why not?" I said. "Why won't they come?"

Alby pulled out his car keys. "Because some things are too far gone to bring them back."

Mr. Broadbent got up and started swaying, transfixed by the light on the screen.

I tried to explain. "I thought he would show us . . . you know, that thing he does with his hands. He loves it up here. Look at him. This is where he tries to run . . ."

Alby cut me off. "When are you going to get it through your head, Jack? You can't bring him back. All we can do is keep him safe. He doesn't feel joy or pain anymore. Two things, Jack: You can't teach him new tricks, and he has nothing to show you. All he does is replay his remaining memories over and over, and half the pieces are missing." He sighed. "Look at him."

Mr. Broadbent balled up his fists and rubbed his eyes. He looked like a child, standing there in his oversize tracksuit and party hat. He glanced at Alby, removed the hat, and held it to his chest, running his other hand across the stalks on his head, as if he was paying respect at a graveside.

Two things, Alby said, but it turned out he was only right about one.

22

Jeremiah took Alby's consent and ran with it. He went to the flat and selected dozens of films, interrogated Alby about procedures, and finished painting the screen.

The drive-in became our not-so-secret project. Locals started turning up to see what was going on. They hung around, telling stories about the first and last film they'd ever seen there, and the number of freeloaders you could fit into a trunk.

On the nights I didn't go, I knew Jeremiah took Roly. We hadn't been in the same space since the morning at Meredith Jolley's house, and I still didn't understand why he was being so hostile. Had I messed up their friendship? Was Roly feeling like the third wheel? Or was it Jeremiah stuck in the middle, mediating between Roly and me—or Roly himself, whose absence was palpable whenever Jeremiah and I were alone?

Over three nights, Jeremiah and I sat through nine films while he checked the sound quality and scrutinized every frame. I watched him closely. I learned how to run the equipment, only much more slowly and with far less care. I'd started to notice that Jeremiah couldn't, or wouldn't, do two things at once: Whatever held his attention took his whole focus. When it wasn't me, I might as well not have been there at all.

On the fourth night, I was dozing in the front seat of the car while Jeremiah pulled apart an old refrigerated chest from the kiosk. We hadn't spoken for two hours, and my thoughts were somewhere else, when he leaned through the window.

"We should have a premiere night," he said.

"Nobody will come. Why do you think Alby shut it down?" I muttered, fanning myself with a newspaper. "God, this car is an oven."

"I think you're wrong. Now what do you want to watch tonight?"

I leaned back and closed my eyes for a moment. "I get a choice? Definitely something with kissing." I opened one eye.

He wrinkled his nose. "How about cyborgs and time travel? The apocalypse?"

"Kissing, broken hearts, and a fire escape." I sat up.

He stared at me blankly. "I can't think of anything like that."

I laughed. I thought he was joking. But then I realized his attention was wholly, solely on me, and he hadn't blinked in a while—which could only mean he was going to say something profound or disturbing, or both.

"Jack, there's something I want to ask you . . ."

"I have an idea. Let's invite Roly. The more the merrier," I babbled. "And I'm starving. I need food or I'm going to pass out."

He slumped and nodded. "I already called him before I left home. I told him to bring deck chairs. But I need to . . ."

"Lighten up, J," I said. "You're so serious all the time."

We went to pick up take-out burgers. Roly was waiting when we got back. We hauled deck chairs from the back of his pickup and set them up in a row, using the cooler as a table. Roly sprayed himself all over with a can of insect repellent, and Jeremiah, out of a desire for peace or an instinct for survival, took the seat in the middle.

"*Aahh.*" Roly cracked open a beer and put his feet up on the cooler. "This is the life. Why didn't we do this sooner?"

"Because it was bloody hard work," Jeremiah said.

"And you weren't even here for most of it," I added. "You should pay full ticket price."

Roly bristled. "To watch *St. Elmo's Fire*? Are you serious? You should be paying me."

"Jack picked."

"You picked last night and the night before," I reminded him. "There's only so much sci-fi and time travel I can stand before brain fluid starts leaking from my ears."

"See?" Roly stabbed his finger in my direction. "You two have absolutely nothing in common."

"That's where you're wrong," I said, and folded my arms underneath my boobs so he couldn't miss them, or my point.

Jeremiah turned red and got up to start the film.

"I'll do it," I said, and pushed him into his chair.

Roly clapped his hands together and jigged in his seat.

"What are you doing?"

"Dancing."

I laughed. "It isn't dancing if you don't move your feet."

Jeremiah laughed too. "Agreed. That's slipshod pre-entertainment."

Roly dropped his arms and glared at me. "Stop choosing her side, J."

"There are no sides, Roly." Jeremiah sighed. "And I shouldn't have to choose."

I marched up to the projector room, wishing Roly would leave, even if it meant being alone with Jeremiah and whatever was on his mind. I set the reels and started the film, but I stayed in the booth, leaning in the doorway. Roly and Jeremiah weren't watching the screen at all, but leaning close, arguing. They missed the flash of lights. Three sets of headlights were heading up the road, strobing through the trees.

I jogged down to where they were sitting. "We've got visitors."

"Who is it?" Roly held up a hand, shielding his eyes from the glare as the cars turned into the driveway.

Empty bottles were tossed out of the windows and smashed on the asphalt. We heard loud music along with the breaking glass. *Just kids looking for something to do,* I thought, then realized the "kids" were Ben, Becca, and Cass, plus some townies from Burt. They were our age, they were drinking, and they were looking for trouble.

"J, press inflate and tell them all to piss off."

"Inflate?" I resisted the urge to hide in the projector room.

"Have you seen him when he inhales? Dude doubles in size." Roly let out a shaky laugh.

"Grow up, Roly. I can't believe you still have so many hang-ups from high school," I said, but I felt sorry for him. I was such a hypocrite.

"I'll never forget," Roly said. "I have huge grudges. My grudges are so big I need a porter." He took a few steps back to stand behind Jeremiah.

Jeremiah just shook his head. "We'll just tell them we're not ready, but they're welcome to come back when it's all up and running," he said.

The cars did a lap around the perimeter of the drive-in, rocking and bumping over the cracked asphalt. The girls screamed. Another bottle smashed close by.

Roly flinched.

Jeremiah stood taller and took his hands out of his pockets.

We stayed in the center as they circled.

The cars lined up along the last row of speakers, idling,

with the headlights trained on us. The occupants went quiet, and the music turned off.

"This is like a scene from *Christine*. What now, Mr. Diplomacy?" Roly asked. "Do you still want to negotiate?"

"Calm down," Jeremiah said, shifting his weight to one foot. "They're not going to do anything."

My palms were sweating, but I didn't feel threatened. I could always look after myself physically—it was the emotional stuff that found a way through. What I did feel—and I was ashamed of it—was embarrassment. In my so-called grown-up life I was hanging out at an abandoned drive-in, standing next to a Barbie car and the biggest drop-out loser in the history of Burt Area School. *And* a guy whose murky legend wasn't of the flattering kind. Did they recognize me? Why did I even care? I covered my face with my arm.

Roly, on the other hand, was terrified. I recognized that "deer in the headlights" expression from way back in our first year of high school. Whenever he was asked to stand up to answer a question, he'd freeze like that.

"Oh, how far we've come," Roly muttered. "We're doomed."

Jeremiah picked up an empty beer bottle and started walking toward the cars.

"J . . ."

"Oh shit." I started after him, shaking off Roly, who'd grabbed hold of my arm.

One of the cars took off. Seconds later, the others followed.

They threw a few more bottles onto the road, but that was it.

I struggled with the feelings left behind.

Roly did too. His face was white. He did a kind of jelly flop onto the ground and sat there, stunned. His was a different kind of embarrassment. I recognized it.

"Are you okay?" I held out my hand.

"Don't," he said, but he accepted Jeremiah's hand when he offered it. "Why did you do that?"

Jeremiah pondered the question. "People I don't care about can't hurt me, I guess."

Roly got back on his feet. "Easy for you to say—you've got the fists to back it up," he said. "They probably thought you were a yeti." He dropped Jeremiah's hand and threw me a rueful smile. "He's always been like this. Nothing gets in. My head would be lodged under some guy's armpit, and J would be, like, *la-la-la,* with his nose in a book. 'Hold your breath, Roly; just let me finish this chapter.'"

"That's bullshit," Jeremiah said. "Your problem is you still insist on mapping your own position relative to everybody else's. It's no wonder you've lost all sense of direction."

"Ha! Ha!" Roly said. "Fuck off, Freud."

Jeremiah frowned. "I'm saying the difference between you and me is that you're always checking who's behind you and who's in front. I just keep my head down and read my own compass."

I smothered a laugh.

Roly glared at me. "And you, you stand for everything we said we'd never be," Roly said. "You're the enemy. J's one of the good ones and you're recruiting for the other side."

"What the hell?" I looked at Jeremiah. "Are you going to say anything?"

He shrugged helplessly. "He has a point. I don't mean about recruiting for the other side—not that—but a lot happened to him at school. The only difference between him and me is that I don't think about it anymore."

"That's because you have a future," Roly said, shaking his head. "I'm seventeen and I haul bricks three days a week for a sadistic bastard who flicks lit cigarettes at my butt cleavage every time I bend over. And I bend over a lot. School sucked, so I ain't going back there. And if I don't go back, it's pretty hard to go forward, isn't it?" He pulled out another beer and chugged it down. "And it's people like your *girlfriend* here who made school suck."

I flushed and fired back. "That is all kinds of screwed up, Roly. What did I ever do to you?"

"You didn't do anything, unless you count looking the other way, which I take very, very personally."

"I didn't . . ."

"Let me refresh your memory."

"I know what you're going to say," I yelled. "Yeah, so maybe I should have sat next to you on the bus or in class or whatever. So what if I *had* said something when you were being picked on? Do you think that would have changed anything? Or would there just be more of us?"

"You're not an us. You're a them."

"I was never a *them*." I stabbed my finger toward the road. "You just lump me in with people like that because it's easier for you to hate everybody. What do you think—I left school because everything was so fantastic for me? Don't you get it? I wanted to be *them*. And you can deny it all you want, but you wanted to be them too. That makes us an *us*."

Roly made a hissing sound and slapped his leg.

"She has a point," Jeremiah said. "And *us* and *them* are weird words when you say them too many times."

"Oh shut up!" Roly and I said together.

I picked up a stick and whipped viciously at the weeds. "Anyway, you'll be glad to know things aren't working out quite the way I planned either, Roly." As I said it, I realized Jeremiah would think I was talking about him instead of my spectacularly unimpressive life so far.

Roly glanced at Jeremiah. "What about you, J?"

Jeremiah scowled. "I'm happier right now than I've ever been," he said, sliding a glance at me.

"Right." Roly picked up the last two empty bottles and skimmed them like stones across the asphalt.

Jeremiah came up behind me and slid his arms around my waist. He'd never touched me like that in front of Roly before. I turned around and put my head on his chest, feeling sorry for myself, sorry for the way my brain worked, sorry for everything I couldn't change.

"Are you done?" I asked Roly when he was finished breaking things. "Because I'm feeling a bit fragile right now and I think I want to go home."

Roly turned around. "One more thing," he said. He caught Jeremiah's eye. "One more thing . . . " He stopped again. Then he wiped his palms on his jeans and reluctantly stuck out a hand. "I'm blaming you for all of it. I'm sorry."

I shook it once and let go. "Yeah. Me too."

At least one thing was clearer to me after that night: Jeremiah was the odd one out. He was the only one of us who'd moved on.

Roly and I were stuck with our compasses still spinning.

23

The next day was almost hot enough to blister. Perfect for swimming. I called Jeremiah and asked him to drive us to Moseley's Reservoir. I had to get out of the house, and the reservoir was the only body of water within forty kilometers that didn't heat up to air temperature. In my possessed bedroom, moisture was trickling down the walls, and the window had swollen shut. I had another motive: I hoped that revisiting the scene of my summer bliss might banish my ghosts. It felt as if I was half in love, with only half my heart to give. Jeremiah was easy; he was safe; he was there. I loved too easily, Trudy had said, but it wasn't easy at all.

We pulled into the parking lot. Jeremiah reversed into a spot, and we put our towels and cooler under the wooden shelter. The reservoir was as still as a glass table, opaque all over, as if it had been stirred with a spoon. The water level had dropped by about half a meter—I'd never seen it that low before.

Jeremiah eyed the reservoir suspiciously. "I've never been swimming here," he confessed.

"How is that possible?" I shook my head. "It's a route of passage, isn't it?"

"Rite," he said. "Let's just say I took the route less traveled and stayed in the shallow end of the Burt Public Pool while my mother held on to the back of my shorts."

"You can't swim?"

"Not even almost. I paddle pretty well. I excel at floundering." He wandered down to the edge and stood on the bank, staring out across the water. "I suspect this reservoir is seething with *Naegleria fowleri*."

"Is that some kind of fish?" I stripped down to my bikini.

"It's a single-celled amoeba. If it gets up your nose, you're toast." He bent down and ran his fingers through the water. "The temperature might not suit proliferation, though."

I threw up my hands in frustration. "Why did you agree to come, then?"

"I liked the idea of seeing you half-naked outside of my sheets," he said without turning around. His ears turned red.

I was half-naked right then, but he didn't seem to notice. I took a long run-up and bombed off the end of the wooden jetty, staying under for as long as I could. When I surfaced, Jeremiah had his shirt off.

"Were you going to jump in after me?" I teased.

"I hadn't made up my mind yet. That would have meant

two of us needed saving." He sat at the end of the jetty, swinging his legs. He was annoyed with me. "You should at least hold your nose when you go under."

"Come in. I can touch here; look." I put my arms above my head and dunked, but I was wrong. It was far deeper than I thought. My hands went under as my toes just brushed the silty bottom. I came up. Already my legs were tingling from the cold.

Jeremiah wouldn't look at me.

"Are we having fun yet?" I snapped, and immediately felt guilty. "Just walk in and cool off at least."

Reluctantly he waded out up to his knees. I stayed just beyond reach to entice him further. "You want this? Come and get me."

"I'm not a fan of venturing blindly where I can't see the bottom," he said.

"It's only mud and a few crayfish."

"You're missing my point." He grimaced.

"As far as I can tell, you didn't make one," I said. But I knew he was talking about us. And he knew I knew.

He stopped where he was. "Aren't you afraid of anything?"

I turned on my back and floated. "Are you kidding?" The sound of my own voice reverberated inside my head. I could almost pretend he couldn't hear me. I closed my eyes. "I'm afraid of everything."

I must have drifted nearer to the bank; Jeremiah would not have voluntarily stepped out where the bottom dropped away.

He reeled me in by my left ankle and suspended my body, his palms under my shoulders and my upper thighs. I opened my eyes. He was looking me over. With the flat of his hand, he followed the path his gaze was taking, skimming my skin, raising goose bumps. He kissed the tip of my nose, took his hand away, and returned to his careful scrutiny. It was unnerving, intense, and somehow . . . physical. Waiting for touch.

Jeremiah's lips moved around the words: *I love you.*

There it was, the feeling I had been waiting for. Or was it? I stared up at the sky with my ears still underwater, willing the desire to take over my mind the way it had taken over the rest of me. And it didn't. My mind stayed clear and detached. Trudy might believe her theory about a guy not being able to choose between the thought in his head and the one in his pants, but I wanted to tell her she was wrong. It wasn't that simple. It worked both ways. To be desired was as powerful as desiring, but it wasn't the same thing—it didn't have the same reach. I couldn't bear to hurt Jeremiah, and so I chose to lie.

"I didn't hear you," I said, raising my head. My feet drifted down and found the bottom.

Jeremiah lied too. "I said your skin smells." He sniffed his fingers. "It's oily."

"Gee. Thanks. What do I smell like this time? *Eau de* duck shit?" I swam away from him. "Way to kill the moment, J," I said.

Regret passed over his face. He wrinkled his nose. "No. It smells like . . . kerosene. Or oil of some description." He scooped a handful of water, and it dribbled through his fingers in strings.

I turned and noticed the spreading slick on the surface, marbled with rainbows, like the last time but more definite. It swirled around us like a living thing.

Jeremiah bolted out of the water and toweled himself dry.

I pulled myself up onto the jetty and stood, rubbing my arms and legs. The water beaded and ran off. The oil stayed. "The water level is way down," I said through chattering teeth. "It's like somebody's pulled the plug out."

"It's spring fed. It's normal to fluctuate, particularly in summer." He wrapped my towel around my shoulders. "Hey, what is *that*?" Jeremiah said, pointing. "Can you see it?"

The sun had gone behind a cloud. I stared at the oil slick, tracing its origin to the widest thicket of reeds. Where once the reeds were dense and green, they were now brown and bent over, leaving a visible crop circle in the center where nothing grew. A pale bubble-shaped shadow seemed to hover just below the surface. The sun reappeared, and the shadow was lost in ripples and reflections.

"Jack . . ."

I handed Jeremiah my towel and dived back in. The unknown presence in the water was somehow less frightening than whatever he might have been about to say.

"Wait!" Jeremiah paced the bank. "What the hell are you doing?"

I swam toward the field of reeds. As I got closer, I put my

feet down and inched carefully through the clustered roots underneath. Here the waterline was still up to my neck. The reeds were tiny swords, slicing into my skin. When I reached the inner circle, I couldn't go any farther. My body hit something smooth and unmoving. I knew instantly what it was.

Jeremiah had worked his way around the outer edge, through the scrub. He stood on the nearest bank, peering over the reeds, about twenty meters away.

"It's a car!" I called.

"Come *on*, Jack."

My toes and the front of my thighs were starting to go numb. I parted the slick with my fingers and ducked under. When I came back up, my eyes were stinging. The smell here was pungent, the slick thicker. The oil had been starving the plants and the crayfish of oxygen—was that why the crayfish had taken their chances on land?

I reached below the surface and mapped the shape of the car with my fingers. *Roof. Windows. Doors. Trunk.* I worked my way around to the hood, and my hand closed over something hard, slimy, and square. I pressed my feet into the bumper and rocked the car, hanging on to the object.

Jeremiah was yelling. "Get out of there! Don't make me come in after you!"

"It's okay!" I yelled back. "I just want to see . . ." But I had stirred up so much mud and oil it looked like I was floating in a bowl of soup. I couldn't see anything.

I rocked harder. A pocket of air, just like the one Luke and I had seen, bubbled up and burst, and the slippery thing in my hands came free. I juggled it madly, but it shot from my fingers, flew into the air, and landed in the soup. *Plonk.* I tried to find it on the bottom, but I couldn't feel my feet. It didn't matter—I'd seen enough.

I gave up and paddled back to the jetty. Jeremiah hauled me out like a greased pig, his fingers sliding on my skin.

"You need a shower," he said. "And some Band-Aids. Your legs are bleeding." He wrapped my towel, and his, around me.

"It's nothing," I said.

"I'll take you home."

My teeth chattered uncontrollably, and I bit my tongue.

You're asking the wrong questions, Mads had said.

Now I knew exactly where to start.

I need, you need, we all need to talk.

As Jeremiah drove, I hunched in the seat, chewing my fingernails. I thought that if I spoke, my rage would sputter out, and I wanted to hold it close.

We pulled up in front of the house—not only was there nobody home, but I couldn't find my keys, and the scent of my own skin was making me feel ill. As Jeremiah cheerfully pointed out, the odors I'd left behind in Meredith's car (Tutti Frutti, Chinese buffet food, and now rank reservoir water and engine oil) were blending and leaching from the upholstery like proof of poltergeist activity.

It was the weirdest thing, showering while Meredith Jolley sat in her kitchen. When I came out draped in her towels, she handed me a loose pinafore dress with a ghastly floral print and some clean underwear. They were too small, and the elastic bit into my waist.

As I finger-brushed my hair in her bathroom mirror, Meredith came up behind me and took my wrist in a pincer hold. She seemed bewildered that she couldn't close the gap between her fingers. Then she opened a drawer and pawed through a tangle of jewelry. She held a pair of pearl drop earrings up to my earlobes and shook her head. She picked up a chunky marcasite watch, undid the clasp, and fastened it around my wrist.

"Yes. It suits you," she said. "You must keep it."

"No," I started to say, but she pushed my arm away.

"Please. I want you to have it." Her eyes were glassy.

I thanked her because there was nothing else I could say without sounding ungrateful, but it felt as if we'd made some kind of deal, only I didn't understand the terms. This moment—being accepted into my boyfriend's family, even thinking of him as my boyfriend, doing normal things like sleeping over and using the shower—it didn't feel normal. It wasn't quite how I imagined it would be.

The watch felt like a miniature anchor. It left dents in my skin.

I stood outside of the Mobius pub wearing the borrowed dress and the gifted watch. I smelled of foreign shampoo. I had begged, borrowed, and stolen, my haven had become a prison, and I was bursting with questions that, should I ask them out loud, might change my landscape forever.

Trudy was behind the bar, cleaning the sticky tops of spirit bottles. There were about five drunks sitting alone with their OTB tickets and beer.

She looked up and froze at the sight of me. I didn't often venture into the pub, and I certainly didn't do it dressed like that.

Trudy laughed. "What on earth are you wearing?"

I went up to the bar and climbed aboard a stool. "It's borrowed. I locked myself out."

"Borrowed from where? *Little House on the Prairie*?" She picked up another bottle.

"Meredith Jolley. And she gave me this." I held out my arm.

Trudy inspected the watch.

"It looks expensive. Why would she give you an expensive watch?" She ran her fingertip over the face. "And what are you doing borrowing her clothes?"

I sighed. "It's a long and winding story," I said.

And because Trudy was a sucker for long stories, she

walked right into it. "I'm on a break." She squirted lemonade into a tall glass and pushed it across to me.

"So," I said. I joined two short straws together and took a sip. "I went to the reservoir with Jeremiah today. We went swimming. Well, I went swimming and . . . wait, I have to go back further."

"Get on with it." Trudy came around to the other side of the bar and took the stool next to me. "And for the record, I'm not sure about this thing you have going with Jeremiah Jolley. He's not your type."

"You're the one who told me if it feels good, do it. And who, exactly, is my type?" I asked.

"Just tell the story," Trudy said. She flopped her head onto her arm and faked a snore. "I'm fast losing interest."

"Oh, you'll love this one." My anger flared again. "The crayfish in Moseley's Reservoir have been dying. I noticed it a while back—way back with Luke. I didn't think much of it. Critters die all the time, right? Mother Nature can be so cruel. But there was something different today, and I swam out to—"

"Oh, for fuck's sake, Jack. Get to the point." She grabbed my wrist and performed an exaggerated reading of the time. "I've got to get back to work."

I thought I was losing her, but her eyes flickered strangely. Was it an act?

"You know what I'm talking about, don't you?" I pressed.

"Go home," she said. "Get out of that revolting dress. Take

my keys. Shit, take my car if you have to." She went back behind the bar, her hands grasping for something to do.

"It's your car, Trudy. Your car is in Moseley's Reservoir." I waited. I couldn't be absolutely sure, and Trudy was giving me nothing.

She turned her back on me and busied herself with the cash register. "My car is parked out back." She took a deep breath and spun around. "Here." She slipped her front door key from its key ring and slapped it on the bar. "Get out of here. Some of us have to work for a living."

"But . . ."

"Out," she said.

I took the key and pushed through the swinging doors. Without proof, all I had was a brief encounter with the slimy hood ornament from Dad's old Ford Falcon, which was given to Trudy the day she turned eighteen. The same car she'd driven off in six years ago; the same car now parked in the reeds at Moseley's Reservoir.

I didn't know what it meant, and I had no clue why it was there.

On a hunch, I sat behind the refrigerator in the parking lot for about twenty minutes. Just when I started to doubt myself even more, Mads drove into the parking lot and went inside. A few minutes later, Trudy came out. She got into her Mazda and burned off, spinning her tires, in the opposite direction from home, heading up toward the reservoir.

24

"There's probably a body in the trunk." I paced up and down Meredith Jolley's driveway while Jeremiah tinkered with the engine of her car. "She came back to hide the evidence." Any attempt I'd made to shake Trudy up had been met with a twirling finger and a two-note whistle. "And she calls *me* crazy."

"Who'd she kill?" he mumbled with a socket wrench between his teeth.

"I don't know."

Jeremiah waved the wrench. "Let's assume you weren't seeing things and it is her car. So where was it the whole time she was away? Or did the car drown before she left?"

"I don't know. I don't know *anything*." I did another lap of the driveway, wringing my hands. "Well, I do know this: I know it's her car."

He popped his head out again. He said, "Why don't you just ask her? Surely that's the reasonable thing to do?"

"People lie, Jeremiah. My sister lies. I lie. Everybody does it."

"I don't. Seems to me all it does is create more trouble." He wiped his hands on a rag. "Where are you going?"

I threw up my hands. "I'm not in the mood for your logic. I'm going home!" I started walking.

He caught up and fell into step beside me. "There's probably a simple explanation, and it doesn't involve a heinous crime, unlike your body-in-the-trunk theory," he said. "I really don't understand why you're so upset."

"That's because I'm a *why* person," I yelled. "And you're a *how*. I can't get my head around this."

He grinned. "I love it when you're angry."

I turned around and walked off in the opposite direction.

"Where are you going now?"

"Home. I mean Ma's. I'm hungry."

"It's you," Ma said.

"It's me."

"Well, you might as well come in. I can't stand here all day. I've got something in the oven."

From the set of her shoulders, she was brewing a fair wicked temper.

"Will you be staying for dinner?" she asked.

If there was a right answer to that question, I couldn't tell. "Yes?"

"Wash your hands. And do me a favor, go get your father and tell him I'm ready to serve."

The glorious scent of Ma's butter pastry was coming from the kitchen. It was the one thing she cooked that made me think of home and happiness at the same time. My stomach growled.

One of Meredith Jolley's cats had made himself at home on the back verandah. I wondered how long it had taken before it realized that Gypsy wasn't there anymore.

"Dad?" I called. I turned the shed handle. "The door's locked." He had the music turned down low.

"It's you," he said, opening the door.

"Don't look so happy to see me."

"I didn't mean it like that. Come here." He wrapped me in a hug. I realized for the first time that I was taller than him. "Has your sister driven you out of the house?"

"Has Ma done the same to you?"

He chuckled. "It's more peaceful out here with my sub-woofer."

"Is there any room for me out here?"

He looked horrified.

"I'm joking. Trudy and I get along. When I can get past the fact that every time she opens her mouth, spiders come out."

Dad laughed. "It's a female trait. I mean family—family trait." He shot himself with his finger. "I've got to get that under control before we go inside." He sniffed. "Can I smell butter pastry?"

Ma had set an extra place where I used to sit, right above Trudy's bubble gum graveyard. I sat down and kept my elbows off the table. I reminded myself that I was a guest: I would not throw myself in Ma's firing line to deflect any attack on Dad, thus ruining my chances of finishing my meal and licking the plate. He was on his own.

Ma stood in the kitchen with her hands on her hips. "I take it you're ready for me to serve. Did you wash your hands?"

Dad ignored her, but I dashed to the kitchen sink and gave them a quick rinse. There was still a space left on Ma's shelf from when I took her china bird. Dad had tracked sawdust from the back door to the table, and he was paring his fingernails onto the tabletop with a small chisel. He'd also brought in a woodworking magazine, which he was reading.

Ma was doing her sorcery in the kitchen. She carried a tray to the table and set an exquisite, steaming, golden meat pie in front of Dad. On top, she'd cut a lattice shape, and rich brown gravy bubbled from each window.

Dad kept reading.

"It smells amazing, Ma."

She waited. Dad ran his finger underneath the words as he read. He was on the first page of a double spread. I watched Ma carefully, wondering whether a flung pie cooked at 350 degrees, or thereabouts, would inflict second- or third-degree burns.

Dad read on.

"Would you like me to serve, Ma?" I stood up.

"Sit down," she said quietly.

I did. My heart was hammering so hard I thought I might bust a rib.

Ma scooped a mound of mashed potato and slopped some onto each of two plates. She used tongs to place baked carrot, pumpkin, broccoli, and sprouts in perfect piles, like miniature funeral pyres. Finally, she pressed the point of a carving knife into the center of the pie. She cut two quarter wedges, slowly and deliberately, and used a cake server to slide one onto my plate, and then one onto Dad's. Her plate was still empty.

She stood in front of Dad and waited.

I froze.

Ma held up the dripping knife with the tip to the ceiling.

Dad reached for the ketchup and smothered the pie without looking up from the magazine. He forked a mouthful, cursed, blew, and tried again.

I waited.

Gravy ran along the glinting blade of the knife, down Ma's forearm, and dripped onto the floor.

I dropped my fork and slid my chair away from the table. The legs made a crude grating sound against the linoleum.

"Dad . . ."

Ma looked like she'd just watched everyone she ever loved

sink on a boat, while she was stuck on the bank, unable to swim. It was as if I wasn't there.

Dad had eaten all his pie and half his vegetables before he realized I hadn't touched my plate and Ma wasn't in the room anymore.

"What?" He shrugged. He wiped his mouth with a napkin, closed the magazine, and pushed the plate aside.

I followed Dad out to the shed. Ma was in her bedroom with the door closed. Dad hadn't noticed the gravy he'd spilled down the front of his shirt. He turned on the radio but lowered the volume.

"I don't mind. Turn it up if you want to. It's your shed."

"Well, thank you." He smiled. "You know, for years it was your sister's music shaking the walls. Then yours. Now it's my turn." He chose several pieces of twisted wood and started sanding.

"What about Ma?"

"What about her?"

"Does she ever turn the music up? Does she dance around the house when nobody's looking?"

"How would I know, if she does it when nobody is looking?"

I frowned. "You know what I mean. Is she ever happy? Does she have anything besides us?"

Dad winced as if I'd prodded a painful nerve. "We are not

a demonstrative family, if that's what you're getting at," he said. "But that doesn't mean we don't love each other. We show it in different ways."

"Like baking pies," I said. "And folding shirts."

Dad heaved a shuddering sigh.

"Dad? Could I have my room back? If I wanted it, I mean?"

"You know you can always come home, Jack," he said, but his eyes went snaky. "You don't have to ask." He picked up a tin of clear varnish and jimmied the lid open with a screwdriver.

"But I do." I sat on a stool in the corner and watched him stir. "It's not a halfway house."

He stopped then. "What is this really about? Is it money? Is it Trudy?"

"I think it's me," I said as honestly as I could. "Dad, are you and Ma okay? Did I make it worse?" My voice cracked.

"Worse, how?" He frowned.

"Worse, like . . . without us here, is there nothing keeping you two together?"

"Oh, Jack." He put the dripping brush down in the sawdust.

He was struggling with emotion. What he really wanted was for me to leave the shed so he wouldn't have to answer my questions. He wanted everything to stay the same. I understood that on more than one level: To say nothing was far less destructive than letting it all out.

"You should have thanked Ma for the pie," I said.

"I should have done a lot of things."

"I'm sorry," I told him. "You're a good man."

Dad shook his head. "I'm the one who let your Ma go cold. It's my fault. Don't you go thinking any other way."

"It's nobody's f—"

"You're wrong," he broke in. "But I don't expect you to understand. You're still a kid."

"I am not."

"You are. You know how I can tell? It's because you ask so many bloody questions—but you might as well ask them before you get so guarded you can't say what's in your heart anymore and your mouth does all the talking. And your mouth doesn't know any better." He slapped his chest. "This gets all dried up and tough if you don't let it take a punching once in a while."

"Stop. You're going to make me cry."

He cupped my chin. "Now, the first time you ask, Ma will say you can't come home. But she'll only say that once. It's not what she really means. You can get all angry and storm off, or you can ask her again. You have to ask twice. Okay?"

"Okay," I said. "I will."

Ma stayed in her room, and Dad drove me back to Trudy's house after I'd cleaned up the dinner dishes. Mads was home, but I didn't tell her I was there. I prowled the front deck, bugs circling and colliding around the sensor light. Inside, the phone rang four times while Mads's bedroom light was still on, and rang out once after she'd turned it off. It was past ten, and Trudy still wasn't home.

I slouched in the hammock and dozed. At eleven, I went inside, tripping over Gypsy, who was curled up on the mat just inside the door. She barely raised her head.

In my bedroom, the window was still open. Somehow the screen had come off and fallen onto my bed. Ma's china bird was in pieces on the floor. The moment I switched on the light, I realized my mistake: Bugs swarmed in, clicking and clacking, fluttering around the lightbulb and dive-bombing onto the bed.

"*Aargh!*" I danced around, waving my arms. I struggled to push the screen back, and the catches broke off in my hand. "Goddamn it!" I gave up and flicked the switch, ran out into the hallway, and slammed the door behind me.

"What the hell?" Mads came out of her room, rubbing her eyes.

"I'm going to sleep in Trudy's room," I declared. I put my hand on the door handle, daring her to challenge me. I opened it. "And by the way, did *you* know Trudy's car was at the bottom of Moseley's Reservoir?"

Mads took a step backward. "She told you."

Gypsy yelped and Trudy stumbled through the front door, swearing. Gypsy skittered across the floorboards out of her way.

"Bloody dog!" She looked at Mads, blinked, and focused on me. "What are you doing in my room?"

"What are you doing to my dog?" I said.

Her eyes were tired and bloodshot. "What the hell is going on?"

"I have to sleep somewhere," I told her. "My room has a plague now. The demonic possession is complete." I waved my arms around to simulate the bug swarm.

Trudy jerked her thumb. "So sleep on the couch. It's custom-fit for your arse now."

"Hey, I have a better idea. Let's all sit up and have an honest conversation. Let's talk about why you didn't bother to stay in touch for five whole years, and then you roll back into town like the freakin' Pied Piper. Let's talk about why your car never even made it out of Mobius. Shit, for all I know, you never made it out either!"

It was a shot in the dark.

Mads closed her eyes and pressed her fingers to her temples. Trudy dropped her handbag, and something inside it shattered.

"She knows," Mads said quietly.

"What? What do I know?"

Trudy's face turned purple. She pointed at Mads. "You . . ."

"I didn't tell her. Obviously someone else did." She sighed. "I'm going back to bed. You can scream all you want at each other, but I've had it with being the meat in this sandwich."

She smiled at Trudy, then at me. "Tell her. Please. And not in the hallway." She slammed her door.

"Am I right?" I whispered. "You never left?"

Trudy shrank. She left her bag on the floor and went into the living room. She slumped onto the couch.

"I knew it was coming. Who told you?" she asked. "Was it Ma?"

I held up my hand. "Wait. Go back. You never left, and Ma knew?" I was so furious—surely I was letting off sparks.

"I left home. I left Mobius. I didn't get quite as far as Europe."

"How far did you get?"

"Williamstown."

I let that sink in and it did—like a stone. "That's, like, two towns away. Less than a hundred kilometers. It's practically next door."

She nodded.

"Do you have any idea how much that hurts?" I yelled. "Everything I believed about you is a lie!"

Trudy's magic lay in the places she'd been, the things she'd seen—places I'd probably never go. Hearing her admit it never happened was like seeing the dust rubbed off a butter-fly's wings and watching it flap on the ground. The magic was gone.

"That's not true," Trudy said. "Some of them were lies you told yourself. I don't know who started the rumor about

Europe, but Mads told me that's what you all thought and I figured it was better that way."

"And the car?"

"How'd you know?" she said. "It sank pretty deep. I thought it was gone forever. I went up there but I couldn't find it."

"The water level was down. The reeds died. Jeremiah saw it and I swam out. The hood ornament snapped off in my hand."

Trudy pulled one of Mads's cigarettes from the packet on the table and considered lighting it. "I was waiting at the reservoir," she said. "I'd told Mads and she was supposed to come, but she didn't. Ma had kicked me out after one of our fights. I had no idea where I was going. I just wanted out. When Mads didn't turn up because her folks wouldn't let her leave, I was so mad and so lost. Then the car wouldn't start. So, I pulled it out of gear and tried to push it backward—to jump-start it down the hill—only it started rolling in the wrong direction, toward the reservoir. I jumped out." She put her hands over her face. "God, it went under in less than a minute. Everything I owned was in it. I had nothing." She laughed. "I walked back into town."

I asked the question, but I knew the answer already. "Why didn't you just go back home?"

Trudy made a harsh sound in her throat. "And prove Ma right? Not likely. I caught a ride to Burt in Ken Watts's truck and from there I called some friends. They helped me get on my feet, no judgment."

"And Ma knew the whole time."

"No. I only told her when I got back." She squeezed her eyes shut. "I wanted you to think I was happy," she said. "I had three different jobs, paid my rent, hooked up with a few guys, and none of them worked out. Five years go by so fast."

"Not when you're the one left behind."

She sniffed and wiped her nose. "It doesn't make you any less important, Jack. It just makes me less honest. I'm sorry. It wasn't about you. None of it."

That hurt. I picked up a cushion and threw it at her. "You sold me this whole stupid dream about living with you and being like, *best pals*, and it was all going to be boys and parties and . . . it's all turned to shit. It's shit!"

Gypsy put her tail between her legs and curled up in the corner.

"Maybe it was your dream." She gave me a hard look and stood up. "Yeah, shit. There's a lot of that. But you're telling me you wouldn't have moved in with me if I had told you the truth? Get over yourself. You couldn't wait to get out." Trudy threw the cushion back.

I punched it. "You didn't give me the choice." I knew she was making sense and I'd forgive her, eventually. I always had. But right now I just wanted to find her weak spot and press it. "You're such a fraud."

She smiled. "You always thought I was a stronger, better person than I really was, Jack. That's really hard to live up to."

She got up. She brushed past me and went to bed, leaving me alone with my shaking dog and a throbbing headache. As she picked up her bag in the hallway I heard the broken thing inside it tinkle. *That's us,* I thought.

I turned her story over in my mind and tried to think of it in a way that wasn't all about me, but I couldn't.

25

"Jeremiah Jolley is on the phone for you again," Mads said, clamping the receiver to her chest. "He called last night, too. Are you home?"

I shook my head. All those times I'd complained about the phone being cut off, and now I wished Trudy would unplug it. I drew my finger across my throat and made an X with my arms.

"She's right here," Mads said, frowning. She offered it to me, stretching the cord as far as it would go. "I'm tired of playing secretary." She yawned and went into the kitchen.

"Hi," I said brightly.

"I have something to tell you," Jeremiah said, his voice a note higher than usual. "Well, ask, really. It's a surprise. I'll pick you up at six tonight?"

Something to tell me. *A surprise.* All perfectly fine words arranged to arouse my curiosity and give me butterflies, except I felt like I had a stomach full of curdled milk. I plucked at the cord and deliberately cut off the circulation in my thumb.

"I have something to tell you, too," I said, thinking of Trudy's revelations, but then I realized I didn't want to tell him about it. He wouldn't understand.

"Oh," he answered.

Immediately I felt more guilt: that I could so easily suck the joy out of him. "Hey. Looking forward to it! I'll see you tonight." If he knew me even a little bit, he would have seen right through it, but to Jeremiah words and truth went together. He didn't know me well at all.

I waited, slouched in the hammock. Trudy and Mads were having a girls' night out, and I would have done anything to trade places, to be laughing, drinking, dancing, even if I hadn't forgiven Trudy. But I wasn't invited.

Mads said we both needed time to lick our wounds.

I gave the hammock a violent twist. One of the ropes snapped. I landed painfully on my side. I just lay there and contemplated life from what I thought was rock bottom. The deck boards were peeling, and several shoots had come up through the gaps, searching for something to strangle. If I stayed there long enough, it would be me.

I got up, untied the hammock, balled it up, and threw it in the outside trash can. Even my possessions were turning against me.

"There's a hole in my bucket, Jeremiah, Jeremiah," I sang to myself.

A car pulled up and did a U-turn on the front lawn: a dark blue coupe with racing stripes and a powerful, throbbing engine.

"What do you think?" Jeremiah called, hanging his head and both arms out of the window. He gave it a rev. "Do you like it?"

So this was the surprise. I was so relieved he hadn't arrived with flowers and a different surprise that I smiled and said, "It's amazing."

He opened the passenger-side door.

I slid into a deep bucket seat that held me like a tight hug. It smelled of frangipani deodorizer and leather. "I am in love with this car," I said, running my hands over the dashboard.

Jeremiah flinched. He straightened out his hurt expression and got back into the driver's seat. "Look." He measured the distance between the roof and the top of his head and stretched his legs out until they were locked at the knee. "Do you know what this means?"

I was too afraid to know what it meant. I whooped and turned up the stereo instead.

Jeremiah grinned and put his foot down.

With the new leather smell in my nostrils and the seats slid all the way back, the mushroom lights glowing, the speakers crackling, and the screen all lit up, the tension was almost more than I could stand. Jeremiah and I were going to make love, in a car, at a drive-in, while the credits rolled. A normal, everyday date. I was stuffed with cold buttered popcorn and Coke. My hand had been held. We were alone and I was cherished.

It was perfect.

We made it almost to the end of the movie before Jeremiah exhaled and spoke, all in a rush.

"Jack, I have to go back to Melbourne and get some things sorted. Then I can come back here for another week, and after that I figure I'll drive home for the weekends. It's only a few hours," he said. "But what I want to know is . . . will you come with me? For a couple of days? We can drive down the coast and my place is small but nice . . . you know, separate from my uncle's house. You can stay. I'll show you around." He glanced at me shyly. "If it makes you uncomfortable we can stay in a hotel in the city." He ran his free hand over the dashboard. "I've been thinking about buying a car but until now I've never really needed one." He let his hands fall into his lap. "I know it's sudden. I've tried to ask you before, but . . . I want you to come with me. What do you think?"

What did I think? I let go of his hand.

I thought that if he had thrown a bucket of cold water over me, I would have been less stunned. I wished we'd gone straight to the last part first. I didn't know what I wanted. Things were moving so fast and in a direction I didn't expect, even though, in hindsight, I had been at the wheel for the whole ride.

"Gosh," I said. "*Now* things are complicated."

He moved his body away from me. "What the fuck is that supposed to mean?"

I sounded like him, and he sounded like me.

"I don't know. I just thought you were here for a good time, not a long time," I said, trying to lighten his mood. "Summer's almost over, and so is the movie." Why couldn't he see? I was letting him off, no strings. He didn't owe me flowers and everlasting love; I wasn't like other girls. I clamped my hand on his thigh and squeezed. "I thought this was what you wanted."

He tensed. "You've never asked me what I want." He gestured to the screen: John Cusack was serenading Ione Skye with his ghetto blaster. "So what was all of this?"

My blood ran hot. Why did everything come down to a *choice*? Why ruin what we had right now by making me *choose*? I was still caught between trying to flush out my lingering feelings for Luke and trying to fix my messed-up life. I wasn't ready to make a choice, and Jeremiah had made a rookie mistake: He gave me his heart too soon, before I knew how to be careful with it. "Something to do," I mumbled, and I wished I could take it back.

"And what am I? Or what was I?" His deep voice cracked, and his eyes were hollowed out. "Jack? Was I just something to do?"

So I leaned over and I kissed him. It turned out I could

fake it. A kiss was the only thing I could think of to make him stop talking, and he was breathing hard and kissing me, too, but not touching me with his hands at all, as if there was a force field pressing him back. I got angry. I got scared. I played the ace. I unzipped his jeans, tugging them down while I held eye contact and lowered myself onto him. He lifted his hips, and he didn't look away; our breath misted the windows, but suddenly his lips were telling me *no*, and in his eyes I saw pain, anguish, confusion, desire. And it was familiar.

"No?" I pulled away and folded into myself. I dragged hot tears away with my fists. "Really?"

I wanted to take his hand and tell him I understood. But I was fumbling around in the dark, half-stunned and blinking, being held accountable for mistakes I'd made before I knew any better; my body said one thing while my heart yearned for something more, and the whole time the answers were somewhere in between, just out of reach.

"No?" I sneered. "Then what the hell did we come here for?" I reached up and switched off the speaker. There was nothing but silence as the credits rolled.

Jeremiah pressed his lips together. He got out of the car, slammed the door, and pulled up his jeans.

I waited, curled into the seat, as he shut everything down. I closed my eyes, but the ghostly silhouette of the screen and the shape of Jeremiah were still there.

As he drove me home, I practiced lines in my head that

might get us talking again, might tell the truth or something like it, but nothing would come out.

Thom and Trudy's cracks were beginning to show. She niggled at him over nothing, and Thom stayed over less often. Mads spent more time in her room to avoid the tension, but I made sure I hung around. I reclaimed my end of the couch and commandeered the remote; I ate whatever I wanted and left dirty plates lying around. Trudy couldn't attack me without running the risk of a very public counterattack, and so she picked on Thom. I used Trudy's lies as currency. Trudy skirted me as if I was a bomb that might detonate without warning.

If I let things play out, Trudy would sabotage herself: She'd deliberately pick the unstable block rather than allow anybody else to knock over her tower. I knew, because we were both becoming experts in self-sabotage. But this was the waiting game, and I was already a master.

On cue, Trudy hissed, "Why don't you ever put your shoes away?" She kicked Thom's boots across the living room floor. She picked up a glass I'd left on the table and took it into the kitchen.

"Sorry," Thom said, and got up. He started putting on his boots.

Trudy came back in. "Where are you going?

I felt sorry for Thom. Trudy's weapons were loaded for me, but she had to fire at an innocent.

"I've got to go and check on this bloke up in the forest," he said. "I'll head home after that. I'll call you tonight."

My stomach dipped. "What bloke?" I asked too quickly. So Thom had seen him too.

At my tone, Trudy raised her eyebrows.

"Camper," he answered. "He's a bit odd, but it's probably nothing to worry about. It looks like he's been there for a while. I've encouraged him to move along. It's just habit. I always check on anniversaries."

"What anniversary?" Trudy and I said together.

Thom frowned. "You know—the young lad. The last one, a year ago. He was—"

"Don't say his name." Trudy put her fingers in her ears. "That's like inviting them inside."

I was light-headed, even though I was sitting down. There had to be a connection. I knew *something* was about to happen, and I wouldn't be able to stop it.

It didn't seem that long ago, but a lot can happen in one year. Trudy had come back home but I felt like we were further apart now than when I'd imagined whole oceans between us. Ma and Dad had disconnected. I'd loved and lost: lost Luke, lost Trudy, lost Ma, lost Astrid, lost my job. And Jeremiah. I reached down and found Gypsy's warm body squeezed under the table next to the couch.

Losing Gypsy.

Losing my mind.

Losing hope.

And if it was exactly one year today, I sensed Pope would be leaving, one way or the other.

Losing Pope.

Thom's car came down at a sedate speed an hour later. I took my chin off my hands. *Everything is okay.* If it wasn't, surely he would have been speeding. Or was it too late to matter?

I let twenty minutes pass, then started walking. My heartbeat was skipping all over the place, and I was out of breath. Halfway there, it started raining; I was dripping by the time I reached the forest sign.

"I hoped I would see you today," Pope called before I came into view.

The air smelled fresh and sweet, but my relief was sweeter. I hadn't made a sound; the earth was spongy and silent underfoot.

"How can you tell when I'm here?"

He was packing up his tent. "The insects. You have to listen. The sound changes—it's as if they're playing elevator music. The real music starts when they think there's nobody around. Like people, really." His stubble had grown into a full beard. His eyes were still sunken and sad. "Hungry?" He held up a bag of barbecue chips in one hand, a squashed iced bun in the other. "One person can't eat all of this." He gestured to a pile of canned food and wilting vegetables in plastic bags.

"Hey," I said warily. "I feed you, remember?"

He threw the bun at me.

I caught it, opened the bag, and broke off a piece. "I suppose you know the ranger knows you're here."

"I do." He stuffed the tent into its bag, dirt, leaves, and all. "We met weeks ago."

"He didn't say anything about you until today."

"I asked him not to. Same as I asked you. The last thing I needed was all of you people conspiring to bring the madman down from the mountain."

I frowned. "You people?"

"What, you thought you were the only one?" He winked.

"I'm sorry—I don't understand."

Pope wiggled a tent peg from the ground and shook off the dirt. "Others came. Merrilyn from the bakery. Alby. Thomas. They brought food, like you. They tried to get me talking, like you. I guess you'd know most of them, living in a place like this." He dropped the peg at his feet and wiped his hands. "I've only had the odd day alone since the day after I got here. You were the first, though." He reached over and plucked a leaf from my hair. "I'm the best-kept secret that everybody knew and nobody told."

I sat down and crossed my legs. I wasn't the only one separating the people in my life. It was a great strategy for keeping secrets, but it didn't make for much of a safety net to catch you on your way down.

"I'm surprised and not surprised all at the same time," I admitted.

Pope reached into one of his pockets and pulled out Alby's spare set of Laundromat keys. "Here." He dropped them into my lap. "I won't need them anymore. So, anyway, I'm leaving."

"Oh."

"I thought you'd be pleased."

"I am," I said, scowling, and he smiled. "What happened? What changed?" As I asked the questions, I looked up. The bottle was gone. Fragments of glass were scattered under a nearby tree. "You opened it?"

"I needed to read it—I was always going to read it on this day, and I was always planning to leave today if I survived knowing what was inside."

I screwed up my nose. "But I thought you wrote it. I thought it was yours." I was so confused.

"It was my brother's . . . Joel." He stumbled over the word. "The car was his but I drove it back here. It was his bottle and his note. He had just turned eighteen." He sat down next to me.

"Joel," I said slowly. Using the tent peg, I wrote the letters in the dirt. "I'm so sorry."

Pope watched, and retraced them with his finger when I'd finished. "Me, too. I don't know why I felt I had to come here. I needed to do something until the world was the right way up again. Does that sound crazy?"

"No," I said. "I count."

He rubbed his dirty hand over his face. "So many times I let the phone ring out when he called. And if he didn't call, I told myself everything must be okay." His breath sighed through his fingers. "It's like what you said about not being able to acknowledge your goldfish—that was me. It wasn't my problem if I didn't pick up the phone. And then he was gone, and we've all been asking *why, why,* but none of us really wanted to know the answers. It's hard to know how much is my fault and how much I couldn't have changed if I'd tried."

I swiped at tears before they could spill over. "What does the note say?"

Pope was dry-eyed, but his expression was haunted. "It says 'I'm sorry' and 'I love you' and 'God, help me'—all the things we never say until it's too late. Imagine if we said out loud all the things we might write down and stuff into a bottle? I wish I'd picked up the phone. I wish he'd waited."

I struggled to find the right words. Whatever I said, it would be wrong. My life seemed so short and untarnished right now. "Waiting is hard when no one comes."

He nodded. "That's the truth."

"So that's it, then. You have closure."

Pope shook his head. "Closure. That's a term people use when they have reasons and answers. I don't have any of those things. What I have is sixty days in a forest and about a million mosquito bites. I have the kindness of strangers."

He touched my hand. "Being here gave me something to do while I obsessed about not being able to change anything." He scratched at a bite on his arm. "So no, I wouldn't call that closure. I call it distraction."

I sniffed. "I hope you're going to be okay. I hope your family will heal. I hope I don't see you here again."

"I don't want your hope, Jack. Hope is something small and weak, trapped in here." He tapped his chest. "Hope is faith without wings. Find faith, instead—it'll carry you further. Hope is nothing if you squeeze too tight and don't let go. It lets you down, every time."

He hugged me awkwardly. I sat on the damp forest floor, letting the rain seep into my pants, watching him pack up the rest of his campsite.

"I hope I see you again," I said softly. *I still hope.*

Without turning around, he replied, "We'll find each other again. We're the lucky ones. We're the kind of people who go looking." He stared up at the pieces of sky above. "Blue skies, Miss Jacklin. Blue skies."

I didn't expect to feel so empty when Pope left. Like the night he arrived, I heard tires sliding on the dirt road to Nula, but I didn't see him go.

I loved too easily. Did I feel love for Pope? It felt as if I did. Anything beyond like felt like love to me; there was nothing in between. But as I left him behind, the emotion had already started to fray, like the bonds made at school camp over midnight pranks and spinning bottles. I'd outgrown my childish love for Trudy, and in its place was something stiff and scratchy that needed to be broken in all over again. Astrid: a bright button, something to hold up to the light every now and then with a shrug and a smile. Ma and me—our love seemed like it would keep stretching and fading until it wore so thin, it tore away; Luke would always feel like someone I'd borrowed but had no right to keep. And Jeremiah—my emotions made no sense, a loop with no end. Life would be easier if I could care less. Love would be easier if it was one size fits all.

The sound of tires on gravel faded. I moved a bead on the abacus to the right-hand side. I wasn't only putting lines through the days, I had started crossing off people, too. I moved beads for Trudy, Ma, and Astrid, and left one poised in the center for Jeremiah. He hadn't called, and I couldn't tell if I was wound up because he might call, or because he might not.

Pope's words rang true. Distraction worked best when your heart hurt so much you couldn't be alone with it. Was that what Jeremiah was to me? A *distraction*?

I ate half a tub of Mobius's World Famous Homemade Ice Cream and made myself more queasy. Trudy and Mads were asleep. Gypsy had sneaked up onto the couch with me and was slowly squeezing me off and onto the floor. Outside, the trees tapped on the windows, and I could hear it, the bug music, the way they played when nobody was around.

I felt the change in beat when a car rattled up and idled in the driveway.

Gypsy pricked her ears and growled.

I rolled off the couch and went to the window, but the car was hidden behind the rainwater tank. A door slammed. Heavy steps on the back verandah. My skin prickled. Nothing good happened at a quarter to midnight.

Gypsy pressed herself against my legs and let out a vicious bark.

I slid the door open a crack. "Who's there?" I called, but I could tell who it was by the shape of him, standing in the shadows, shuffling from foot to foot. Gypsy pushed her nose into the gap. "Stay," I said. I pressed my hand onto her head, and she backed up.

"It's me," Jeremiah said. He stepped forward, and the sensor light came on.

"You scared me." I smelled beer. "You've been drinking."

He had his arms wrapped around his waist as if he was trying to hold himself together. "I didn't drive. Roly's waiting out front. I'm sorry; I know it's late. I just needed to talk."

"Everyone's asleep. I'll come out." I slipped on a jacket and slid the door closed as quietly as I could.

"I was going to call, but . . ." Jeremiah trailed off. He was a mess: His face was haggard, eyes bleary, pieces of hair sticking up like he'd been running his hands through it.

"I know. I should have called you, too, but stuff has been happening, and . . ." I meant that I shouldn't have waited so long to tell him we were over, but he brightened.

"I'm sorry," he said, and dropped his arms to his sides. He moved toward me.

"God, what are you sorry for?" I took a sideways step. I didn't want him to touch me. If he touched me, I might unravel. I'd screw things up all over again. "You didn't do anything wrong. This is my fault. I just can't seem to say what I really mean. Ever."

"You can tell me now," he said.

"It . . . must have been hard for you to come here."

Jeremiah smiled. "Bravest thing I ever did. Say it, Jack. You're shaking. You're breath-holding and slow-blinking. It's pointless. Eventually you'll have to open your eyes and breathe out. Look at me. Just say it."

Cruelty, kindness, truth, lies—they all hurt in the end. It was better to say nothing at all. I squeezed my eyes shut and wished there was an easier way. When I opened them again, he'd moved closer. As hard as I tried to look at him, my eyes kept sliding away.

Love is a pie. Of all the things my sister could be right about, it was that.

I shrugged.

Jeremiah drew himself up to his full height, stuffed his hands into his pockets, and stepped back. "I'll go. I'm leaving tomorrow night. I'll wait at the house until five. If you want to come with me for a couple of days, meet me there. If you don't, well . . . I'll see you when I see you, Jack."

When I heard tires crunch on gravel, I went inside. He'd given me the easy way out, and he was gone. The wrong wishes always came true.

26

Tick-tock. Never had a minute hand moved more slowly than this. I watched five o'clock come and go, curled on my side, spooning Gypsy, feeling her uneven heart-beat beneath my palm. How long would Jeremiah wait—at which point would he decide I wasn't coming? Was he already making excuses for me? Would his waiting be measured by his perfect logic, or blind faith? Would he just wait—endlessly, hopefully, irrationally—like I had, so many times?

Gypsy stirred and lifted her head. She stared at me as if I'd made a sound. Her breath gargled in her throat. I wiped her drool and rubbed her ears, but she sighed and moved away—she knew what kind of person I was, and she didn't approve.

My bedroom door opened.

"I didn't hear you knock."

"I didn't," Trudy said. "What's wrong with you?" she asked, like an accusation. "You can't stay in here all day." She sat on the end of my bed. "Thom and I nearly broke up last night. You don't see me wallowing in it."

"That's because you have no heart."

Trudy's bottom lip quavered. Her eyes filled.

"I'm sorry," I said. "I don't mean it." I started crying too. "And what do you mean 'nearly'? You know when it's over."

"It feels like it is."

"If you don't want it to be over, you should fix it."

Trudy spread out beside me on the bed. Though it was still an island, we could both touch the walls on either side with outstretched fingers. "You can't swing a cat in here."

"Tell me about it."

Trudy grabbed my hand. She laced our fingers together. She gripped so tightly I got the start of pins and needles. For once, we were in balance—as if we'd both jumped off the seesaw at exactly the same time—just the right amount of wasted love and useless pain, a dash of good but mostly bad, and nobody to blame but ourselves.

"This falling in love malarkey," she said, sniffling. "It won't work. I'll be doing him a favor. At least the damage is contained. I've never told him how I feel."

"Congratulations," I said. "Crisis averted."

"Hey, at least we have each other." She squeezed my hand. We both stared up at the stained ceiling.

"There's that," I said dully.

"You and me. Hearts in tatters, dignity intact."

"Amen." I crossed my heart.

"It could be much worse."

"Yeah. Close call," I said.

"We should have kept it simple. I wish he could have left it at sex and the occasional movie."

"God, stop!" I exploded. I swung off the bed. "Who are you trying to convince?"

"What do you mean?" she said, blinking.

"I don't see the problem! He cares about you. You seem to care about him. Do you know what the chances are of that happening to two people, at the same time?"

"It's not that simple." She jerked away. "It's bound to end—I might as well end it now. You'll understand one day." She got up to leave.

I picked up a pillow and hugged it. "See, I don't want to be brittle like you. I don't want to hold everything inside so I never get hurt. The falling is the best part, isn't it, in love? But how would you know—you never let go."

"You're just a kid," she said.

"I'll be eighteen in nine months. I expect I'll know it all then." I sat down heavily. "I think you're kidding yourself. You're upset anyway. Tell him how you feel. What's the worst that could happen?"

She balled her fists and pressed them into her eye sockets. "I can't. It's too hard."

"No. It's not."

Trudy had such a long way to fall from the pedestal I'd built. I liked this new Trudy: messy, vulnerable, and scared, like me. For the first time ever, I could see right through her.

"You liked him," Trudy said. "Jeremiah."

"Yeah, I did. I do."

"He seems like a nice guy. He was good to you."

"He was."

"Tell me the best thing and the worst thing," she said.

I ground the heel of my palm against the ache in my chest. "The best thing . . ." I stopped. There was no way to separate a whole tangle of emotions into best and worst. I let my body go loose and fell back onto the bed. "I liked him. I loved the way he made me feel." I tried to make sense of my thoughts before I let them out. "But . . . I think the problem was . . . I loved the way *I* made *him* feel more than anything else." I glanced at Trudy. "I suck."

She nodded. "Yeah, sometimes you do. Sometimes we all do." She lingered in the doorway. "Maybe you just weren't ready. It's too soon after Luke. Dust yourself off and move on."

"Jeremiah *was* my version of moving on. How do you *steer* this thing?" I yelled and thumped my heart.

Trudy gave me a peace sign and closed my door.

Something screamed outside.

"Fuck off!" I screamed back.

I leaned through the open window and caught a glimpse of Ringworm skulking underneath the bushes. He shot out and glared at me from a safe distance with his yellow eyes, tail swishing. I looked down. The smell was stronger here. I parted the leaves, and beneath the bush there were at least thirty empty cans of tuna, crawling with ants, fermenting in the heat.

I didn't know whether to laugh or cry, but I should have known that my sister would always say one thing and do another.

Trudy had been feeding the damned cat too.

Two days after Pope disappeared, the morning after Jeremiah had left, Gypsy wandered into my room. She stood at the foot of my bed with her front legs splayed and lowered her head between them, blowing so hard that her jowls ballooned on each side.

I sat up groggily and rubbed my eyes. I'd left the window open all night, and the rotten smell had almost gone. A cool breeze lifted the curtains and swayed the bare lightbulb on its cord. Ringworm yowled nearby, but Gypsy didn't react.

"What's wrong? Are you hungry? Do you want to go outside?"

Gypsy turned around, went back into the hallway, and came into my room again. It was as if she'd forgotten what she wanted, and the act of passing through the doorway would remind her.

I snapped my fingers and stretched out my hand; she found it, snuffling.

"Do you want to come up?"

I got out of bed and put my arm around her middle. Her hind legs slid out from under her, and she fell heavily onto her side, pinning my arm underneath her rump. The floor was wet. I lifted her onto her feet, but her back legs wouldn't hold her; she turned her head and glared at them. I yanked my arm away and took her whole weight, heaving her onto the mattress. Her pee ran along my forearms and I ignored it, but with her one remaining sense she sniffed and knew it was hers. She looked away.

I settled her on the bed and made a nest with the quilt.

Trudy swore at the other end of the house. Instantly I knew what it was for. I headed to the laundry and filled a bucket with scalding water and lemon disinfectant. Trudy stood over the stain on the living room rug, still half-asleep. I plunged my hands into the water and brought the cloth out, dripping. My skin turned red. I started scrubbing without a word.

"Jack . . . ," Trudy said.

I put up one of my stinging hands. "Don't." She walked away.

I heard the shower running.

When the rug was clean, I went to the fridge and took whatever looked good, ignoring the Post-it notes: a whole rump steak, cheese cubes, bacon rashers, and leftover meat pie from Ma. I diced it and scraped the lot into one of Trudy's blue-and-white china bowls, which probably wasn't from Holland, and even if it was, I didn't care. In the bottom of the pantry, the box of tuna was empty. It was clear to me now: The box had been a ticking clock all along. A stray cat had grown fat as my best friend faded, like they'd exchanged souls.

I hated that cat. I wanted Gypsy's soul back.

Trudy came out of the bathroom with her hair in a turban. Mads went in. I squeezed past them in the hallway, holding the sacrificial bowl. Neither of them said a word.

I hand-fed Gypsy, who reclined like Cleopatra and found every dropped morsel in the folds of the quilt, while I made deals with gods I didn't believe in. I listened to the radio, knowing I'd never be able to hear those songs again without being reminded that I was selfish and cruel, and about as useless as a hung jury. But every minute I didn't act was another minute I could feel my dog's warmth and her heartbeat, though every moment was an ending of some kind.

Gypsy fell in and out of sleep. I stayed awake, watching her whine and twitch in her dreams.

After lunch Trudy poked her head around the door. "Jack ..."

"I know."

"Do you want me to call Ma?"

Ma would take over. She would still be my shield, if I let her. Ma could make the decision, and then it wouldn't be up to me; she wouldn't hesitate to approach the fishbowl. She'd handle it the way she handled everything: straight-backed and steely-eyed, saying all the wrong things at the very same time as she did what was exactly right. But in the time it took for Ma to get there, I knew I would change my mind a thousand more times, and I would hate her after. It was my decision.

Gypsy sighed. She looked so helpless, yet peaceful, and I knew then that she was ready even if I wasn't. I could leave her now, or I could take her as far as I could.

"No. Don't call her."

"Do you want me to stay home?"

"Yes."

"Okay. Do you need anything?"

How could doing the right thing feel so wrong? I took a deep breath and started counting down. "I need you to call the vet. Ask him to come here. We're ready."

I ran Gypsy's velvet ears through my fingertips. I strummed her ribs. I picked one song to match my grief and played it over and over in my head until the vet came an hour later. Gypsy didn't stir. I didn't let go.

"Trent is here to pick up the bike," Mads said. "He's had a look and dropped his offer to three fifty."

"I'll take it," I said. I didn't bother getting up.

Mads stood in the doorway. "Don't you need to . . . ?"

"It's unregistered. Tell him it has no fuel and it starts without a key. There's a red helmet hanging under the carport—he can have that, too."

"Okay." She disappeared outside.

I flicked between channels without paying any attention to the screen. When Mads came back, she threw a wad of fifties onto the blanket draped over my legs. She and Trudy had been tiptoeing around me for three days while I slept on the couch and watched television. Thom was back in Trudy's life, and she was happy again. There was no good reason for me to leave the house: Jeremiah had left, and Pope was gone too. Gypsy was buried under two feet of mud near the back fence. As Thom had dug, I'd been at the window in my old room, my elbows in the groove, watching the dirt fly.

Trudy came home a few hours later, carrying groceries. She bustled in, smiling. Her face fell when she saw me still on the couch, and she remembered we were supposed to be in mourning.

"Why don't you take us up to your drive-in tonight?" she said. "We could pack dinner and watch something."

"It's not mine. And it's raining."

"It won't rain forever."

I shrugged and changed to a local channel: It was a live news broadcast of a crew filming the attempted rescue of a stranded humpback whale. Juvenile, they said. Washed up overnight. It was in good health, and there was no apparent reason for it to beach itself. They were trying to keep it alive until the next high tide. In the bottom right-hand corner there was a timer, ticking away: five hours and fourteen minutes.

Trudy sighed, went into the kitchen, and started putting the groceries away.

"What on earth are you watching?" Mads asked. "God, you'll make yourself feel worse. The poor thing. It's so depressing."

I changed channels again, but when Mads went away I flicked back. I was fascinated by the depth of nothingness I felt—usually this kind of thing would have had me sobbing into my pillow. Was there a place beyond feeling? Was I there?

The "Whale Watch" segment became my obsession. The whale became my whale. The seaside town, Fowler's Bay, was only about three hours from Mobius. Occasionally the broadcast would be interrupted by other news, and I waited impatiently for it to come back on. As the timer ticked over into the eighth hour, Trudy grabbed my ankles and swung my legs onto the floor. She confiscated the remote.

"I'm going to work in an hour. You're not having this back until you've been out of the house for at least that long. Get some fresh air."

I gathered up the fifty-dollar notes from the floor and went to my bedroom. I hadn't been back in there since Gypsy went to sleep forever on my quilt. It still held her shape, but not her warmth. I touched the fabric; it was then that the nothingness burst open.

I ran out, down the hallway, into the living room. Trudy and Mads were sitting there. I kept running outside, slamming the sliding door behind me.

"Where is she going?" I heard Mads ask.

"She's getting some air."

I gasped on the back deck, my head between my knees.

Where *was* I going? I shouldn't have gone into that room that wasn't my room. Grief had muddled my thinking. No matter where I looked, that lump of dirt by the back fence was at the edges. When my breath came back, I sneaked around the side of the house and sat on the front steps, hiding like a little kid who couldn't run away without having somebody drive them.

In another part of my mind, that timer kept ticking.

I went back inside, stuffed clothes into a bag and money into my jeans pocket. I straightened the quilt, erasing Gypsy's shape forever. I took the bag into the bathroom, showered, and threw yesterday's clothes back on in record time. I waited for Trudy to leave, then asked Mads if she would drive me to the bus station in Burt.

Pope said hope was nothing if I squeezed too tight and didn't let go—he said I should find faith instead. But he was wrong. To find faith was to believe in something that wasn't mine, something I couldn't control, something without any evidence that it existed. Hope was different—I knew I had to hold it tightest when it seemed it might float away.

Hope was personal. One day I would tell him that.

27

Fowler's Bay seemed like the edge of the world: a ragged strip of high, white cliff and a broad sloping beach that stepped off into the endless blues of the sea and the sky. I'd been there an hour, and people were still coming. There were about a hundred of us now, spread out along the beach, cliffs at our backs, huddled against a shrill wind. It was unbearably bright as the sun set directly in front of us. I'd left my sunglasses behind on the bus.

I was stupid to think I'd be the only one.

When I first arrived, I found shelter in a shallow scoop in the cliff face. The sand was hot and gritty against my legs, the air briny and sour. I avoided catching anyone's eye. I tried not to fidget and draw attention to myself.

Down on the beach, it was like a crime scene: six men and three women wearing orange-striped wet suits, standing inside a flimsy barrier of yellow tape. Outside, a couple of camera crews inched closer, grumbling when they were ordered back. A helicopter hung lazily overhead; below, a cluster of seagulls hovered, just the same. Offshore, a tuglike boat seemed anchored to the spot though the waves surged and chopped around it. Along from me, an old woman, wearing a floppy blue sunhat and faded harem pants, defended her patch of shade beneath the cliff overhang.

And down on the beach my whale was dying, her fins two useless black wings at her sides. She'd dug herself into a trench, and her sounds of despair—clicks, sighs, deep-chested groans—were coming at intervals further and further apart. When I'd first heard them, I felt so hollow I thought I would cave in. Soon she would stop thrashing and be all pause.

There were so many of us—couldn't we move her? Couldn't we roll her like a giant hay bale until the deeper water took her back? Wouldn't she know we were helping her, and wouldn't she try harder? Wouldn't she fight?

I refused to look at the man who droned "That's it. She's gone now," each time the pause grew longer or the trench got deeper and the waves retreated.

The light was different here, the colors, too. When I'd stepped off the bus, the light was blinding, everything faded like over-washed clothing. The sun seemed much closer to the earth. In Main Street, Fowler's Bay, the shops were cheerful and open for business. The heat wasn't warm air that settled around you, but a burning haze that shimmered above. My skin was pink within minutes. The ice cream was plainly Häagen-Dazs in Häagen-Dazs containers, and the people on the street didn't stop to talk. It felt like the sun never went down in this town.

I stood and slipped off my shoes. I took a few steps out onto hard sand.

"You can't go any closer," the old woman said. "They don't want anybody down there." She raised a pair of binoculars hanging from a cord around her neck. Her skin was creased, toasted a deep brown.

"I know."

"She's hanging in there." The woman nodded to herself. "The tide's going out. She knows it. She's resting, conserving her strength."

"I've come a long way," I confessed.

She lowered the binoculars. "Are you upset?"

"I'm tired." I sank back into the soft sand and dug my feet in.

"I'm Nat," she said, and moved over to make room. "Come on up here."

"Jack," I said.

Nat refolded her towel and made a cushion for me. "You're burning. Here." She rummaged in a bag and handed me a bottle of aloe vera lotion, a flask of cold water, and her binoculars. "Look. See for yourself."

I searched through the lens for the whale's eye and wished I hadn't: It was dark, pain-filled, and intelligent, with a rim of white, like a human eye. The eye tracked the people around it, watching. I wondered if she understood that we wanted to help, or did she believe that these busy, black figures were the enemy. Was she terrified? Was she in pain? Were her insides being slowly squeezed by her own weight?

"Why do they beach themselves?" I asked.

"I prefer to think it's not a choice," Nat said. "Maybe she was lost, disoriented, or chased by a predator. This is the ninth I've seen wash up here in the last twenty years. The inlet creates some strong currents this time of year, so it could be that, too."

"What happened to the others?"

"Some died. The fully grown ones usually do. They're too heavy to help us to help them."

I shook my head. "She looks so weak."

"She has a better shot than most. She's stuck right where the drag is strongest."

"But couldn't we all move her?"

Nat smiled. "She's heavier than you think, and one swipe with her fin could cause serious injury. Her tail could kill. She has to do it herself—they can't save her, they're just keeping her alive."

"Are there more out there? Are they waiting?"

"No."

I let that sink in.

"It's the wrong time of year for migration. She doesn't need them. She knows where to go—she just took a wrong turn."

The team of rescuers backed away and spoke in a huddle. One man stayed, pouring seawater over the whale's glossy back, but the skin on her tail was already turning dull and gray. *Crayfish lose their shine like that,* I thought, *then other creatures move in and eat them from the inside out.*

"What are they doing now?"

Nat took the binoculars. They were damp from my tears, but she didn't seem to mind. "Something's happening."

"That's it; it's over," said the doomsayer, and somebody, finally, told him to shut up.

Apart from the lone man with the bucket, the rescuers moved away to sit inside the vehicles parked farther up on the flat, away from the shifting sand. The helicopter had gone. The boat was heading farther offshore.

"They're stopping," I said. Many people were packing up and leaving. I wanted to run screaming at the seagulls, which had settled in a semicircle around the whale. Were they waiting for her to give up?

"They're resting," Nat said, and put her sun-browned hand on my arm. "They've been here for two days straight. Where have you traveled from, Jack?"

I told her, and, gently, she asked more questions. She was trying to distract me, I knew. When the whale sighed, her grip tightened and she didn't let go.

"Won't be much of a moon tonight," she said. "It's going

to make things more difficult. How old are you anyway?"

"Seventeen," I said.

"Seventeen. I'm seventy-nine," she told me with a wry smile. "This is all I can do now—wait. I've lived here my whole life. I'm almost too old for anything but watching and praying. Doesn't seem like fifty years since I was waving placards in outrage and only eating orange food."

By sunset, Nat knew that I came from a place that was green all year round and that I'd never seen the sun slip over the edge of the earth like it had right at that moment. She knew about Ma and Trudy, about Trudy's car floating in Moseley's Reservoir. I told her about Pope, and Jeremiah, too—how he loved me but I wasn't whole enough to love him back. Nat said that sometimes all you could do was acknowledge the gift. She told me that she grew up in an even smaller town and she knew firsthand how everything you did left a ripple. And she asked me why I'd want to be on a beach far from home, with a crowd of strangers, an old woman, and a stranded humpback whale.

I didn't answer. It was too hard, and I was too sleepy to explain.

I wanted miracles.

The moon came out from behind a sheet of cloud. Nat was right: It wasn't much. But it was the same moon, wherever you were, and the stars made up for it. As I watched, one fell.

This time I was very careful what I wished for.

Nat dozed in her deckchair next to me. The wind had dropped, and the only sound was the gentle slap of waves. I stretched my stiff legs and brushed sand from my cheek. I slipped on a jacket. A faint stripe of pink was showing above the cliff face, but daylight was still a little while off. It was quiet.

This can't be how it ends.

I listened and strained to see any movement. There was nothing for the longest time, and I was already mourning when the whale shifted and blew. Torches flickered down near the shore. A floodlight came on, illuminating a circle of black sea, the half-submerged hulk of the whale, the bodies in the water.

"Nat." I shook her shoulder. "Nat, wake up."

She struggled to her feet. "The tide's back in."

"That's good, right?"

"It's good if it doesn't leave her stranded higher up. They'll have to try to hold her position now." She topped up my water flask and opened a packet of cookies.

"This is it," somebody else said.

"A week ago we had the mother of all king tides," Nat said. "She could do with one now."

There was a flurry of activity, and the boat edged its way in. The helicopter had come back, and a lone cameraman shot from a safe distance. Ropes were flung and tied. The rescuers began digging. As light broke, the tide fell short of its last line and receded. I watched, counting the waves as they broke farther and farther away, measuring the inches in increments of lost hope. The humpback was floundering in the deep hole she'd made, agitated now, spitting seawater through her blowhole with each sharp burst of breath. One fin turned circles, batting at the shallow water like a broken oar.

"They've got the ropes under her," Nat said, patting my arm.

Nat and I pressed closer, and the broken line of people behind followed. The rescuers ran clear of the water, away from the whale.

"They've missed it," said a woman. "There's nothing more they can do."

My hands bunched into fists. "No!"

The exhausted rescuers jerked around to stare. One man raised his arm in a final salute and barked into a walkie-talkie.

"No," Nat echoed. Her head bobbled on her thin neck as if she was struggling to hold it up.

I watched, silently praying they would go back to help.

Offshore, a giant wave built. A wall of dirtied water swelled. When it finally curled and broke, the wave smashed over the humpback whale. For a moment, she was lost to us. The tide surged in, lapping our toes, its powerful drag sucking the sand from under my feet. The boat's engine screamed; the man lowered his arm. She'd turned. Her great tail smacked the water, making it boil and churn. Just then the ropes snapped and flung back. The boat rocked. But she'd turned.

The next wave carried her backward. She was thrashing now. The cradle of deeper water held her as she surged forward onto the sandbar. She flopped helplessly until another wave gave her just enough lift to propel herself forward again.

"Let her go!" Nat shouted. "Go. Go, you beautiful thing!"

"Go," I whispered. I put my hands over my eyes. "I can't watch anymore. Tell me when she's gone."

I counted to seventy-six.

"She's gone," Nat said.

I opened my eyes. Nat grabbed my hand. We joined the others, hugging and high-fiving each other.

Way out, past the sandbar and in deeper water, the whale breached, and her underbelly flashed silver.

Nat and I took the long way back to town, wandering along the shoreline. I helped to carry her things, and she talked about her family. I had a bad case of sunburn and a lump in my throat too big to swallow.

We rounded a point and came to a horseshoe cove where the waves had pounded shells into fine grit and the tide had dredged up huge piles of rust-colored seaweed. I picked up a knotted piece of driftwood and a perfect cowrie shell. I put them in my pocket to take home.

Nat smiled at me. Her teeth were outrageously white in

her sun-browned face. She looked like something the sea had thrown back too.

"Nat?"

"Yes?"

"Do you think she'll catch up?"

"I think she'll do the best she can," she said.

She approached one of the mounds—over half her height and shaped like a giant mammoth—and slipped off her shoes. I did the same, and we kicked every one of those mounds, because you never knew what might be underneath.

There were still so many mysteries left.

28

I got off the bus in Burt at two o'clock and spent the last of my cash on a taxi back to Mobius. I watched the meter tick over until it matched the number of dollars in my pocket, then I asked the driver, Nick, to stop. We'd made it halfway along Mercy Loop. He pulled up in the truck stop, the last point where you could still turn around before Pryor Ridge came into view.

Nick offered to take me into town. "I can't leave you here." He shuddered and crossed himself. "I could never forgive myself if you turned that corner and were never seen again. You know what they say about the ghosts."

"I've run out of money," I said.

"I'm not worried about the money."

"I'm not worried about the ghosts." I got out of the taxi and let the familiar pulsing beat settle into my bones. "People only disappear in Mobius if they want to."

He crossed himself again. The taxi idled in the truck stop

until I turned the bend, and even then I think he was still sitting there.

I trudged along Main Street, matching my steps to the beat. A choppy breeze picked up dead leaves from the gutter and whipped them into whirlies; outside the bakery Barb Tuckey and Terri Walsh clutched menus and held on to their hats. Terri was the follower and Barb was the leader, and together they were all shit and no sugar, so Ma said.

"All right, Jacklin?" Terri said. "Don't you look like the weary traveler."

"I'm fine, thanks. I'm just headed back home."

I went to leave, but Barb Tuckey put her hand on my arm. "It's not right," she said. "We've been spreading the word. Alby will not be getting our business until he sets things right. We look after our own."

"The sooner he comes to his senses, the better off we'll all be," Terri agreed, and pointed her finger. "Since that one took over, the roadhouse has gone to hell."

I stopped. "What do you mean?" I followed the finger and saw Astrid, all legs and billowing skirt, attempting to hold down items of stock as the wind peeled them away and tossed them onto the street. It looked as if she had half the store on the sidewalk. Even from where we were, we heard her swearing and spitting hair.

"Hips like a harlot," Terri said.

Barb nodded. "Mouth like a trucker."

"I have to go. I'll see you later."

My bad temper returned. I realized you can't have a life-changing experience, waltz back into town, and have folks notice, as if you were wearing a pair of new shoes. Ten years from now, Barb and Terri would be waiting for their scones and tea, waiting for their husbands to haul in from the field, waiting for the outsider to put a foot wrong.

I started to cross the street so I wouldn't have to pass Bent Bowl Spoon. I kept my head down. My toes were still crusted with fine sand, and the tops of my feet were sunburnt. A couple of tiny, floaty white spheres got caught underfoot.

I looked up. More were coming, thousands, tumbling and dancing, spinning in flurries and taking flight over rooftops. I held out my hand and tried to catch them. A few stuck to my skin and dangled from my eyelashes. I felt like I was inside a Christmas snow dome. Astrid was emptying a couple of old beanbags from the lunch room into the Dumpster next to the roadhouse. It was a Styrofoam-bean blizzard.

"I hope you're going to clean that up," Terri yelled.

"Disgraceful," Barb called. "It's littering. That would have to be a five-hundred-dollar fine."

Mrs. Gates came out of the salon and clapped her hand over her mouth. Down the street a few drunks holding pints wandered out of the pub to watch the beans roll past.

Barb and Terri abandoned their table, marched up to Astrid, and let loose a mouthful of abuse.

Astrid opened her mouth to fire back, but she couldn't get a word in.

I stood in the middle of the road—trying not to laugh at the two women, sprinkled with white beans, bristled up and spitting venom—willing Astrid to stand her ground. The wind blew, her skirt ballooned, but she didn't bother trying to push it down. She dropped the bag and put up her hands as if to protect herself.

The beans were almost all gone now, just a few stragglers trapped in the gutter or caught in the trees. The snowstorm had lasted less than a minute.

I crossed the street and stood on the opposite sidewalk, staring at the wreck of Bent Bowl Spoon, the leaning stacks of diamond tiles resting against the side of the building. I could count them all right now, if I wanted to. Or I could accept that I saw things differently now from how I had seen them seven years ago. I just got stuck. Jeremiah was right.

Mrs. Gates shook her head and went back inside.

Barb plucked beans from her cleavage and threw them, along with some more choice words, at Astrid, as if they were stones.

"Leave her alone," I said.

Terri shot me a glance, but Barb's mouth was still running and she didn't hear.

"Shut up," I said. My voice carried clear across the street, but I was trying not to laugh. I wanted snow; I got snow.

Nothing was turning out the way it was supposed to, but maybe I had to change my expectations or just go around being disappointed all the time.

Barb's head swiveled slowly. "What did you say?" she said, her eyes bulging.

"I said shut up." And some of the rage under my ribs was gone. "Let it snow."

Alby opened the front door of Bent Bowl Spoon and stuck his head out. "What's going on?"

Barb and Terri retreated, muttering and shaking their heads.

Astrid lifted her chin. She bent down, picked up another beanbag, and unzipped it. A slow, glorious smile spread across her face, and she gave me a wink, snapped the bag like a wet sheet, and let the beans loose on the wind. She kept shaking the bag, until it was empty.

I walked into the blizzard. "How's Adam?" I stopped in front of her.

"He starts school next week."

"So you're staying in Mobius, then?"

Astrid looked uncomfortable. "I've said a lot of things I don't mean. And it's not like I have anyplace else to go." She fixed me with a stare. "You're lucky, you know."

"Lucky?" I screwed up my nose.

"Yeah. You belong." She reached out and put her hand on my chest. "Dare I ask about this?"

"Stricken. But still beating."

"Well . . . if you ever want to talk about it." She folded the bag into a tight bundle. "Jack? What happened to us?"

I looked down at my feet. "I don't even know."

"Trudy told me to stop hanging out with you."

My head jerked up. "She told you what? When?"

"Back when you were still working in the roadhouse. Something about a special place in hell for me." She smiled and held up her palms. "Don't get mad."

I thought about how Ma had gone out of her way to say the same thing to Trudy, and I wasn't mad. I *did* belong.

"Well, I'd better get back to work." Astrid gestured at the mess on the street.

"Still modernizing, I see."

"Yeah. Sometimes you have to make a big fucking mess before you can start over," she said.

Right then, I decided that Astrid was some kind of genius.

Homecoming. Coming home. I hadn't been gone that long or that far away, but I had an inkling of what Trudy must have felt the day she came back: a strange mixture of nerves and resignation. Home isn't where the heart is at all—it's where you can bunker down with your regrets without paying rent. I had nothing left to count but mistakes.

My tire swing was dangling from one chain. The other chain lay in a snake on the ground. The second tire was missing. Across the street, Meredith Jolley was sitting on her front verandah, her legs bare and her feet hanging over the edge. Jeremiah's Ford was parked in the driveway in front of the Barbie car. My stomach dropped away.

Using both hands, Meredith gestured for me to come over.

I crossed but stayed on the sidewalk, waiting for her to stop pretending and stab me through the heart.

"How are you?" she said.

"I'm good."

"Sit." She moved over to make space. "Stay awhile. Let's talk." She watched my expression carefully. "He's not here, Jack."

I breathed out. And because it had been a long time since anyone had invited me to stay, I sat down.

"I liked your eggs," I said to avoid other talk.

She smiled dreamily. "I crochet now. Some might call it making knots, but it keeps me busy." She looked down at her hands and spread her fingers. They shook ever so slightly. "The medication keeps my mind still, but not these. They're always twitchy."

"So you feel better?"

She groaned. "What's better? Can I function? Can I cook a meal without forgetting there's a pot on the stove? Yes. I promised Jeremiah I'd keep taking the pills so he wouldn't worry and he wouldn't have to check up on me—not for a while at least."

"Why . . . ?" I pointed at the car. "I don't . . ." I gulped. "I'm sorry."

"I know you are, Jack." She put her hand on my arm. "Honestly? I think he left the car behind so he'd have a reason to come back. Other than the obvious reasons, I mean."

"I'm really, really sorry. I want to give you your watch back. And I wanted to talk to him, but . . ."

"No. It's good that you let him go." She shushed me when I started to make excuses. "Jack, one of you had to make a choice and he couldn't do it. I thank you for that. I'm being selfish here too—he needs me right now, when he's sad, and in turn that's exactly what I needed, to be needed, if that makes sense. We've been pushing each other away for years."

I shook my head, but at the same time I thought of Ma and the push-pull of our love. I was uncomfortable, being invited into this secret adult world of straight talk and confessions.

"You must hate me," I said.

"Only a little bit."

"I hate me."

Meredith waved my comment away. "Jack, the last thing I wanted was for my son to be the nice boy who turned into a good man who lives in his shed. Do you understand what I'm saying? Now, I've known your mother a long time. We were never friends, but when you grow up in a town this small you can't help brushing up against other people's business."

"Are you friends now?" I asked.

"She's shown me kindness when I didn't deserve it and she helped me when I didn't know how to ask. We're both different now from when we were young." She cocked her head as if she was listening to a whisper in her ear. "Yes. I think you could say we're friends."

"Do you think Jeremiah hates me?"

"No. He loves you, Jack, and that's far worse. I've had to talk him out of calling you. He wants an ending of some kind. He needs to know there was nothing he could have done differently and that he's still worthy of love. We all need that."

"Will you give me his number?" I blurted. "I want to tell him I'm sorry." I was the toxic part of our relationship. He deserved to hear that.

She shook her head. "Not yet. He's not ready. Give him some time." She stood up and let go of my hand. "I want Jeremiah to love somebody who loves him back," she said. "You did the right thing, but you did it the wrong way. I'm not telling you that I forgive you. I'm telling you that I understand."

"I know."

Meredith nodded as if we'd made another deal. She opened her door. "Come back and see me. I mean that. When I think he's ready, I'll give you his number."

"I will."

"This is why we adults tell you not to grow up so fast," she said, as I walked away. "You think we have all the answers. But the truth is that we just get better at avoiding the questions."

Ma stood with her back to me, facing the kitchen sink. Her shoulders were tense. I heard the familiar clink of her gold bangle, the one she never took off, hitting the steel as she washed and rinsed a cup I'd barely finished using. A small suitcase stood in the corner near the dining table. I eyed it with a sick feeling in my stomach.

"Trudy tells me you took yourself off on a little holiday. To the coast," she said, without turning around. "That's nice."

"Nice" and "lovely" were words Ma used, I'd learned, in place of "selfish" or "ridiculous" or to indicate that she didn't understand or agree with your choices but didn't care enough anymore to say what she really thought.

"I did. I caught the bus. I saw a whale."

"Lovely."

That was it: I'd officially crossed over. She was done ranting, accusing, ignoring me, or telling me how to live my life. It was the same cycle she'd gone through with Trudy and Dad: separation, then bored, numb acceptance.

At that moment, the volume in the shed increased. The vibration rattled the trinkets above the sink. Ma steadied a crystal bell that was walking off the shelf and stomped to the back door, shouting at Dad to turn the music down. While she was gone, I reached into my pocket and left the driftwood and the cowrie shell to replace the china bird. I could see how Ma had to keep plugging spaces that we all left behind.

She came back, muttering. A crash near the front door made us both whip around.

"Goddamn it," she said, and went to investigate.

Ma picked up the splintered frame of her wedding picture. She slid the photo out and kicked at the glass on the floor. "That's it. That's the last one. Goddamn it," she said again, curling her lip and shaking her fist in the direction of the shed. She ran her hands over the scarred wall.

I went to the laundry and got a dustpan and brush. Seeing the evidence—the picture falling and smashing, not being taken down in spite, as I had imagined—it made me want to hug her. But how did you hug someone like Ma? The woman was a stonefish, all murk and camouflage until you put your foot in the wrong place.

I cleaned up the glass and wrapped it in newspaper before stuffing it in the trash.

Ma got out the vacuum cleaner. She stabbed the carpet with the nozzle until the glass shards stopped clinking, then kicked the barrel of the vacuum back along the hallway. Flakes of plaster floured her hands.

"Ma?"

"Just let me put this thing away."

I followed. "I could patch up the wall for you, if you like."

Ma stopped and cocked her head as if it was a trick question.

"I'll paint it too, and glue the picture frames back together. Dad can put some new hooks up." I was pretty sure, after watching Jeremiah, that I could do it. But she was right to be suspicious. How long since I'd done anything to please her?

"What are you after? Do you need money?"

Her expression set, her battle face, the one I hated so much it made my hackles go up every time. The battle face always, always, preceded an argument.

I crossed my arms over my chest.

Ma mirrored the action.

"I can do it."

I pictured that tense rope, like the one between Trudy and me: *tug, tug.* The way we hammered up our defenses and tried to shoot each other down, all the times we chose hurtful words instead of truth, played dirty tricks, betrayed trust, used secrets, told lies, made war. We fought over the land between trenches as if it was a prize: Every inch gained was an inch lost on the other side. But it didn't feel like winning anymore.

"It'll just end up being something else I have to fix," she said, frowning. "If I want anything done around here, I do it myself."

The old emotions kept bubbling up—seventeen years of this and my programming ran like clockwork.

Ma straightened up and puffed out her chest.

My skin tightened and my blood ran hot in response. It hit me: *God, love is so close to hate*—but I took a deep breath and counted to ten, tapping my fingers on my forearm, and I did something I'd never done before: I dropped the rope.

"Ma, I want to come home."

She blinked slowly. The flush on her chest spread to her cheeks, and before she could blow, I said it again.

"I want to come home."

Her shoulders drooped, and she pressed her fingers to her temples. Suddenly she stepped forward and dragged her fingers through a knot of my hair, tugging my head along with it. "When was the last time you brushed this?"

"Three days ago."

She tutted.

"So, is that a yes?"

Nothing but the sound of our breathing and a dull *thunk* as another piece of plaster fell off the wall. I gave up waiting for an answer and turned to leave.

"I saw you on the telly," she said in a rush. "I was watching the live updates on the whale. I didn't get off the couch for a whole day—I couldn't seem to turn it off. I forgot what time it was, and I ended up telling your dad to make his own damned dinner. I fell asleep on the couch. In the morning, I woke up and I had this awful feeling in here." She touched her chest. "I trust that feeling. I got it the day Trudy left, but I was too busy yelling to pay attention. Just so you know, if you hadn't walked in when you did, I was damned well coming after you. And if I was younger, it would have been me on that beach."

Ma pushed past me and returned to the kitchen sink.

Clink, clink went her bangle. I trailed after her. I looked at the suitcase and saw it differently.

"You knew Trudy never *really* left."

She made a half-turn, but her hands kept cleaning. "Your dad and I didn't find out until after she got back. I've been nagging her to tell you, too. Let it go, Jack. Blame me if you have to blame anybody. She still left—the rest is just geography. It's in the past now." She spoke evenly, but one corner of her mouth had a telltale twitch.

"Next time maybe you could come with me," I said.

"Next time?"

"Next time there's a whale."

The clinking stopped dead.

29

It didn't seem to matter that we gave him a horrible name and cursed at him all the time—Ringworm stayed. Trudy and I were the consolation prize, but then a bad-tempered, people-shy orphan didn't have too many options. On the nights before I moved back home, we set a trail of cat biscuits along the railing leading to a ratty wicker basket on the rear deck. In the mornings, the biscuits were gone. I didn't know if Ringworm ever slept in the basket, but he sure as hell marked it with his scent. We tried to give him a kinder name, but he wouldn't answer to anything else. Over time, he stopped screaming at us and we stopped screaming back, and that was as close as we got to owning each other.

The same thing happened with Ma, Trudy, and me.

Two weeks after moving back home and I was working three part-time jobs: looking after Mr. Broadbent, sweeping hair and rinsing colors for Mrs. Gates on Saturday, and showing back-to-back films at the drive-in on Friday nights.

Astrid started calling me Jack-of-All-Trades; I called her Wrong Turn Astrid to her face. Since I wasn't hiding anymore, I ran into the old crowd from school more often. It mattered less and less what they thought of me, or if they were even thinking of me at all.

Alby let me keep a third of the takings from the drive-in. It wasn't much to begin with, but after a few weeks word got out. On a good night I sold around forty tickets. On a bad one it was just Roland Bone and me, drinking beer on the platform and arguing about everything from high school politics to what love really was. And each time I hit the switch and the old projector sent out its beam like a miniature lighthouse, I stuck up my middle finger at Pryor Ridge, the dark place. I waved to the ghosts, saluted the screen, and made careful wishes.

Mr. Broadbent had slipped further into his own dark place, and the void he stared into was moving closer. Sometimes I had to remind him to eat, and he'd forgotten how to smile. The only time he showed signs of life was when I took him to the drive-in—it was like sight was his one remaining sense, like smell had been Gypsy's.

Alby, in his own way, had already let him go. Whatever roads Mr. Broadbent and I were traveling, we'd passed each other way back, headed in different directions. But, on leaving the flat one afternoon, something made me turn and look up. Mr. Broadbent had taken his place at the window, gazing down at the street.

I wondered if he was young in his dreams. *What are you looking at, Mr. Broadbent? What do you see?*

I waved at him.

His gaze shifted. He raised his arm. He waved back.

I stood there for ages, one foot on the curb, staring up at the window. Alby was only right about one thing: I may have had nothing to teach Mr. Broadbent, but that day it struck home that I'd tolerated, humored, cajoled, berated, force-fed, placated, entertained and ignored him, and treated him like a child, but I'd never thought of him as adult and human. Not until that moment.

Alby took Mr. Broadbent away from the window and closed the blinds, and there it was again: the flicker at the edge of my vision, the glitch in the frame. Time was slippery. His wave was already in the past, and my whole life so far was history; the future was always out of reach, and the present was gone in a blink.

Maybe the best part was the waiting.

In the weeks after Jeremiah left, I played mind-control games with the phone, willing it to ring, and every Thursday afternoon I sat on Meredith Jolley's verandah. We talked. Slowly it started to feel as if I had clawed my way back to something resembling a life. It was such a relief to know that I hadn't finished chang-ing—I wasn't an hourglass that had timed out, all the grains fallen through. I wasn't stuck, too soon the best I could ever be.

That's what hope was, I decided: believing an old man waved, waiting for the phone to ring, gripping the watch in my pocket on Thursdays.

"You're a shit driver," Trudy said. "Move over. You're in the middle of the road."

"There's nothing coming." I edged Trudy's Mazda back over too far, and we fishtailed in the dirt. I steered out of it and straddled the white line again. The car sputtered and backfired. It sounded as if something metal had come loose in the engine.

"I should have let Dad teach you." Trudy put her hands over her face. "We're going to die."

"Not today," I said, and patted her knee.

Trudy dug her fingernails into the dashboard and held on until we reached the outskirts of Burt and the restricted speed limit.

"Are you nervous? I should drive so you don't sweat."

"I'm not nervous," I said, and I meant it. It was just a job interview for a reception position in a chain motel, and not even close to the job of my dreams, whatever that might be. "I've had three in the last two weeks, remember? I'm an old hand at this."

"Well, I feel sick for you," Trudy said. "We'll have lunch at the Burt Hotel when you're finished. Okay?"

• • •

She was waiting for me after the interview, sitting in the foyer, chewing her nails. She looked up. "How'd it go?"

"They said they'll let me know. The woman who interviewed me kept staring at my hair. I don't think I'd recognize her again if she sat on my lap and introduced herself." I untucked my blouse and unbuttoned my skirt once we got in the car. I let my breath out. "Ma's feeding me too much."

We sat in a corner booth at the pub and ordered counter meals, and Trudy bought us both beers. I sipped mine, leaving a frothy moustache on my upper lip. I pretended I didn't know it was there to make Trudy laugh.

"I miss you like crazy now you're not there," she said.

"If I was, we'd drive each other nuts."

"You can come back and live with us, you know."

"Maybe. Anyway, you and Thom might move in together one day."

"Never." She shook her head. "Uh-uh. Nope, no way," she said, which meant she was considering it.

"I like Thom," I said. "He's . . . nice."

Trudy looked alarmed. For a moment I thought she was going to argue with me, but she stiffened. Her stare locked on to someone across the room. Her smile disappeared. "Well, look what the cat dragged in. He's coming over," she hissed.

"Who?" I jerked around.

"Don't look!"

"Okay. Jesus, what?"

"Don't you dare give him the time of day." She arched her eyebrow and sat back in the seat, crossing her arms over her chest. "Tell him where to go."

I knew who was coming without turning around, based purely on the particular disdain Trudy had in reserve for one person. Luke.

A familiar and unwelcome emotion rose in my chest, the shreds of a feeling I couldn't name, something I couldn't stop no matter how hard I wished. Was it hope? Was it love? Is it only love if it comes back to you?

"Don't you need to go to the ladies'?" I whispered.

Trudy tucked her hair behind her ears and folded her arms. "No."

"Please."

"*Fine.* Just remember everything I've ever told you." Trudy downed the last of her beer and flounced out of the booth.

"Jack?"

Finally, I turned around. I found myself shaking. This obsession wasn't brittle at all—it was still fresh. Maybe I would never get over Luke and I'd only ever be left with my side of the story. How would I reconcile what had been with what might have been? How do I end it? How do I protect myself?

"What do you want?"

Luke took a step back, unsure. He thrust his hands in his pockets and rocked on his heels. "I went to the reservoir on Sunday."

"Oh?" I swallowed. "Why did you do that?"

He shrugged and smiled. "I wanted to see you." His teammates catcalled him from the other side of the bar. He waved them away, then shoved his hand back in his pocket. "I thought you might be waiting."

I made my heart a fist. "Well, you were wrong." I delivered a slow performance of twisting the cap off my middle finger, applied an imaginary coat of lipstick with the tip, and offered him the finger when I was finished. "I won't wait for you anymore."

Luke's mouth flattened. "Did I do something wrong? I thought we . . . I thought you were . . . look, forget it. It was good to see you, Jack." He walked away.

I heard a chorus of unsympathetic *ooh*s.

"*Slammed,*" somebody said.

I pushed my beer away. I couldn't stomach it, not when I was choking on words I couldn't say.

Trudy canceled our orders and ushered me into her car. "What did you say?" she prodded once we were out on the highway. "You told him, right?"

"Yeah. I told him," I muttered.

"That's my girl." She fell silent, satisfied, as if that was the end of it.

I waited for the ache to ease, counting flickering telephone poles and white silos and the endless brown fields.

It wasn't the end of anything. Just because you couldn't see a bruise didn't mean you couldn't still feel it underneath. I thought about Jeremiah. He'd seemed so wrong for me, but he'd been so right. Luke had felt right, but he was all wrong. Maybe, in my fucked-up world, it all made perfect sense, and, if I couldn't have either of them, I'd still have to choose.

"Could you stop the car, please?" Louder. "Trudy, please. Stop the car."

Trudy slammed her foot on the brake and pulled over. "What? What's wrong?"

"Turn around," I said. "Turn the car around."

"The hell? We're halfway to—"

"I know. If we get all the way home, I'll never do this."

"Do what?"

I peeled Trudy's hand from the gearstick and linked her rigid fingers with mine.

"You know you can't protect me forever, right?"

"Says who?" Trudy snapped. She sighed and spun the wheel.

It took long seconds for my eyes to adjust to the shadows of the bar. I lingered in the doorway, one foot on the threshold, one hand on my skidding heart. I found Luke exactly where I'd found him the first time we met: leaning over the pool table with the cue drawn back, a glass balanced on the edge.

He jabbed the cue, and the balls split and scattered. He

watched, resting the cue on his foot. His head fell back and he laughed. I laughed a lot when I was with Luke, I realized, but I didn't smile that often. *Smiles are more real,* I thought.

"Luke."

He looked up as I moved forward, but he stayed where he was. It took the longest time to cover the distance between us, and if anyone stared, I didn't notice; I tripped on the carpet, which felt like quicksand, and stumbled the last few steps. Above the pool table, a neon sign flashed purple and red. For a moment I thought about turning around—but I knew exactly what would happen if I kept it all inside. What I didn't know was what might be possible if I just let go.

"I forgot to tell you . . ." I brought up my hands.

Luke braced himself as if I was going to hit him. I cradled his face and I kissed him instead. He gave into it and pulled me against him. We found the rhythm that came so easily to us, and I held on longer than I should have, until the bar noise intruded and the lights seemed far too bright, even with my eyes closed.

I released him and stepped back. Suddenly I was so cold. "I loved you," I said. "I really did."

He blinked. He struggled to say something. I knew, if he found the right words, they would hurt.

I found my way to where Trudy was waiting in the car. I got in and buried my face in my hands.

"Are you going to tell me what happened?"

I couldn't tell her. My lips were stretched into a soundless howl. I tried to reroute the pain by pinching the skin inside my upper arms—it worked whenever I stubbed a toe.

Trudy turned sideways in her seat and stared. "Jesus, Jack! Stop. Are you dying?" She smacked me hard on the back.

I hiccupped. I might have giggled.

"Are you laughing . . . or crying?"

I couldn't answer; I didn't know.

"I'll kill him," Trudy said. "He's not worth doing time for, but I'd do it."

"I know you would." I gave her a shaky smile. "Let's go home."

It was an ending—not the kind my traitorous heart wished for, but the one I needed. Like an exorcism, minus the holy water and all the thrashing. What had once been a ragged wound became a clean hole right through.

30

Friday. FridayFridayFriday.

I stopped at the pub to heckle Trudy about how nice Thom was and to pick up an illicit six-pack of beer; I rode out the four-thirty routine of Mr. Broadbent slapping my cheek and yanking out a few strands of my hair. I left the hair in Mr. Broadbent's fist because he couldn't let go. I forgave him because I could let go.

I walked home from Bent Bowl Spoon, swinging the beer in one hand, my shoes in the other. I stopped to give directions to a carful of out-of-towners on their way to the drive-in. Roly was flying solo tonight. All around the bugs hummed and clicked. The waffle-cone smell faded. I breathed in the scent of greenery growing at a rate you could witness if you stood still long enough.

Meredith Jolley's verandah light was on, but she wasn't there.

"Over here," she called.

They were sitting on a patch of grass in the park across the street. Meredith was rugged up in a jacket, even though it was still warm. Ma had her shoes off, her hands at rest in her lap. Her dress and apron were hitched above her knees. There was something strange on her head.

"What's that?"

She whipped it off and held it up. "Oh. This. Meredith made it for me." Her mouth pursed.

Meredith laughed. "Don't take it personally," she said, and punched Ma's arm. "It's all I can make. It's a doily."

"Shit," I said. Ma hated doilies and cuckoo clocks, and swearing. Nobody punched her arm and lived.

But Ma didn't seem to mind. "Do you hear that?" she said.

"What?"

"Exactly." She smiled and cupped her hands over her ears. "He's fixed my wall, and now he's wearing the headphones you gave him."

"I am a genius," I said. "What's for dinner?"

"You've got jobs first," she said. "And perhaps you could make dinner tonight."

"What do you want me to do?" I said it in my new, most careful tone.

Meredith and Ma shared a look that shut me out. Meredith hid a smile.

"It's okay. Tell me what you want me to do, Ma."

Ma huffed. "I've tried both being in your life and staying out of it, Jack. I tried the same thing with Trudy. Now you're asking me what you should do?"

"Yes." I ground my molars together.

"I think you should go back to school."

"I'll think about it," I said through my clenched teeth, even though the thought made me feel sick.

"Good."

"Anything else?"

"You should clean your room and empty the dishwasher. And you should get the washing off the line." She was warming up now.

I put the beers down next to Meredith. "Here. Help yourself." I put my hands on my hips. "Is that it?"

They looked at each other again.

"Tomorrow you should put that new license into action. Have some fun."

What? "Why?"

Ma smoothed out her dress. "Because one day you're hot in a string bikini, and the next time you blink you're Mrs. Doubtfire." She leaned over and took a beer, twisting the top off with her apron. She handed the beer to Meredith.

Ma made a funny. I didn't quite know how to react.

"It's a lovely doily, Meredith, but I hate it. Thank you." Ma placed it in Meredith's lap. "Go on, then."

"I'm going," I said.

"Not you. Her." Ma nodded.

Meredith reached into her jacket pocket and drew out a set of keys. "Here. Congratulations on getting your license. Your world is going to open up now." She tossed them to me.

I caught them. "Well, if only you'd told me that before. You're letting me drive the Barbie car?" I wished they would stop looking at each other.

"Nooo," Ma said slowly.

Meredith laughed. "Come on. Fair trade." She held out her arm and wiggled her fingers.

Automatically my hand went to my pocket. The watch wasn't there.

"Looking for this?" Ma reached behind her ear and held up Meredith's watch.

"What, are you a magician now?" I said.

Ma sighed. "I just do the washing. You should take more care of other people's things, Jack." She handed the watch to Meredith and got up, dusting her backside.

"They're the keys to Jeremiah's car," Meredith said. "And before you get the wrong idea, I'm only asking you to deliver it. What happens after that is up to you."

I fell quiet. I shuffled the keys in my hands.

What do I do? What do I say? What if I get halfway and turn back? Shouldn't I have the answers before I say yes? What if I make things worse? How do I feel? What do I want? Is there a way of knowing before I get there?

"Come on, Jack. Didn't you ever just want to get in a car and drive?" Meredith said.

What if he rejects me? Can my heart take it? Should I call first? He loved me. He hates me. Do I love him? I miss him.

"Make it up as you go, Jack," Ma said softly.

He deserves better. I am better.

There was no way of knowing until I got there. That would have to be enough.

But what if he's changed? I've changed. I haven't changed enough. I've changed too much.

I was closer now than when I started, whatever that was.

I'll see you when I see you.

Closer.

There was a battle happening on my face. I could feel it. I screwed my eyes shut and held my breath; I made a wish, nothing fancy.

I put the keys in my pocket.

Eventually you have to open your eyes and breathe out.

I started from there.

ACKNOWLEDGMENTS

My books are village-raised and I'm blessed to have stellar human beings in my life. They're patient people too. I take the long way around everything, but they never stop cheering.

I'm incredibly grateful to Christian Trimmer, Catherine Laudone, and the team from Simon & Schuster, for giving my stories their American wings. The thrill of holding a hardcover will never get old.

Thanks to Guy Shield for his sublime and spot-on cover illustration.

As always, thanks to Penny Hueston for the conversations, countless readings and endless support. Without Penny there is no book. Thanks to Text Publishing, champions of Australian literature, and to my agent, Sheila.

I'm grateful to the people who float this passionate and inclusive YA community, especially to my fellow YA authors and our fierce, funny, and passionate readers.

To Allayne, Bec, Paula, Liz, and Fi, thank you for reading, for listening, and for being there when the wheels fall off. You inspire me every day.

And to Russ, Mia, Roan, Mum, Dad, Michelle, and my family and friends, my love and thanks. None of this works without you.